THE RiPPLE EFFECT

Best wishes
Gavin Mayer

Published by the Perera-Hussein Publishing House, 2019
www.pererahussein.com

ISBN: 978-955-8897-31-7

First edition

Printed and bound by Replika Press.

 To offset the environmental pollution caused by printing books,
the Perera-Hussein Publishing House grows trees in Puttalam –
Sri Lanka's semi-arid zone.

THE RiPPLE EFFECT

Gavin Major

PERERA-HUSSEIN PUBLISHING HOUSE
COLOMBO

To Thushy, because she shot-gunned it, to Max who listened and to Ben, who was too busy living his own adventure to know I was writing it. And of course, to Therssy. Everything I am is because of you.

All the characters in this book exist only in my head. Any resemblance to real people is just a spooky coincidence. If you think you recognise yourself in these pages, you are wrong. The characters are a mishmash of everyone who ever lived.

Thalagamma is a spelling mistake.

Ordinary is not a narrow band on a spectrum. It is the spectrum. Conjoined twins are two ordinary people in unusual circumstances. We are all ordinary. Some of us are just broken.

1

S am Benson was 56 years old and lived on his own on the Isle of Skye. Sam thought the Isle of Skye was the most beautiful place on the surface of his planet. He loved the hills and lochs, the birds and the trout in the burns.

People? He could take or leave them as his mood dictated. He had friends, but most of all enjoyed his own company.

His children, a boy and a girl, had grown up and left home long ago. He was reasonably pleased with the job he and his ex-wife had done in raising them. They appeared to be well-balanced, ordinary people showing no more than the average tendency towards being broken.

Sam and his wife separated seven years ago when their youngest child, the girl, left home. It seemed to him that their duty to their genes had been served and both had lost the ability and the inclination to procreate further. The biological deceit called love had lost its ability to deceive. That tingling excitement a new relationship brings had vanished and been replaced by something people tried to say was stronger. But Sam knew it wasn't. Their relationship had followed a very ordinary pattern. Biologically, they were spent. Sam felt content that he had done his job. His genes were out there mingling in the gene pool of humanity. He hoped that his mingled well.

For as long as Sam could remember, his wife's default response to any contentious issue had been to crank up the volume. It was a fantastic strategy, but it left little room for compromise. The family home had become a mosh-pit for two antagonists. He felt they might as well live the rest of their pointless lives separately. Not in a quest to be happier, but simply to be somewhere quieter. Luckily, his wife felt the same.

If you could plot Sam's life on a graph it would most accurately be described by a slowly descending straight line where time was on the X-axis and enthusiasm for life on the Y-axis. Very little rocked his boat. The joys and sorrows of life passed him by and left as much impression on him as drops of water on a newly polished car.

Sam lived modestly. He had been in business throughout his working life and had done well enough to keep things comfortable for those around him. It had not always been easy, but he had managed to maintain a respectable distance between his family and hard times. The effort had taken its toll. As well as being biologically spent, life had left Sam feeling emotionally jaded.

When he and his wife had sold the business, they set off independently on their own terminal paths. Like Pacific salmon after spawning, they left without purpose or direction. Sam's meanderings had brought him to Skye where he bought a small house outside a small village and now lived amongst ordinary people. A few of these people were badly broken, mostly by whisky and cheap vodka. For about a year Sam had been broken by whisky, but he was fixed now. The only things ailing him were the cumulative effects of age and a growing insensitivity to the suffering of other people. But since his genes were out there doing their bit, he didn't really mind, and he knew that this was just what nature had intended for him all along. Some of the ordinary people he knew called it fate. Sam called it biology. Sam's faith in biology was absolute. Its complexity and beauty pleased him. Biology to the exclusion of everything else helped him pinpoint precisely his worth in the great scheme of things. Having sown his seed, he knew his worth was zero. And far from troubling him, it infused his consciousness like a desensitizing balm.

One of the things that Sam did enjoy, was riding motorcycles. Not fast or aggressively, which he considered to be an act of questionable morality, but steadily and for long distances. Unusually for his age he had the urinary constitution of a camel and if fuel tanks could be made big enough he could probably ride for twelve hours without a break.

He entered a kind of meditation the moment he sat on a bike and this got deeper and more therapeutic the longer he rode. Cold and rain were things to be accepted and then, ultimately ignored. He never challenged them because there was no point. If it was raining, he got wet. There was nothing he could do about it, so he concentrated instead on the road and its surface unrolling beneath his boots.

He concentrated on his position on the road, pulling out wide towards the centre on unsighted left-hand bends and tight into the verge for right handers. He rode to make himself more visible and to increase his own forward visibility. He rode well and defensively and the satisfaction he got from doing this to the best of his ability trumped any discomforts the journey might throw at him. If it was wet, he rode better. If it was cold, he concentrated more.

The bike Sam rode was made by ordinary people who were famous for being punctual and efficient and who supposedly loved beer and sausages above all else, but who allegedly had no sense of humour. That was fine by Sam. There were two main things he looked for in a bike. The first was reliability. The fewer times a bike broke down, the more he appreciated it. His bike seemed bomb-proof. With the appropriate nourishment and care it went on and on and rarely gave a hint of its own limitations. At its heart was a 798cc parallel twin engine made by a company who also made engines for aircraft. Sam guessed reliability would be an important consideration for the people who used these same engines to defy gravity.

The other thing he wanted in a bike was entirely subjective. It was simply this – how much did the machine make him smile?

There were many motorcycle magazines on the shelves of the newsagents over on the east coast in Inverness. Some catered for people like Sam who liked to explore their world on bikes. Others pampered the egos of individuals who hooned around like demented gremlins, spending as much time on one wheel as two. The thing all these periodicals shared, and without which they would all quickly have been out of business, was their futile efforts to describe and quantify how much different bikes made them smile. The universally accepted term for this was the 'grin-factor'.

An important thing to understand is that if the grin-factor was at all quantifiable, there would probably only ever have been three of four different models of bikes in the world.

Sam's bike had such a big grin-factor for him that sometimes at night he would go out into his shed, turn on the lights and just smile at his bike. Some might have described Sam's feelings for his bike as love, but Sam knew it was just appreciation. There was no deceit.

If it wasn't for something small being where it shouldn't have been, things might well have carried on for him in this way, straight-lining inexorably to a point where something in his body gave up the ghost. It was something so small most people would probably never have noticed it.

Sam used Italian oil in the Austrian engine of his German bike to ride in Scotland. There were many good reasons why he could have chosen this particular oil, but in truth it was because of the fantastical logo on the oil can. It was a fire-breathing dog with six legs. Sam discovered it was designed in the 1950s by a man called Luigi Broggini, who cleverly died before telling anyone what his magical beast was supposed to mean. The dog made Sam smile. It too had a grin-factor. Sam imagined Luigi had been pleasingly eccentric.

He was decanting the oil from the second of his three, one-litre cans into a long-spouted jug. If he didn't use the jug, he ended up spilling the oil over the bike and the floor.

He kept the plastic oil cans on the workbench at the back of his shed. He bought them in packs of four – three for an oil change and one as a spare to top up as and when necessary. The Austrian engine makers were so clever that his bike almost never needed to be topped up. So, after three service intervals Sam had three spare oil cans which he liked to think of as a free oil change. He enjoyed these more than the others and this time was one of the freebies.

Sam felt satisfied as he watched the steady flow of the synthetic lubricant from the can into the jug. He stared into the translucent liquid in the way a jeweller considers the heart of a perfect gem stone. And, like the jeweller, he saw no flaws.

And then he did. The viscous amber flow was interrupted. A ripple passed down the arc that the oil described. Soot in the sugar bowl. He stopped pouring and put the oil can down on the workbench. His movement was tentative as he raised the jug and tilted the top of it towards him to see the offending inclusion. What he saw was like a slap in the face. The virtuous cycle of man, oil and bike had been breached. For an emotionally jaded man, he felt remarkably indignant.

At the bottom of the jug, resting insolently in the angle between the tilted base and the side, was an olive stone. An olive stone in the oil, even Italian oil, was anathema. This was not like the surprise you might get when cracking an egg into a frying pan and seeing a double-yolker. This was like cracking an egg into a frying pan and seeing a hamster leap out. It shouldn't happen. It was inexplicable. Worse, it was a fracture in the bond of total trust that Sam had in his bike and the nourishment he put into it. It exposed his vulnerability.

When he came to Skye, Sam had welcomed the freedom from his marital responsibilities. It had made him selfish. But increasingly, this lazy, hollow, new-found freedom was turning out to be, unexpectedly, far from liberating. It brought with it a new responsibility – that of accepting the consequences of his choices and he was beginning to understand that only by accepting this responsibility, was there any chance of changing his life for the better. Blaming the oil company would be a forfeit of this right to change.

So in pursuit of true liberation, he obeyed his soul and his soul told him that the best thing to do was to go to Italy and give someone their olive stone back.

2

A five-year-old Nokia with a cracked screen rang jarringly in the corner of the otherwise silent room. Laxman answered it on the third ring. The language Laxman spoke had words which were approximations of the English 'hello,' but he used none of them. He only listened.

The room was bare even by the standards of the country Laxman lived in. The walls were of un-rendered brick and the floor of concrete, made smooth by the skill of the mason who laid it, and from being swept regularly with a coarse broom made from the mid-ribs of fallen palm fronds. Above him were coconut roofing timbers which supported terracotta tiles. Laxman had cut the timbers with an axe, five years ago, from a tree he felled in his garden. The timbers were preserved with used engine oil which blackened them and gave them an apparent weight they did not possess. White smudges covered the wall next to the planter's chair he had been lying in when the telephone rang. These were made by fingertips that had been dipped in slaked lime which Laxman added to the betel leaf, areca nut and tobacco he was fond of chewing when he wanted to relax. This mixture, when chewed, made him spit red juice and gave him a deep mellow hit. One day it would also make him die from oral cancer.

The room's single window had no glass. Instead, the edges of a crude metal grill had been screwed into the uprights of the wooden frame. In two of the screw holes, nails had been hammered and bent over. Inside the grill was a dusty fine-mesh nylon curtain, torn where it had repeatedly rubbed against the sharper parts of the poorly made grill.

The world outside the room was held at bay by a Ginnisappu plank door. The door was open, as usual, but the light from a centrally hung forty-watt bulb barely penetrated the heavy black night outside.

The only other items of furniture in the room were three crimson plastic chairs, a small, blue-painted wooden table and a simple glass display cabinet. The back was broken off one of the chairs which left a dagger-like piece of plastic sticking up with the maker's name still intact. The name was Nilkamel. In the corner opposite the door were five greasy cardboard boxes, made fragile by age and ants. They were stacked neatly in two piles. Leaning against them were four rolled-up reed mats on which Laxman, his wife Shani and his children Rohan and Rassika slept.

Rohan stood up and approached Laxman as he listened to the voice in the phone. Shani turned away from them all and stared at the wall. She knew. It was ten past eight at night. Nobody else would ring at this hour.

Laxman put the phone down on the display cabinet. Shani turned to look at her husband. Rassika sat on the floor and continued writing in her school book.

"Now," Laxman said. "We must go."

Shani quietly slipped out of the house and into the darkness. Rohan opened one of the cardboard boxes and took out a soft sports bag into which he carefully put his clothing. There was no room for anything else. This was not a problem. He owned nothing else.

By the time the bag was zipped shut, Shani had returned in a three-wheeler. The headlight shone into the room through the door, glowing brighter, then dimming as the driver blipped the throttle to keep the bad tempered two-stroke engine from stalling. The extra illumination exaggerated the starkness of the surroundings which had been hidden in the sympathetic glow from the dim bulb.

Rassika put down her homework and came up to her brother. She pressed her palms together then knelt in front of him and touched both his feet with her open hands. He touched the top of her head and helped her to her feet. She was about to go back to her homework but a glance from her father told her to stay where she was. Rohan repeated the blessing his sister had given him to his mother. Shani stooped and held her son's head as he touched her feet. She cupped her hands and brought them to her face and inhaled deeply. She was breathing in her son. Not a word was said.

Laxman went out into the night carrying Rohan's bag and sat in the back of the three-wheeler. When Rohan joined him, the vehicle turned sharply and was quickly lost in the darkness. The buzz from the engine could be heard long after the light had disappeared. The sound of Shani weeping could be heard long after the noise of the engine had faded.

Poverty, and the burning desire not to be, meant that straight lines in the emotional graphs of Laxman's family were luxuries they would constantly be denied. Their lines were big-dipper rides.

Poverty and imagination can make a cruel combination.

3

Sam took just over an hour to pack. First the tools went in the left-hand soft pannier. They were heavy. It helped the bike's handling to keep the weight low. Then his clothing, which was minimal, since he had learned long ago that woollen T-shirts and underwear didn't need washing so often. Two of each were enough, regardless of how long he was away for.

Before discovering the virtues of wool, he used to buy a bag of hideous synthetic socks that sparked with static. He would wear them once or twice and then discard them. The idea being that there would be no washing and the space in his bag would increase the longer he was away. Now, he had perfected the sock situation. He used three good quality woollen socks which he rotated in strict order. Day one: sock A was on his right foot, sock B was on his left foot and sock C was unused in his bag. On day two sock B was on his right foot, sock C on his left foot and sock A was washed. And in such a manner the sock juggling continued for the duration of the trip.

He carried an old pair of Gel Kayanos, which he liked to wear after pitching his tent and when he went on an early morning run. Sam loved running into the rising sun. It made him smile.

In the right-hand pannier, he kept his food items and cooking equipment. His stove was powered by the same fuel as his bike which, in Sam's mind, made the two inanimate objects deeply connected. He would have preferred the simplicity of his Kelly Kettle, which he took to the hills when fishing on Skye. But the Kelly Kettle was bulky and there was no place for it in his pared down touring kit. The Chinese liquid-fuel burner, was as noisy as it was brutally efficient and, when folded, could be held in the palm of his hand.

Sam's habit was to top up with fresh items of food as he went along. He tried to make sure that by the middle of the afternoon he had enough food and water for the night. If it was important to stay hidden, he preferred not to cook where he camped, so would eat before he found a quiet place to stay. When there was no food to be found, he could go most of the day on a few coffees, which he always tried to make himself. One of his most valued items he packed was an insulated plastic coffee mug with a mesh plunger.

Over the years, Sam had tried and enjoyed many kinds of coffee. Since the supermarkets started putting numbers indicating strength on the packets, he had decided he preferred the ones above three and didn't see much point in drinking the ones and twos. Whilst he had to admit that drinking the ones and twos wasn't exactly the sign of a broken person, there was something a bit suspicious about it. Sometimes the fives had been a bit stark and what they clearly had in raw punch they often lacked in roundness. But recently Sam had found a five that ticked all the boxes. It was a French blend. A disproportionate part of his right-hand pannier was taken up by half a dozen large packets of this. He imagined these would last the trip and would mean that, wherever he was, he wouldn't have to drink any foreign stuff.

His tent and sleeping mat were rolled up and fixed across the seat where a pillion might normally sit. After many hours riding, they gave him some support and added to the arm-chair comfort of the bike. His favourite telescopic spinning rod was safely tucked inside the sleeping mat. There was also a dull green lightweight tarpaulin which he used to disguise his bike if he was camping near a road.

A top box was mainly for small personal bits and pieces, including a fishing reel and a few spinners. He always left enough room to put his flip-front Schuberth C3 in. In Sam's opinion, it was the Rolls Royce of protective headgear.

Sam was unusual in the way he got from A to B. For him the journey was his reason for being on the road, so he rejected the idea of being lost. He was never lost. He might go by an unusual route to get somewhere, and it might take him twice as long as the next man but lost was something he just didn't understand. If he was moving forward, he was heading in the right direction. He had never owned a sat-nav. For this trip, he didn't even pack any road maps. He had a Students' Atlas which he had bought for a pound from a charity shop in Inverness.

On a morning, whilst he was sipping his coffee in the door of his tent, he would consult the paper-backed atlas. There were five pages devoted to Europe, so Sam would get the general idea of which direction he wanted to set off in. Then the atlas would be put away in the top box until the following morning. When he saw the sun rise over the horizon he knew where to go. If it had been a clear night, he already knew where to expect it having checked on Polaris before he went to sleep.

So, with no ceremony whatsoever, Sam tucked his passport and a coloured photocopy of his bike's registration certificate into his inside jacket pocket and filled his wallet with as much folding money as he had lying around. The original V5 lived under a foam sheet at the bottom of his top box together with £260 in brand new Bank of England £20 notes.

Sam had learned that notes from the Scottish banks were not accepted abroad. Sometimes they were refused in England despite being legal tender. This annoyed him and accounted for his habit, when down south, of filling his bike with petrol and paying with Scottish notes. If the person at the cash register said they couldn't accept the notes, Sam would shrug and say, "OK, thanks, then," and turn around to walk away. Three steps were the farthest he ever got before the cashier had revised their opinion of the desirability of Scottish notes.

His driving licence and European Health Care card were in his wallet together with a Visa Debit card. He started the bike, did a walk-round check to see that all was as it should be, put on his helmet and gloves and, in the early morning sun which was rising over the Isle of

Raasay, he rode slowly out of Portree. It was the middle of May. Life was on the right side of tolerable.

By the time he reached the inn at Sligachan, nestling by the river at the foot of Sgurr nan Gillean, his tyres were warm and the early summer camper vans, bristling with satellite dishes, were still parked up. He accelerated through the left-hander over the river and took a bit more off the little that remained of his chicken-strips. He passed the deserted golf course at Sconser and, apart from the odd disinterested sheep, he had the road to Broadford to himself. Although he had half a tank, he filled up at Sutherland's and took the opportunity to check the security of his load. Spot on, as he knew it would be.

Round the delightful bends at Eilean Donan and on up to the Cluanie Dam, the only vehicles coming his way were the delivery lorries for Skye and the Outer Isles beyond. There were a couple of newly mangled deer which focused his attention on any animals near the road. This waste of good venison saddened him. More than once he had helped himself to a prime cut from fresh road-kill.

At the far end of the dam there had once been an impromptu art installation of various coloured latex gloves, put randomly on top of fence posts in a long colourful line. It was community art at its best and Sam thought it more relevant and pleasing than anything he had seen in a gallery. But it had long gone. No doubt cleaned up by a council worker operating under instruction from a suit in a gloomy office in Inverness. The Marigolds had touched Sam. Even now he smiled at the memory of them. No Art Council funding. No lottery grants. No money to be made. Just the imagination and involvement of a few individuals doing something for the fun of it to the benefit of all. For a laugh. If Sam had to define what art should be, that would pretty much be it.

He defined lots of things as he rode. It was part of the meditation of riding long miles alone. He lived in the moment and the moment was vast. Being on the road removed the limitations that life put on his imagination. What psychedelic drugs supposedly did for musicians in the '60s, riding a bike did for Sam now. Sam's drug of choice? A litre of unleaded.

The weather was calm and mild, like it so often is in May in the Highlands. He could see a few cumuli above the hidden peak of Ben Nevis which turned the pale blue sky into a scene like the one from the credits of the Simpsons. There were still a few patches of winter snow covering the tops, looking fresh and coolly inviting.

He decided against stopping in Fort William and carried on through Ballachulish and up Glencoe. At the top of the glen he passed the house of a badly broken man whose past deeds had resulted in the house being vandalised with bright red graffiti. The man, a cigar-chomping DJ, was dead. Sam wondered what the house had done wrong.

Glencoe was such a beautiful setting, haunted by memories; one from a long time ago which was part of the folklore of the area. The savagery of this ancient 'slaughter under trust' of the Glencoe Macdonalds by the Earl of Argyll's Regiment of Foot, had been air-brushed by the romance of its antiquity. The other more recent, with the paedophile DJ, had been sharpened by the focus of the law and the spotlight of the media. A communal nerve had been touched and it was still raw. Despite the regular repainting of the house, the graffiti kept coming back and probably would for a generation. Here, ordinary had been pushed beyond the extremes of understanding.

But the wide-open splendour of Rannoch Moor beckoned, and Sam pushed the mph to what he thought a decent plain-clothes police motorcyclist would accept. He knew that they too were bikers, and they understood the pleasures of rubber on the road and the twitchy responsiveness of a high-performance machine. Sam was aware of his responsibilities and he would not abuse them under any circumstances. But, in a legal landscape, barren of emotion and common sense, Sam applied his own interpretation of it to speed limits on empty roads.

He pulled into a lumpy parking area, the entrance of which was partly hidden by large boulders put there to deter travellers. There was a hillock between the parking area and a loch that Sam knew well. From the top of it he could see the road stretching back to Glen Coe and the broad expanse of an empty wilderness. On the hills behind the loch, the West Highland Way wove its unseen path through twists and turns and rocks and sheep. It was here that he liked to put his kettle on and brew a coffee. Much cheaper than the 'Green Welly' a few miles down the road and somehow much more suited to the start of a journey. It was a statement of intent to make his own coffee and enjoy it in the wilderness. When he was finished, he could pee on the ground rather than stand with all the coach party holidaymakers, relieving their ancient bladders in a choreographed line-dance of slow dribbles. He would call at the 'Green Welly' on the way back for a cullen skink and have a blether with the other bikers.

The traffic down Loch Lomond was getting heavier and the road works slowed him down. He carefully filtered past the queuing cars and vans and got to the lights at the front of the line. He was soon joined there by a young guy wearing Crowtree leathers, on a red VFR. They nodded to each other but neither felt the need to talk. When the light went green the VFR shot off, ignoring the temporary 30 mph limit and Sam never saw him again. Which was fine.

Just north of Glasgow he managed to squeeze twelve litres into the tank and have a sandwich from the petrol station which he ate whilst sitting on a wall overlooking a used car lot. The contrast with Rannoch Moor pleased him. What was life if it was not rich with variety?

4

The three-wheeler passed the small village school Rohan had left the year before and joined the main road to Colombo. The journey took almost two hours. The roads were dry and the evening rush of traffic leaving Colombo was almost over. Drunks, dogs and an occasional wandering cow kept the driver alert. Negotiating potholes in a three-wheeler required specialised skills that a car driver could never understand. In order to survive, three-wheeler drivers needed nerves of steel, lightning fast reflexes, and a large daily dose of luck.

The three-wheeler Rohan and his father were in had only one of the three front lights working and none at the back. Any life in the indicators was nothing more than a distant memory. Where bright flashing bulbs once were, there now was only dust and the beginning of a hornet's nest.

The torn plastic seat at the back slid off its shelf every time the driver braked or swerved violently. This was no big deal. All Sri Lankans who travelled in three-wheelers were used to it. Visitors to Sri Lanka called them tuk-tuks. The Sri Lankans knew what the tourists meant, but to them they were always three-wheelers. They were a way of life. People ate, slept and died in them. Babies were born in them and sometimes even made within their beige, biscuit-tin-thin, bowl-like shells. David Pieris, the sole agents in Colombo for a popular Indian brand, sold over fifty every working day.

The one Rohan and Laxman were travelling in was taking them to a rendezvous at a busy city junction with people neither of them had ever met. They were sending Rohan to another country. His father had borrowed money and paid it to them via a broker. A lot of money. These men had the power to bypass the normal formalities of entering a country. Formalities that would preclude young men like Rohan from standing a chance of ever succeeding. For this service, they were paid well. In a world of shadows, they operated in the darkest corners.

Thanks to the skill of the driver they made it to the designated junction fifteen minutes before their due time. They pulled onto a paved area under some shabby apartments, carelessly painted orange and yellow. The smell of spices, exhaust fumes and poverty filled the humid city air. Across the road was a sacred bo tree and a large, white, sitting Buddha. The Buddha's look was serene. He had been given a halo of concentric flashing lights. The chaos of the lights illuminated the Buddha's face and was at odds with the calmness upon it. Disco Buddha. Laxman would travel past this same Buddha every time he caught a bus to Colombo. A number 4 from Puttalam.

Laxman's phone rang.

"Are you there?"

"Yes."

"Get out."

Laxman did as he was asked, stepping over Rohan's legs and onto the paving. The driver spat betel juice through pursed lips in a red gob that splattered on the heavily-stained floor beside Laxman's feet. The phone went dead.

Less than a minute later a white van pulled up on the wide paved area between the road and the three-wheeler. The engine ticked over. The side door slid open noisily on metal runners clogged with dry sand. A voice from the front seat told them to come in.

There was no internal light. Dark plastic tints had been stuck on the inside of the windows. This was not unusual. It was peeling and torn at the corners where time and inquisitive fingers had picked at its edges. The seats were stained and there was a strong smell of kerosene and sweat. In Laxman's world, this too was not unusual.

The man in the front passenger seat turned around and asked Rohan if he had anything that could identify him, "Identity card, driving licence?" He did and was told to hand them to his father. When the man was satisfied, he passed over a new passport and told the boy to look at the name-page at the front. The photo was of Rohan. It was taken two months previously in the modelling studio in his village. Under the photograph was a name. A name that Rohan was not yet familiar with, but one that he was told to memorise, along with his new date of birth, before they reached the airport. His new name was H.R. Malinda Hettiarachchi and his new birthday made him almost four years older than he really was. He was given a new address to go with his new name, in an area and a village he had never heard of.

It was not uncommon in rural Sri Lanka to have an address with no street name or house number. The most important part of the address were those two letters 'H-R' before the name. They were part of the family name and families tended to stay in their traditional locality. The postman or Grama Niladhari would know at once where the H.R.'s lived.

In the back of the passport was an airline ticket in a card wallet together with a handwritten letter on a page torn from a lined school book. The card was crisply folded and the printing was sharp. The letter was from the sort of book that every village shop sold for a few rupees. It was a love letter to Malinda from a girl called Nilanthi. It was well handled and worn where it had been folded. Rohan was told to put it in his back pocket. It was evidence, should it be needed, that he was who he said he was. Mr H.R. Malinda Hettiarachchi. Casual evidence to be found only if he was searched. Laxman raised his eyebrows in admiration. These city men knew things that a fisherman like him would never know. The stamps in the passport showed Rohan that he had been to Italy before.

The man in the passenger seat motioned silently to Laxman that his involvement was over. The boy knelt on the dusty concrete at his father's feet. He touched both feet, bare, in old rubber-thonged slippers, and brought his face very close to them. The father reached down and touched his son's thick, oily hair before raising him to his feet. The city life around them went on uncaring. But for the two of them, frozen in this moment of respect and love, the ground beneath them pulsed. Life was wound up as tight as it could possibly be. Laxman quietly ended the torture and went to sit in the three-wheeler. Rohan climbed into the van and the door was slid shut. On a moment... on a son... on a life.

5

Sam made it as far as Shap when he decided to pull off the M6 and camp for the night. He had stopped there before and knew a secluded spot near the end of the slip road. He pulled his bike out of sight and onto a hard-standing. Within two minutes of leaving the motorway he was hidden and ready to put up his tent. After a moment's hesitation, he decided against the tent and made a lean-to with the tent's fly sheet. The evening was fine and he had left most of the early season midges behind in the highlands. From the lean-to, he could enjoy the night sky to the west. There would be no visible sunrise but the sunset should be worthwhile. He cooked a simple meal of pasta with a tin of tuna. He drew comfort from the fact that his needs were few and his simple sleeping requirements needed only moments to prepare. Before the water for his pasta had boiled, his sleeping mat was unrolled and his three-seasons bag laid out on it. He had a simple travel pillow which compressed into almost nothing. He supplemented its meanness with a towel.

He ate his food, sitting on a rock, beside the tent. It was hard for Sam to imagine anyone more content. His food was simple, but warm and nourishing. There was no embellishment that could have made it taste better. He knew that taste was nothing more than electrical impulses fired from chemical receptors in his mouth and nose to a part of his brain which then had the tricky task of deciding which impulses should be tasty and which should not. What a responsibility, thought Sam, as he took pleasure in giving his mind the freedom to wander.

When it wandered too close to anything too deep or dark, through practice, he consciously thought of something else. Sam often thought of the stupidity of tattoos. That always did the trick.

The light faded just after nine that evening. There was no sunset, just the slow death of a day. Sam enjoyed it all the same and lay there watching the stars come out. The noise from the motorway faded away until he no longer noticed it. He slept soundly and woke, by habit, just before five in the morning.

He drank from a plastic water bottle and slipped into his running kit. All of it was well used but comfortable and functional. None of it chafed. It didn't flap in the breeze behind him. It fitted him and did what it was supposed to do. He ran on a bridge over the motorway and did a couple of miles on roads that got smaller the further he went. At last he came to a reservoir and toyed with the idea of going back for his fishing gear. When he remembered he was south of the border, he changed his mind. Scotland did not require a rod licence, England did. Anyway, he told himself, there were very few waters in England filled with as many wild brownies as he was used to on Skye.

A wild brownie. Probably the perfect fish. Nature had some wonders but was there really anything to match the shivering yellow splendour of a brown trout leaping for a fly in the fading pink light of a Highland summer evening? If there was, Sam hadn't yet seen it.

At 5:15 A.M. the first sliver of the morning sun rose tentatively above the horizon. It was at this point Sam turned away from the reservoir and ran back to his bike. He ran east, directly into the rising sun. There was a faint sweet smell of agriculture in the still air – unseen farm animals in a nearby field. The rest of the run uphill was easy. Sometimes his body felt like a bag of washing, but this morning his joints and tendons and all the other bits of meat and gristle were warm and worked smoothly.

Sam grabbed the towel from under his pillow and walked down the hill, away from the motorway. Around the trees that had given him cover last night and along a fence was a burn bubbling gently from the north. He had a smile on his face and a bar of coal-tar soap in his hands. He bathed in the sharp bite of the cold water and kicked up a stink with the coal-tar.

When he got back to the bike and put on his riding gear with the socks-de-jour, all that remained was for him to make a coffee and pack. The first coffee of the day was always a special moment and Sam would never rush it. There was no need to. Life was just a question of priorities and right up there near the top was making the most of a decent cup of coffee. He smelled it. He sipped it. He closed his eyes. The spot was hit.

He knew England well enough not to get the atlas out. It was all downhill. Today, the south coast was his target. Unless he changed his mind. He hadn't decided if he was going by ferry or the tunnel. He was sure ferries sailed from Dover but was not certain where the tunnel started and was vaguely apprehensive about it anyway. Statistics proved it to be as safe as houses, but the idea of being so far underwater for so long made him feel slightly claustrophobic. Someone with an attitude problem and a working knowledge of explosives could ruin his day. The route he eventually took to France would probably depend on which sign he saw first.

He made good time and, on a whim, he turned left before Manchester and took the M62 over the Pennines. Long before the motorway was even thought of, Sam's father had worked putting overhead telephone wires over these hills. Through the razor sharp, black mornings of midwinter, when the wind blew wild tunes through the dry-stone walls, his father had struggled up wooden telephone poles wearing two woollen jackets, a Bradford Park Avenue pompom hat and heavy leather tackety boots. He had tightened the new cables and fixed them to the poles. In those sepia days of the early '50s, telephone wires were uninsulated, and poles had to route the wires directly from one subscriber to the next. They also had the task of keeping them apart over their entire route. That could be from Thurso to London, almost seven hundred miles. Imagine that.

The bare wires were anchored to porcelain insulators which were fixed to wooden arms via steel spindles. Just as each snowflake is unique, so were the telephone poles. Every one of them was erected and assembled by men like Sam's father. Every man would put a bit of himself into his work. Looking back down a hillside to see the line and arcs described by the poles and wires, Sam's father could not help but feel proud. It was his art. The glow of satisfaction he got from admiring his work probably kept him as warm as his two old coats.

Sam grew up with stories about the extremes of Pennine weather and the solitude of the landscape. As a boy, Sam had imagined his father was more like Scott of the Antarctic than the head of the household at 5, Naseby Terrace, who worked for the GPO. That is a good thing. A boy should admire his father.

In the days before synthetic fleeces and technical layering, Sam's father had lived in a beer-drinking, rugby-playing, war-fighting working class ethic which had no energy to spare for what he had called 'poncing about.' It was these roots that kept Sam's feet firmly planted on the ground... and the uncritical simplicity of it which he envied.

It was still too early to eat, but Sam found it difficult to pass so close to an icon of taste and style without calling in to pay homage. So he turned off the M62 and took the road into Bradford. The centre had changed beyond anything he could imagine, but the hills surrounding the city were the same. The topography of Bradford was pressed into his being. Sam knew that when he saw the starling-splashed Town Hall he should turn left and let the momentum of his descent carry him up the hill past the Alhambra, now with trees growing out of the gutters, past the ice rink (was it still in there?) and onto a small cobbled street between rows of anonymous back to backs.

The Karachi Social Club. He ordered a keema and chapattis and wallowed in its ancient familiarity. As a boy, Sam had been a regular. The lino tables. The sliced onion and chopped tomato and a spoonful of yoghurt in a stained white saucer. The greasy glasses and a jug of tap water. Only the old man stirring the curry in a pot the size of a jacuzzi was gone. Everything else was the same. Reassuringly and happily so.

As work supposedly expands to fill the time available, Sam found curry did with chapattis. He could order two or twenty-two of them and the curry would be finished only when the last torn piece was used to wipe the plate clean.

It was more than thirty years since Sam had eaten at the Karachi. Since then he must have become used to simpler ingredients because, as he rode out of the city, there was a little rebellion going on in the battleground of his stomach. Nothing serious, just dark and unexpected rumblings like distant thunder from an unseen storm. Maybe in the city of Karachi anyone who used a helmet on a bike would sensibly have an open-faced one, because nobody could reasonably expect to survive the smell of second-hand curry that filled the intimate environment of his full-face Schuberth. He flipped the front open and rode out of Bradford with his mouth open, looking like a cross between a blow-up doll and a plastic knight in a cheap chess set.

Icons? Who needs them?

6

The journey to the airport took thirty-two minutes. The man in the passenger seat had done this trip many times. He had forgotten the name he had given this boy already but, as he looked back, he could see the boy closing his eyes trying to memorise it. The man knew it would not be necessary. He knew that the passport was good to get out of Sri Lanka with and should be good enough to get into Italy. That was all that was necessary. When this boy walked through customs at Milan airport his job was done.

If Rohan was caught before he left the airport in Milan he would be arrested and flown back to Sri Lanka. And it was supposedly part of the unwritten contract that existed between the boy's father and him that he would have to let the boy try again using a different name. The man did not want this to happen because it would cost him more money and take time to set up another attempt. He took pride in the fact that, of all the boys he had flown to Italy, not one had ever been caught. If one day one was stupid enough to be, there was nothing that could come back to him.

Many years ago, it had been harder. He'd had to send people in containers and then to organise overland trips through countries with names he could not pronounce. Many people he didn't know were involved in the organisation of these trips and his share of the profit was small. People died in the containers or were discovered, by bored Italian police, being led over quiet border crossings. But now it was easy. All that was needed was a passport with a rubber stamp on the right page. These he could buy. The Italians were lazy. They never checked things too carefully. He loved the Italians, though he had never met one."

At the airport, the van crawled past other vehicles unloading passengers with their bags and belongings. Just beyond the drop-off zone, a man appeared from behind one of the white concrete pillars. He had a black number seven written on a fluorescent orange vest. Above the number was the word 'Porter'. The van stopped beside him.

He opened the sliding door and took Rohan's bag and placed it on a metal trolley. There was already one suitcase on the trolley – a fabric one with a chequered pattern on it. It had a small brass padlock fastening the zips together. It was not new. Rohan had seen bags like this before at the stalls next to the central bus station in Pettah. The thing that made this bag different from the ones in Pettah was that it had his new name clearly written on silver-grey tape stuck on the side. Rohan was impressed. The man in the passenger-seat had thought of everything. If Rohan hesitated when questioned, his address was on the suitcase as a reminder. The man turned around to face Rohan and handed him an orange one hundred rupee note.

"Follow the porter, do as he says and, when he leaves you, make sure you are seen giving him this money."

"All of it?"

The unsmiling face of the man in the passenger seat looked at him. "Yes, sir."

The porter led Rohan across two lanes of traffic to a double glass door manned by a military guard who took Rohan's passport and looked cursorily at his photograph.

"Ticket?"

Whilst the guard checked the details, Rohan ran the tips of his fingers inside his back trouser pocket to make sure the letter from Nilanthi was still there.

The porter pushed his trolley through the glass doors and into a brightly lit room with three long machines onto which passengers were loading their bags. The bags went on rollers through a metal box whilst a man in a blue uniform looked at a screen. Rohan was fascinated and wondered what they were looking for. When he tried to lift his bags onto the rollers the porter firmly pushed him aside. Rohan leaned forward to see the screen as his bag went through. With no discernible change in his expression, the porter quietly kicked Rohan's shin and guided him towards a metal frame through which he had to walk. An alarm sounded as he passed through the frame and a large man, with the shiniest shoes Rohan had ever seen, put his hand up for Rohan to stop.

"Coins? Keys?"

Rohan patted his pockets and said there were none. The guard was unimpressed and instructed Rohan to remove his belt and try again. Rohan put his belt on the rollers. It fell through them. The metal buckle made a noise on the tiled floor which attracted the attention of those nearby. If anyone was paying very close attention they would have seen the porter glance at the guard. The guard caught it but, like the accomplished actor he was, the porter subtly squeezed his lips into a thin smile changing his expression from apprehension to one of conspiratorial amusement at the expense of the stupid village boy. A woman behind the rollers picked Rohan's belt up from the ground and put it into a small plastic tray. The disdainful look she aimed at Rohan missed its mark by the length of a cricket pitch.

They entered a long corridor that was open to the evening breeze. The porter looked straight ahead and walked with a hurried step. He was a dark man with receding grey hair and had the slight stoop of one who has been damaged by too much manual labour. Rohan knew that skin as dark as the porter's came from a life in the paddy fields and was not a curse from his ancestors. His feet were dusty grey and his toenails were long and broken.

"Uncle, why did you kick me?"

The porter looked briefly at Rohan and held his gaze with an authority unbecoming his position. He mouthed the word 'modaya,' which roughly translates as 'idiot.'

Beyond a second glass wall, at which another man wanted to see his ticket, was a row of stalls with coloured signs above them. Behind each one was sitting a man or a woman in uniform. The girls were very smart and wore as much make-up as a village bride. The men were young and had smart jackets and oiled hair, like Colombo schoolboys.

There was a queue in front of each desk. The porter chose the one with the shortest line. The people in this queue were all Sri Lankans and Rohan could see that a notice board behind the girl managing the desk told him that the people in her queue wanted to go to Milan. In other queues, some of the passengers were well-fed red-skinned foreigners. The Sri Lankans were dressed smartly. The foreigners wore hardly anything at all. He had been warned repeatedly by his mother about foreign girls. They were diseased. He guessed she was probably wrong, but he couldn't help staring as he shuffled forwards. He had never seen such an inviting display of flesh. It was all a funny colour, but the shapes were mostly the same as the ones he constantly dreamed about.

The porter pushed Rohan in the back and urged him towards the girl. She smiled at him and ignored the porter. She was pretty and Rohan was glad she was not dressed like these white girls.

"Ayubowan."

"Ayubowan," replied Rohan. And he waited.

The porter caught Rohan's eye and nodded briefly towards the pocket where he kept his passport and ticket. Rohan passed them to the girl.

"Are these your bags, sir?"

The porter gave the tiniest of head wobbles that Sri Lankans are famous for.

"Yes, Miss."

"Have you packed them yourself, sir?"

A slightly bigger wobble.

"Yes, Miss."

"How many bags are you checking in today?"

"Just this one, Miss," said the porter, lifting the bag with Rohan's new name on it onto the rollers.

The girl put a tag on the bag and asked some more questions. She had started the conversation in English but quickly reverted to the language Rohan understood. Dumfounded by her sophistication, Rohan mumbled his replies almost incoherently. The girl didn't mind.

There is a typical look village boys have that Colombo girls can recognise at a hundred metres. Maybe it is their haircuts, which are always too perfect. Or maybe it is something about the earth they walk in barefooted all day long that is drawn into their bodies and grows up through them like an invisible spectre of compost and decay. Whatever, this girl saw it and knew that speaking English would be futile. So in a language that allows for every nuance of respect and politeness to be employed abundantly, she turned it up to the max. A city boy would have seen through the shallow charm to the contempt that lay beneath. Rohan was clueless.

His mumbles impressed her enough to press a button and the bag with his new name on was lost from sight as it passed noisily through some plastic curtains. She handed Rohan his passport and a new piece of paper that she told him was his boarding card. Her eyes and her mouth told contrasting stories, but the one that could make a noise said, "Thank you," and, "Have a pleasant flight."

The porter picked up Rohan's sports bag and walked towards another row of desks. He stepped aside and beckoned Rohan close to him. The desks at the far end of the hall were deserted but the first seven had people sitting behind them. All but one were men who wore white shirts and trousers. Some had silver decorations on their shoulders. The solitary lady wore a red sari in the Kandyan style. It was the kind of cheap sari school teachers wore and gave off sparks if they tried to run.

"Go to the man beyond the madam. Join his queue and give him your passport. When he gives it back to you follow the others and go up the stairs. Find gate number 4 and wait outside. When it opens, give the person there your boarding card. Don't talk to anyone. Gate number 4. *Haride?*"

"*Isthuthi*, Uncle."

Rohan remembered the hundred rupees note. He also remembered a sentence in English he had been forced to memorise as a child. He wasn't entirely sure what it meant but it somehow seemed appropriate.

"Good day to you, good sir."

But the porter was gone before the echoes of Rohan's obsolete textbook English had bounced back at him from the bare walls of the customs room.

7

Southern England felt like an old friend to Sam. He was so far inside his comfort zone that it made him uncomfortable. He rode on into the evening, keeping the sun on his right until it set, and then continued down the tedious M1 until the M25 crossed its path. On a whim, he turned left. Clockwise seemed preferable. He imagined tearing around the M25 leaning in to his right and accelerating in faster and faster M25-sized circles until the right side of his tyre was worn down to the canvas. It was at this point he knew he needed a coffee.

There was a service station, the name of which reminded him of a clinical reference guide. When he started to imagine that the service station buildings were made of pill-shaped blocks, he knew he would go no further tonight. The car park was quiet. It was that empty time between people going home to get out of working clothes and putting on different ones to head back out and spend the money that had just been earned.

He killed the lights on the bike and rode quietly between the main service blocks, which offered a smorgasbord of American bad taste, and sterile-looking accommodation. He was riding on a footpath, but that was of no consequence. If he was stopped, he would limp and say he was trying to get as close to the entrance of burger-central as he could. But he wasn't, so he passed the indecently lit buildings and made instinctively for some trees on the far side of a gravel path.

The trees bordered a field in which wheat was growing. The flag-leaves were visible and Sam knew the farmer would not be paying much attention here for another couple of months. He would set up his camp, unseen and undisturbed on the far side of some large oaks. No tent tonight. A simple ground sheet and a sleeping bag would suffice. When in stealth mode he preferred to be able to make his camp in less than five minutes. If there was any chance of being seen he would not use the stove. It was not ideal arriving after dark but he had done it many times before.

He secured everything out of sight and casually sauntered back along the lane to the service station. In the gents, he used the toilet, then spread his soap, hotel-sized bottle of shampoo and micro-pore towel out beside one of the counter-sunk basins. He set about washing himself the best he could. There were bits of him that it would not be decent to wash in a public facility, but Sam was not a shy man and he usually managed to get himself satisfactorily cleaned without upsetting too many people. There was a hand-dryer that made a noise like a rocket and Sam tried drying his hair under it. He made two young men smile when they came in and found him standing in his underwear on one leg drying his left foot.

"Evening," said Sam, and returned their smiles. They emptied their bladders then left without washing their hands, to find Security.

Supper was a coffee, a pot of instant noodles and two bananas he bought from the shop in the service station. He felt he owed them that.

The constant background throb of urban life did nothing to spoil Sam's night. When his children had been small, his life had felt like an experiment in sleep deprivation. He believed that the parents of new-born babies were the nearest thing in his world to zombies. But since then, sleep had come easily to him.

In the morning, he ran repeatedly up and down the lane behind the service station. He saw the sun come up over the wheat field and briefly glimpsed a flash of the brilliant turquoise of a kingfisher.

Afterwards, he had his coffee with his back against a tree. In the service station toilet, he was at ease, confident that there would have been a shift change since his brief conversation with last night's security man. Then he was back on the M25, riding clockwise against the growing early morning rush of people doing their thing in their metal boxes of choice.

8

The customs man took Rohan's passport as if it had been soaked in something leaking from a garbage bag. He glanced through it in a way that would have made rudimentary seem interminably long and gave a blank page a brutal 'kerchock' with a wooden-handled stamp. Rohan was through. The customs man had just made the equivalent of two months' salary. This would almost be enough to convince the headmaster at the school he wanted his ten-year-old daughter to attend, that her presence there was a good thing. Almost, but not quite.

The walkway was quiet. Opposite gate number 4 was a kiosk which served sweet instant coffee. Next to that was the door to the men's toilet. A uniformed attendant stood in the door waiting for the next foreigner to enter. When one did, the attendant would run a basin of water for the man to wash his post-peeing hands in. When the gentleman was unable to find a paper towel, the attendant would thoughtfully open a cupboard in the wall and offer a handful from the pile he had earlier hidden. The gentleman would be overcome with gratitude at the gesture and give the contents of his wallet to the attendant. Surprisingly, it worked on about one out of five occasions.

The English rarely gave him anything but the Americans almost always did. Russians tend to scowl at him, then give him a day's wages. Any manual job which brought an employee into such close contact with tourists was highly prized. The attendant earned approximately twice as much as his brother, who was a maths teacher at a private school in Colombo. He knew small talk in fourteen languages and would never willingly give up his job as a toilet attendant. Rohan saw it all.

The last time Rohan had seen a coffee kiosk like this had been at an uncle's funeral. He imagined that when he returned to Sri Lanka a wealthy man he would be able to afford a kiosk coffee any time he wanted. He might even have a machine installed in the kitchen of the two-storey house he would build. But for now, he would be satisfied to look on with respect at those white people who could afford such a liquid status symbol.

Security at the gate was brief and functional. He was asked to remove his belt and shoes. Nobody explained why and when he tried to hand his shoes to the uniformed lady she cut him down with a look that was sharper than his father's filleting knife. Then he joined a queue which filed past two smiling attendants dressed in peacock-coloured saris. One of them tore off a part of his boarding card and handed back what was left. This made Rohan relax slightly. It was the first thing tonight that was familiar to him. He had done it a hundred times at his local cinema.

The glass-walled room was filling up with passengers. Some were resting their heads on the shoulders of the people they were with. There were white people going home after having laid on a beach for two weeks. Some were brown, others red. None were white. Some had got bad sun burn that made their skin flake off. Rohan wondered why anyone rich enough to afford a kiosk coffee could not afford sunblock.

There were groups of young Sri Lankan girls with an up-country shyness about them and Tamil girls from the north who avoided eye contact. Sri Lankan men in suits talked noisily on mobile phones. An elderly white man with long hair read a book and laughed out loud. People near him started slowly moving away. Rohan saw a Sri Lankan boy about his own age with an empty seat next to him. As he sat down the boy looked away.

"*Kohomeda*?"

The boy ignored him.

"*Machung*?"

The boy's silence was eloquent. Rohan guessed he was either deaf or, more likely, doing the same trick he was. They would both have been told not to speak to anyone. Same rules, different interpretation. So they sat together in a common bubble of fear and excitement and sadness... and communicated none of this to each other. They missed a chance.

Eventually instructions came over an unseen loudspeaker, first in Sinhala and then in English. Rohan joined the queue of people waiting at a door which led down a sloping corridor to another door where two more smiling people, a man and a woman, stood greeting everyone. Rohan was surprised when the man took what was left of his ticket, glanced at it and welcomed him by his new name. He indicated Rohan should follow the man in front of him through a small pantry. Then he turned right and stared in amazement at what he realised, for the first time, was the aircraft.

A lady in a peacock-patterned sari stepped from between the seats ahead of him and asked to see his boarding card. If Rohan had entertained the idea that the lady had singled him out because she admired him in some small way he would have been mistaken. Seven years in the job had taught her that if she wanted the flight to leave on time, seating those walking towards her with wide eyes and open mouths should be her priority. Rohan was as wide eyed and open-mouthed as anyone she had seen in a long time.

When she had started the job, it used to trouble her to see such naïve youngsters leaving, unaccompanied, for places they knew nothing about. She feared for their futures and wondered what toilets they would end up cleaning. Now she didn't care. She just wanted them to sit down and be quiet and, if possible, not to get too drunk.

Rohan's seat was the middle one of three on his left. The lady took his bag and put it in a cupboard above his head then, gently, with her hand on his shoulder, guided him to his seat. In a culture where open intimacy is forbidden, and every corner has a tut-tutting aunty peering around, secret touches take on a significance they don't have in the West. Rohan looked directly into her eyes. But in a moment, so brief that it occurred between racing heartbeats, she was gone.

The seat next to the aisle, was taken by a young Tamil girl. She had a gold ring through her nose. The girls in Rohan's village thought nose jewellery was beneath them. The yellow embroidery on the edges of her purple shawl was coming loose, and byssus threads stood out like flags of poverty and defeat. If Rohan wanted to see a shawl without loose threads he would have had to look forward. About twenty seats forward, in another world.

A small, suited man eventually took the window seat and when the passengers had settled down, the flight attendant and her colleagues told everyone to fasten their seatbelts. Rohan willed her to look at him and rekindle his excitement, but she breezed past and their eyes never kissed.

An amplified voice spoke and the man who had said his name at the door did a small show, waving his hands around in a way that reminded Rohan of his priest giving a benediction. A few minutes later, there was a deafening roar as the plane accelerated forwards. He had not expected this. Was it normal or was he about to die? He didn't breathe from the moment the captain applied full power until the surging, bowel-loosening moment when the aircraft began to rotate. His knuckles were white from gripping the ends of the armrests. He didn't want to be the first to scream.

The bumpy acceleration of the runway turned into the ghostly silken hollowness of the air. He looked at the other passengers and was not surprised to see they also were too embarrassed to scream. When the pain in his lungs reminded him he needed to breathe, he exhaled then sucked air in with a violence that made those around him stare. It was only later when a man's soothing voice came through the speakers that he thought things might actually be OK. Others started unfastening their seat belts and one or two people stood up. They were not rushing anywhere. They were calm. Things were all right after all. It must have been a narrow escape.

Rohan was given a plastic tray containing food with names he recognised but tastes that he didn't. When he finished it, he wanted to ask for more. The Tamil girl next to him quietly pushed her tray towards him. She ate and drank nothing throughout the eight-hour flight to Milan.

He saw a Sri Lankan man in the row in front drinking steadily and achieving a level of inebriation that was normal amongst the fishermen in Rohan's village, but one he had not expected to see on board a flight to Italy. The drunk man pestered the girl sitting next to him and Rohan saw his sophisticated chatter and high-class way of talking were only crude excuses to touch the girl on her shoulder and arm. The girl inched as far from the drunkard as the arm at the side of her chair would allow. After twenty minutes of flirting, the drunk gave up and fell asleep with his head lolling over onto the mortified girl. An attendant noticed the girl's distress and pulled the man back to an upright position and then moved on through the darkness and fuggy warmth of the after-meal cabin.

The man fell back over onto the girl a moment later. This time the girl pushed him away. His head flopped over into the empty aisle. There it stayed until another attendant pushing her aluminium trolley back through the cabin cracked it sharply. Nobody minded and the Tamil girl giggled. The man slept on unaware but, on arrival in Milan, the Italian customs officers would be so alarmed at the incoherent state of the drunken Sri Lankan that they would refuse him entry to their country and put him on the next flight back to Colombo.

Rohan had almost forgotten he was flying when an announcement asked everyone to sit down and fasten their seatbelts. The aircraft began to point downwards. Nobody seemed worried and so neither was Rohan. This sensation carried on for a few minutes. The drunk man was gently pushed upright by the attendant. Rohan wondered if her more caring approach had anything to do with the fact that the cabin was now well lit. The sun shone in through the Rohan's window. He saw the world below him. The mountains were topped with snow. He had never been so excited in his life.

When the aircraft eventually came to a stop he joined everyone else in retrieving their bags from the cupboards above their heads. The drunk did not move. The Tamil girl could not reach her bag and so Rohan passed it to her with a smile. She took it without acknowledgement and made her way forward to the queue that was forming behind a drawn curtain. Rohan followed her.

When the curtain was opened, people began filing forwards and out, past an attendant who thanked the passengers as they left. Rohan didn't understand what he was being thanked for, but it felt good that a fair-skinned man in a suit took the trouble to speak to him. Italy was going to be just fine.

He followed the crowd which walked quickly through corridors and tunnels. At last they came to a hall where there was a row of desks behind each of which were uniformed men and women. A line of people slowly snaked their way to the front. Rohan saw that as the passengers were called forward, one at a time, they showed the uniformed person their passports. Some were asked questions but most quickly received a rubber 'chock' in their passports and moved on. When it was Rohan's turn, he nervously offered his passport to the man. The customs officer had the hairiest hands Rohan had ever seen. They were also the cleanest. His nails were cut as smooth as an office girl's and they were white at the tips like a Burgher's. He was still studying the hands when they unexpectedly returned his passport and the man turned his attention to the person behind. And, just like that, he was through. He was in Italy. Bella.

Rohan imagined that one day he too would have a job like the Italian customs man. Any job where you could keep your hands so spotless had to be important. And how hard could it be? He would learn Italian and get a job with a uniform where he only had to stamp passports and at the end of the day he could go home in his own car and drink coffee with his wife. His clothes would be unsoiled by sweat and earth and fish scales. The job would be so easy that he would quickly grow fat and make his mother proud. Life would be one long poya day. This was his dream. But, you could drive a bus through the yawning gap between his dream and reality.

Following the flow, he came to a revolving rubber belt. There were bags moving on it and people with metal trolleys waiting. Rohan was surprised there were no men with orange vests and numbers on the back. The porters must all have been busy.

Rohan felt important when he saw Malinda's bag come down a chute onto the belt. He wished his father could see him now.

The next bit was confusing. He took his suitcase and hand luggage and followed a group of people he recognised from the flight. They approached two large openings. Above one was a green sign with some words on it he didn't understand. Above the other was a red sign.

Everybody went under the green board. The corridor zigzagged out of sight. Small groups of men stood behind steel tables that lined the walk. They glared at the passengers as they filed past as if they wanted to start a fight. Rohan had no idea what they were doing but it was intimidating. One man, who looked like a Tamil, had been pulled out of the flow and was being asked questions. He was told to open his bag on a table.

Rohan was fascinated by its contents. It seemed that all his clothing had been used as protective wrapping for bottles of spirits. Rohan recognised the black and silver labels from a very expensive brand of Arrack. The Tamil man looked worried, but the group of men who were going through his bag were smiling at each other. The happier they looked, the more wretched the Tamil man became. Rohan stopped his trolley and tried to join in the happiness of the Italians as they rummaged to the bottom of the man's suitcase. The Italians temporarily brought their glee-fest to a halt and, as one, glared at Rohan. The mood had changed. The Tamil man briefly looked relieved that the focus of attention had been diverted. Rohan quickly pushed his trolley away and left the over-emotional gathering behind. And then he was out of the corridor and into a large hall with glass walls down the far side through which he could see Italy. It was beautiful. He was as proud as a young man could be.

Passengers were being met by happy family members or by people with little plastic boards with names written on them. None of these names looked anything like Malinda Hettiarachchi and there was no smiling family there to greet him. Rohan didn't know what to do next. Nobody had gone through this bit. All his attention had been focused on getting to where he was right now. Italy had been the only destination and now he had arrived he was lost.

It was at this point that a small man with a denim cap and very dark round sunglasses walked closely past Rohan. He didn't slow down or change direction, but as he was at his closest he said in Sinhala, through lips that barely moved, "Malinda, follow me. Don't talk."

The small man walked easily and smoothly at the pace of the crowd. Rohan quickly pushed his trolley and tried to keep up. They walked the length of the hall to an exit where a few people stood around smoking cigarettes. Then the small man was gone. Their walk had been carefully watched by an Asian man across a road, by the entrance to a car park. He knew Rohan would look for the small man. And he knew that it was only a matter of time before the boy would notice him standing there. When he did, the man would give a quick gesture with his right hand which the boy would understand meant he had to come to him.

Rohan looked. The gesture was given and Rohan crossed the road. This was not the first time such a scene had been played out. The Asian man had a shiny leather coat on and a cigarette between his lips. He too wore sunglasses, which impressed Rohan. He looked at the cigarette and wondered if he might start smoking.

The leather-coated man opened the rear, right-hand door of a small red car and beckoned Rohan in. He lifted Malinda's bag into the boot and slammed it shut. He threw the sports bag onto Rohan's lap and got into the front passenger seat which, Rohan realised with a shock, was on the wrong side. There was a driver who looked Italian and said nothing. Rohan started to talk, but the driver caught his attention in the rear-view mirror and slowly brought a black leather-gloved finger to his lips.

9

Even before the engine on Sam's bike was properly warmed up, he saw a sign for the M2 to the Eurotunnel and, without a moment's hesitation, took it. He remembered one of his favourite sayings about travel: 'When there is a fork in the road, take it'. Sam wished he could have said something so utterly profound.

In the past, poor people travelled to get to war and, otherwise, probably didn't venture far from home. Wealthy people travelled the length and breadth of their imaginations in coaches and carriages fit for royalty. In fact, they often *were* royalty. Quality was built into whatever mode of transport they used. Romance and panache were de-facto inclusions in any journey a lady or a gentleman might make.

Then poor people decided they wanted to go places and, for the first time, cost was a consideration. This resulted in the mass transport systems Sam was so familiar with. Efficiency necessarily displaced grandeur.

The worm-hole under the English Channel, made to connect the land masses of England and France, was brutal in its single-minded functional ugliness. There is more imagination in the National Anthem, more romance in a used car lot. But the Eurotunnel is nothing if not efficient.

The human population of the island that Sam called home was roughly nine thousand. He probably knew a couple of hundred of those. There were entire island communities and villages he had never been to nor met anyone from. The Eurotunnel carried a daily average of around six times the entire population of Skye. No room there for romance and very little space for imagination. The terminal was just a giant car park with a hole at one end of it that people, cars, lorries, trains, and Sam were poured down.

After just over half an hour of electric light, the French sun shone through the windows. The warmth of it on Sam's face made his skin tighten. Outside, everything looked like England, but the experience was in reverse. It felt like a regurgitation. All the paltry romance a single British man in his mid-50s was capable of feeling returned to him the instant he fired up his bike and saw the concrete and tarmac of the terminal shrivel to nothing in his mirrors.

It was midday and the sun at its zenith. His shadow was directly beneath him as the rays stuck to his sides like molten wax from a burning candle. He filled the tank with cheap French petrol and himself with a rather good French coffee. Normally he would have brewed his own, but he was keen to keep moving and uncharacteristically decided he might as well try their version of French blend.

He rode on motorways with no soul. They were predictably grey and grimy, but the fact that it was a foreign grey gave the dirt a slightly exotic hue. England did grime so well. Anything else was an improvement.

By the time he reached the northern outskirts of Riems, the A26 morphed into the A4 and a toll had to be paid to facilitate the morphing. The A4 ran from Paris to Strasbourg. Sam took the road in the opposite direction to a sign that pointed to Disneyland. He passed through rolling countryside where another sign told him that Strasbourg was three hundred and fifty kilometres ahead. Another four hours of riding, so he should arrive just before sunset. He disliked turning up in large, unknown cities after dark. It made the task of finding somewhere to sleep so much more difficult. An element of chance was introduced, and chance was not desirable when stealth camping. When he had bought his tent, he made sure that it was low profile and dull green in colour. He removed all the labels and reflective tags that the manufacturers seemed so proud of.

Sam was good at many things, but he was brilliant at blending in. If he was in the middle of nowhere, he chose a site that gave him the best view of the sunrise. When he was in a built-up area, he liked to do a recce without attracting too much attention. He preferred places on higher ground above any obvious hot spots. People so rarely looked up. Once he was satisfied with a site, he would hang around doing nothing whatsoever to attract attention and, fifteen minutes before darkness, he would strike out for his pitch. He could make his camp in five minutes with no need to use any give-away lights. Then as the darkness covered him in its cloak of invisibility, he was all set. The early morning light was no concern to him because he was gone by the time most city dwellers put a foot over their thresholds.

This evening Sam saw a wooded area to north of the A4, about twenty kilometres before Strasbourg. It looked promising. He took the exit to his right and swept back over the road finding himself in an agricultural area of fields and foliage and low buildings. There were some thick, broad-leafed trees that might conceal him from any night-time traffic, but they were a little too close to the road. He rode on, looking for the perfect spot. Then he saw it. A minute after passing a small, empty, chocolate-box cottage, there was a turn to the left which went into woodland thick enough to stop any light coming through from the other side. The path looked unused. No signs of vehicles, bicycles or booted feet. No signs of anything. The lack of signs was a good sign.

Sam knew with certainty that he could have an undisturbed night in the cocoon of this dense woodland. He rode on until he came to a village where he stocked up on a few essentials. Fruit and a salami would be good for tonight and water for his coffee in the morning. There would be no need for any night-time cooking.

If it was ever necessary, he could pack his tent and be away in two and a half minutes. Usually it took even the most psychopathic farmer at least that long to work himself into a frenzy. And if one ever turned up, Sam would be gone before the crimson flush from his bulging neck even reached his ears. Bye-bye.

The night was predictably uneventful. For his morning run he continued down the deserted path where the ground was soft and cool. The track disappeared in places and was blocked in others by fallen trees and branches. He climbed over these or took a detour around them into the woodland where the undergrowth was stunted by the dark. After twenty minutes, quite suddenly, he came out of the other side of the woodland and saw an opening vista of treeless fields.

The sun was barely up but he didn't want to be seen, so he headed back to his camp. He was riding down the road half an hour later and nobody had noticed the happy man quietly sliding out from his wooded lair. If he had been spotted, and someone had gone to see what he had been up to, other than some bent grass and a small clump of wet coffee grounds, they would have struggled to find anything. Precisely as it should be.

The atlas had told Sam that he could head south into Switzerland and then carry on tumbling down the continent into Milan. It would be possible in a day. But it also showed if he turned left at Basle he could carry on to Austria and Innsbruck. That sounded like a much better route and one that could only be suggested by looking at the world on a scale used in a child's school atlas. Sam was enjoying himself too much to think of reaching his destination yet. Innsbruck would do as an attractive diversion.

A gently-curving, four-lane motorway took him through the centre of Strasbourg. He rode past parks and railway lines and immaculate cemeteries that bore hallmarks of obsessive military precision. They were beautiful. An expression of art in death. Sam, though, would not be seen dead buried in a place like that. He would rather die in the hills at the back end of summer when the vegetation was thick and strong and would hide him until the icy blasts of winter killed it back. He would be halfway towards being recycled when walkers found him the following spring. And what was left of him by then, they might just as well chuck away. The only downside was that he disliked the idea of spoiling someone's day out on the hills. He could appreciate how finding his remains would take the edge off their morning.

The traffic was building up on the opposite carriageway as he passed through Strasbourg and Sam was as relaxed as a man could be. The airflow through his helmet was cool and refreshing and the engine sounded sweet between his knees. There were two new countries to ride through before he found a place to sleep tonight. How much better could a man's life get?

Then, out of the blue, the thought hit him that he missed his wife. Where the heck had that one come from?

In the six years since their bubble of union had divided into two separate, shimmering, delicate spheres, they had not bumped into each other. If they had, both might have burst. He had no idea where his old partner was but was pretty sure she wasn't travelling down the A35 between Strasbourg and Basle. So how had she entered his head? And, now that she was there, why did he miss her? This could take the rest of the morning to sort out. But it was all part of the joy of being alone on the road. His imagination was his responsibility and there was no higher being on his radar to answer to.

Maybe there was a void in his head that memories of his wife had somehow settled in? Was it the onset of Alzheimer's leaving ex-wife-shaped fissures as it started to pull apart the tissues of his brain? What a miserable end to a life Alzheimer's was. If it ever happened to him, would he know in time to orchestrate an alternative end-game?

How long would it be before the Co-op started offering Dignitas-type packages and aging Co-op customers would be seen with toothless wicked grins, waving Dignitas coupons at their kids saying, "Don't worry about us, we've got everything sorted." He briefly wondered about stopping off at Lake Zurich to see if he could find any Dignitas urns bobbing around.

He was enjoying his mental wanderings but was aware that he was in danger of not sorting out this business with his wife. So he reigned his mind back to the job at hand, which was to find out why he missed her. What exactly was it he missed? Their separation had silenced the constant background noise to Sam's life. The source of the noise had gone forever. His life had not significantly improved, although, initially, he had profoundly appreciated the quietness. He had left his wife in search of a more peaceful existence. A life that should have been more rewarding and less stressful. But had he achieved that? Probably not.

What, then, had been the source of the constant irritation he had felt in the later years? Why had he wanted to leave her after bringing up two children and spending over 25 years together? When he had a stone in his running shoe he took the stone out. He didn't throw the shoe away. Had he been hasty in walking away? Could some mental adjustments on his part have helped bring them back together, if not as loving, then at least as caring partners? What use had he made of his new freedom that he couldn't have done with his wife still there?

She never fussed when he took off and was happy so long as he told her when he would be getting back. He remembered now that he had even been irritated by the fact that she wanted to know roughly what day he would be returning. It occurred to him it wasn't such an unreasonable request to make of a partner. Were all the other irritations so critical when looked at from her point of view? It was a frightening thought. At the time, he never considered he was the problem. But, looking back, he could see it was a view others might justifiably take. His experience of the world depended on how he reacted to a situation. And, on reflection, the evidence seemed to show that he might have reacted unwisely. Maybe he had been worn down by the constant attrition of his domestic circumstances, but he knew that was no excuse. It just meant he had been reacting badly for a long time.

He supposed the reason he missed his wife was because somewhere, deep in his own biology, he had known all along that he was at fault.

It was good to put thoughts in order. Sam wanted a simple life. He felt it was the ultimate achievement to be satisfied owning nothing. He knew he would never get there, but he was aware that possessions brought responsibility. They required constant maintenance otherwise they became damaged and useless. How much easier would a natural life be? Only in a natural life is decay acceptable.

Basle came up before he had thought about lunch so he pressed on to Lake Zurich. The roads were beautiful and the traffic none too bad.

The miles, or kilometres, flew by without being in any way demanding, so he gave full reign to his wandering mind. Days like this were not common and he made the most of it. The land he was travelling through was like a giant park. Postman Pat vistas and blue postcard skies with fluffy white clouds here and there.

When Lake Zurich came into view, it looked like a stretched version of the Lake District. Everywhere was Ambleside. Quaint, but uninspiring buildings with gabled roofs and walker-friendly paths beside the lake. The sun was high overhead and the grassy banks of the lake demanded that he sat and enjoyed the view. It would almost have been rude not to.

He bought some crusty, knotted bread, a few slices of a pale meat that was probably unethically produced, a cooked sausage that was satisfyingly gnarly and, of course, a block of cheese. With a large apple to finish, it was as much food as he had played with in a long time. He was looking forward to it with the appetite of a man who had dodged breakfast and ridden two hundred and fifty kilometres on no more than a cup of coffee.

He was spoilt with possible places to pull in. Experience had taught him that carrying on looking for that perfect spot was a folly. In the past when he had spotted a good place to stop, on seeing the road ahead, he had always carried on. Often into a long urban landscape that offered little in terms of beauty or convenience. But over the years he had learned to pass the first suitable place and stop at the second. It usually worked out OK. This time the second was a small gravel car park devoid of vehicles. May was still a relatively quiet time of the year.

His uncharacteristically large lunch was uninterrupted. He liked this place. The world ignored him, which was the relationship he most wanted with it. The fewer people he saw, the less contact he had with the difficult ones. He didn't read the news. It tended to be nothing but stories about catastrophically broken individuals that he didn't need to know about.

After lying on the grass for half an hour, he decided to go for a quick swim. It was enjoyable and had the added benefit of giving him a thorough wash.

Later, when his body had dried in the afternoon sun, he decided to try his luck with the rod. He looked at the surface of the lake, but it gave no clues. He was fishing blind and decided on a gaudy yellow lure with sets of treble-hooks trailing from its belly and tail. If anything took it there was a good chance it would stay on. He chose not to use a wire trace as his experience with trout in the Highlands made it unnecessary. But who knew what was lurking in here? The water would be warming up by now and the fish might already be feeding hard, so a lure was a good choice. The chance of a fish swallowing it deeply was small, which meant if he did get something, he should be able to unhook it and release it unharmed.

The joy of casting a line in an unknown water is one of the greatest feelings for an angler. Sam took on board every detail of information the water offered whilst setting up the tackle. Then planting his feet firmly and smoothly uncoiling all the wound-up tension in his core muscles, he swung the tip of the rod in a long accelerating arc directly overhead. He released the line at exactly the right moment and watched the lure fly in a looping curve and land in the calm, dark water with a minimal splash. Sam had done it thousands of times and every time was special. Was there a predator beneath the surface? The hinged lure morphed into a distressed fish as he snapped the bail-arm on and wound the reel to bring it home.

Fishing for Sam was poetry and, like poetry, it had the ability to take his breath away. From adolescence onwards, people from his side of the world rarely felt the contentment he was feeling now. The power of that feeling, the overwhelmingly vital innocence and simplicity of it, changed the way a man looked at life. It is doubtful that anyone under the addictive influence of such blissful contentment could knowingly go out and start a war. Start a war? It is doubtful that, paralysed as he was by such ephemeral joy, Sam could even make a sandwich. Drop fishing rods, not bombs.

The fact that the lure returned to the rod untroubled by the snapping jaws of some monster of the lake made no difference. After a few more casts to get the feel of the lure's weight, he could drop it within a ripple of where he wanted. His accuracy came from endless days of practice on highland rivers where a bowhair too far would send the lure onto the far bank to be lost in the vegetation. A costly waste but, worse than that, an unwelcome trinket of barbed debris in an otherwise pristine environment. Sam never left broken lines by the lochs or rivers. He never left anything other than the obvious, squelchy, welly-shaped footprints and an occasional whoop of delight ringing through the glen.

From his spot on the shore, Sam methodically fished the area in front of him, fanning out an arc from right to left. On the fourth cast, just as he started to retrieve the lure, something took it. It was a hard take. No sucking and teasing the bait. Just a hammering strike that bent the end of the rod. Sam struck, but the violence of the take meant it wasn't necessary. Whatever was out there was already hooked securely.

The fish went deep and fast, directly away from him. He quickly adjusted the drag on the line. He firmly pulled the rod to his left, parallel with the ground, and gently wound the line in on the reel. The fish's head was turned and, reluctantly coming towards him. Slowly and carefully Sam played it. When it headed back out to deeper waters swimming strongly away, Sam let it. He applied just enough pressure on the line to keep it tight as the fish swung about on the end, like a kite dancing in a storm. Slowly the distance between the fish and Sam reduced. The fish was tired but, as the water got shallower, its vigour returned. Sam knew this was the most critical time. He would not rush it. On the contrary, he would be happy for it to have lasted forever.

Then he saw it. A long, slim, blunt-nosed torpedo. Dark green, streaked with yellow flecks as it flashed on its side. A pike of about three pounds… and perfect in every way. He was lucky to have landed it without a trace. A pike's teeth are numerous and razor sharp and could easily have cut the line.

Sam didn't have the luxury of an unhooking mat and, without a landing net, he decided to try and unhook the fish in the water to minimise any distress. Keeping the line tight, he grabbed it behind the head and, seeing that the hooks were near the front of its mouth, slid a couple of fingers under the impressive gill covers and gently took control of the fish. When fishing, Sam always tucked an old pair of dental pliers in his back pocket. They were beautifully made with a quality and precision that commercially available angling tools didn't share. The fish was quiet once Sam lifted its head and, with the pliers in his right hand, he quickly twisted the hooks loose. First the back ones and then the front.

After taking a moment to enjoy the beauty of the animal, Sam waded out until the depth was enough for the fish to be comfortably covered. He gently held onto its tail and pointed it out to the deeper water. Then he did nothing. Just patiently waited for the gills to start working and the lactic acid in the pike's muscles to dissipate. Once the gill covers were moving fluidly and regularly and the fish was comfortably able to stay the right side up, Sam released the tail and it swiftly swam out into the lake to be instantly lost in the magic of its underwater world.

What a fantastic day. But he realised he was on the wrong side of Lake Zurich to get to Innsbruck quickly and anyway, the mountains above him looked inviting. So, he decided to nap on the shore then head up into them for what he hoped would be a cracking sunset over the lake. He struck out just after four o'clock and headed upwards on whichever roads pointed in the right direction on the slopes of the Pfannenstiel.

He was impressed by the sight of a canyon that wound its way back down to the lake. The scenery was spectacular and primitive. Unspoilt but well-tended in a way that only the Swiss are able to pull off. It would require investigating later. But for now, Sam was happy to lose himself in the landscape. There were countless small roads and paths and very little housing.

The fields between the woods seemed to be mostly crops. Crops needed less attention from the farmer than livestock, which meant he was less likely to be disturbed. After about half an hour of gentle cruising, he spotted a suitable target. A small path went uphill from an already narrow road. The path was ungated and there was no sign of anyone around. It was early evening and the walkers and tourists from earlier in the day had gone down to their hotels and holiday homes beside the lake.

Sam pushed his bike off the path where it was quickly lost from sight in the thick of the trees. He was hidden well before dark so, after he had put up his tent, he thought it an acceptable risk to light the stove and cook a pan of noodles. He added what was left of the sausage and meat from lunch, a couple of tomatoes and a generous pinch of pepper. When the simple meal was ready, he took it back to the edge of the woods and sat on the grass overlooking the lake far below him. The pike was in there. Sam wondered if it remembered anything at all about what had happened to it earlier in the day. Do fish remember like that? Sam would remember the fish and the part it took in his perfect day for the rest of his life. Simple things make the best memories. He went to bed early and dreamt of fish and asparagus.

In the morning, the good feelings from the day before had not left him. He had his coffee and skipped breakfast. It was still early when he found the gorge he had seen the day before and he emerged from his bike gear like a mayfly from its pupa and slipped his running kit on. He didn't like leaving things on the bike, but it was Switzerland and they had a reputation to maintain, so he risked it and set off down the trail. The path was well-made and well-used. It hugged the banks of a river, which looked perfect for trout. There were fire pits beside the path. Sam guessed it would soon be busy. The woodland was a modern-day primeval rainforest.

Despite all the pampering around the path, a recent landslip and huge glacial erratics showed that it remained untamed. There was a cave that looked like a dragon should live in it and steps built into the trail which he ran down. Small steps and a high cadence ensured he would run surefooted and very rarely be caught out by uneven surfaces or hidden obstacles. After about three quarters of an hour, when a change in gradient suggested he was getting close to the bottom, he turned around and effortlessly ran back up. He wasn't surprised to see that his bike remained untouched. He quickly bathed in the stunningly cold water of the river and felt invigorated and ready for anything the day might bring.

His atlas had showed him that after Innsbruck, which he should reach by midday, he would have to head south through Trento and Verona, then on to Milan. He had mixed feelings about getting there because then he would have to turn around and head back home. Any anger about finding the olive stone had disappeared long ago. But he would still return it, just to give the journey a minor meaning beyond pointless hedonism.

A purpose was important to Sam. It was the starting point of all good things.

10

The drive from the airport was as smooth as an oily sea but Rohan's discomfort was growing. He was unfamiliar with the concept of an uncomfortable silence. In his life, if there was something to say, he said it. If not, he stayed quiet. He couldn't imagine any other way to behave. But now, he badly wanted the two men in the front to speak. To tell him a bit about Italy maybe, or explain what it was he should be doing next. He was giddy with curiosity. But each time he started to speak, the man in the leather coat would half turn in his seat and raise the palm of his right hand in Rohan's direction, like a policeman stopping oncoming traffic. After a few attempts, Rohan stayed quiet. The quietness outside amplified the silence inside the car.

It was mid-morning and the sky was a dry, powdery blue. The open ground around the airport began to close in and was slowly lost to buildings. Most were box-like, with many windows, few of which were open. Between the buildings were parks, like the ones he had seen in Colombo. People walking on the streets and pavements looked unhurried and some walked with dogs on ropes. At first Rohan thought they must be blind, but then realised there were too many of them. The only time he had seen a dog on a rope before was when the dog doctor came to the shop in his village. He would set a table up beneath a coconut tree and all day long the villagers would bring their dogs to see him. He would stick his long needle into the animals and make them squeal. Then he would put a blue plastic collar round their necks and give the man or woman on the other end of the rope a piece of paper.

Small children would try and catch the dogs to cut the blue collars off and put them on their own necks. When they succeeded, they would run about laughing and pretending to bark. But Italy was different. There was no dog doctor and no coconut trees. These people were walking with their dogs for no reason. What a strange thing to do.

Rohan saw a woman waiting patiently whilst her dog squatted in the middle of the pavement. People walked around her and the dog. When the woman reached into her handbag and pulled out a plastic bag and bent down towards what the dog had deposited, Rohan looked away in horror. He did not want to see what she was going to do. He gagged. His life so far had not prepared him for anything so depraved. If someone tried to do this in his village, there was a good chance they would be tied to a lamp-post and beaten with sticks. And quite rightly so. The men in the front seats must not have noticed because their expressions never changed.

In a small street between two anonymous-looking buildings the driver pulled to a stop in a space between parked cars. He said something which Rohan didn't understand. The man in the leather coat dramatically slapped the top of the plastic lining of his door. He told Rohan they had a flat tyre and asked him to get out and check which one it was.

Rohan was happy they had started talking and quickly put his bag on the middle of the back seat. Both tyres on the near side were OK. He leaned into the open back door and told the men the good news.

He was surprised this seemed to irritate the man in the leather coat, who told him to go back and check the other side. As he walked to the back of the car, his door was suddenly closed and the car shot forward with a squeal from its perfectly inflated tyres. As the car gathered speed, his hand luggage was flung carelessly out of the passenger's window. The red car turned sharply right behind the corner of a building and was gone. Rohan thought it was a game. Anything else was unthinkable. He smiled and waited for the car to reappear from behind with the driver and Leather-coat grinning and laughing at him. He picked his bag up whilst he waited.

Realisation came slowly to him he had been cheated. When he finally accepted it, he felt idiotically helpless and wondered if it was possible to be more alone? He stood there, not daring to look in any direction but up. Upwards he could see the sky and the sun. The same sun that shone down, even now, on his proud father as he baited his hooks. The same sun that dried his sister's school uniform as it hung on a line strung between the corner of his house and a coconut tree beside it. He could be there with his family, so long as he kept looking at the sky. He didn't notice the pedestrians who walked past him or the cars that drove by. He stared at the sky, slowly being blinded. When he finally collapsed, it was late afternoon. If he had been noticed by passers-by, he had been dismissed as yet another crazy immigrant. Rohan had no idea how long he had been there. All he knew was that his family had gone and this strange, lonely country had taken their place.

As the afternoon sun dropped lower in the sky and his eyesight slowly recovered, he wept and cursed his luck in fisherman's filth. He sat on a small wall beside the road and gathered what remained of his shredded thoughts. His father had always taught him that in dangerous times he needed a plan. His father had been talking about storms at sea and being a long way from the shore in a small fragile boat. But a plan seemed like a good idea here on the pavement in the suburbs of Milan. So Rohan sat and he thought.

The first thing he needed was water. The sun was not as hot as in his village, but the air here was dry and that, combined with the after-effects of the flight made his throat so parched he could hardly make a sound. If he could find a shop, he had no money and didn't know what to say. In Sri Lanka it is the act of a devil to refuse a man a drink of water. So even in the hardest droughts, the last well in the village, deep enough to have a remaining drop of water, was made available to everyone. Even though this well was behind the walls of the house of the richest man in the area, a doctor at the Base Hospital, it was free for all to use until the water ran out or the rains started. Water was never owned, it was just stored for you and other people to use. In any Sri Lankan village, more than a dozen people would have offered him a drink by now. If you saw a thirsty person, you gave them a drink.

Italy was very different. He began to walk with no purpose other than finding a drink. After a few minutes, shuffling along with his shoulders dropped and his bag trailing on the pavement behind him, he saw a park to his right. In the park, was a large stone fountain. The water gurgled out of the mouths of stone animals and into a trough that ran around the fountain. From this trough, it cascaded down into a deeper and wider sculpted pool that was contained by a stone wall. Young couples sat on the wall. An old man smoked a cigarette as he read a book. Rohan only saw the water.

He threw himself head-first over the wall. The splash he caused as the algae-green water rose in a frothy plume attracted the attention of the lovers and the smoker. Kisses and cigarettes suddenly became of less interest than the Asian boy doing a header into the fountain. Their interest increased as Rohan remained face-down. He was like a dried-out amphibian that needed to rehydrate through every dusty limp pore in his body and only when he had done so did he feel inclined to take a gulp of air. His metabolism was so slow that oxygen seemed unnecessary. But when he did come up, he felt rejuvenated. Born again. He was no longer a lost innocent.

The water had lubricated his thoughts and gave him the ability to make a plan. His mind raced with a new-found vigour. He drank deeply from the upper trough of the fountain, ignoring the spectators. His plan was simple. He would survive. If that meant he had to become like Leather-coat, then he would. The hardest part was the thought of letting his mother down. Of becoming the sort of man she had always warned him not to be. But he had a growing belief in himself. He would succeed in Italy. And if that meant doing bad things to achieve success then that would be OK. Rohan was fortunate in belonging to a religion that easily forgave its followers for doing bad things. He could do all his misdemeanours quickly, then do good things to make up for them, for the rest of his life, if necessary. But now, his priority was survival and drinking water from the fountain was an important step towards that.

His father had once been adrift in a boat, lost at sea for six days. His kerosene outboard broke down and the currents off the west coast of Sri Lanka had taken him quickly away towards the Maldives. Within hours, he had lost sight of land. The boy who crewed for him had cried. Laxman felt swamped by a crushing feeling of helplessness and resigned himself to his fate. He felt grief and guilt for his helper but for himself, nothing. There was no food other than a crust of bread left over from their morning meal. It was soggy and salty in the bottom of the boat. But there was enough water. It was over the next days Laxman learned that with water alone they could survive. Food was a luxury, at least for the first few days. But water gave them the vitality to keep poking death away.

The winds changed after three days and blew them back into the embracing shores of mother Lanka. A fisherman repaired their engine and, after a meagre meal, they set off back up the coast towards home. They were almost as good as new. But Laxman made sure his son knew never to do without water. And so he drank his fill and more. His body tingled with thoughts of the challenge that lay ahead.

Rohan had lived with the flow of the ocean since he was born and instinctively knew how to read the waves and the currents. The long shore drift of coarse grainy sand would build up the beach in his village and then take it away again with the changing seasons. When Rohan arrived at a busy road, he read the flow of people as he would the ocean. He knew if he turned to his right he would find the centre of the city. What else he would find there he was unsure, but he hoped to discover someone who spoke his language. His people were naturally generous and he had no doubt that a Sri Lankan, when asked for help, would not refuse. It was their way.

As he walked, he dried out in the early evening sun. The buildings grew and eventually the streets became narrower, tightening in on themselves, like touch-me-nots when brushed against. There were brightly-coloured sunshades above the windows of the shops and cafes. He grabbed half a loaf of bread from an empty table outside a café and quickly stuffed it into his shirt. The waiter saw him but couldn't be bothered doing anything about it. "Bloody immigrants," he thought.

Eventually Rohan came across a huge graveyard. There were thousands of headstones and tombs made of crumbling rock, all above ground. Rohan guessed these were the resting places of very rich and important people. Stone tombs were not welcome in his village. The small graveyard was beside the church and had served the community for as long as anyone could remember. When you had someone to bury, you dug a hole. After a few minutes digging, you would often find another body. So you had to throw the sandy earth back and find a new place to dig. Some lazy people just pulled the old body up and threw it to the side in the bushes that grew thickly there. It was not uncommon to see bones and rotting garments lying on the surface. Nobody minded. You buried your body and piled up the sand neatly into a long pyramid above it. After a few weeks, or months, when the coffin collapsed, the pyramid of sand would cave in. Then you would go and make the sand pile neat again. Very rarely, someone would put a wooden cross at one end of the grave. But mostly, after the second or maybe third time of tending the sand, you forgot about it and left biology to do what it would until the next person came and dug a hole for their body.

It was natural. Things got put back to where they came from. But this place in Milan with all its marble gravestones and elaborately carved boxes above the ground was just selfish. How could you fit any more bodies in there with all that stone around? A graveyard like this would have to keep growing. There could be no end to it until people stopped dying. And by then there would be no room left for the living. It was unnatural. Rohan walked past the graveyard, pensively chewing the last of his bread.

After half an hour, he came to the centre of the city. The setting sun had been cut off abruptly by the tall buildings and the streets cooled quickly in the shade. There was none of the magical mercury light his sister loved so much. In his village, though twilight was brief, it was long enough to see the setting sun extinguished through the coconut trees, reflecting off the ocean and giving a special quality to that time of day.

But if the city evening was robbed of its twilight, the electrical lighting, around the most fabulous building Rohan had ever seen, more than made up for it. There was no doubting it was a railway station, but on a scale and grandeur that dwarfed the Fort Station in Colombo. The white, stone columns grouped together shimmered in a cool blue light. Between them were arches, lit from the cavernous space within. Above the arches was a balcony like the one the Pope came to wave from, lit in turmeric yellow. Above the balcony were windows and carvings and walls that went high up into the night sky. It was breath-taking.

People sat on wide steps surrounding the station. Couples leaned on metal lamp-posts and embraced without shyness. Nothing about what he saw was normal and everything about it was to envy.

To the average Sri Lankan, litter and garbage are invisible. A non-issue. But here, their absence screamed at him. He had never seen such a large area devoid of man-made debris. Suddenly, everything at home seemed dirty and backwards. Being here made him feel important. Italy was washing away the layers of his sun-browned, salty, Sri Lankan skin. And he liked it.

When Rohan's mother needed to remove any tooth-shattering stones that inevitably came with raw, unwashed paddy, she put the rice with a cupful of water, into a nambilia, a notched clay bowl, and swished it around. The action of the swishing would make the stones settle to the bottom of the nambilia from where they could easily be removed. Gravity and the swishing, did that.

If Milan was the clay bowl, and the rag-tag, counterfeit watch-selling, mock-gypsy scam merchants, the stones, then a railway station is the bottom of the bowl where the stones gather. If you wanted to find the red-light district, you generally wouldn't have to look far from the station. The same with drugs. The most popular place to sleep rough? The station. Want to get your pockets picked? Head to the station. Unaware of this, Rohan walked into Milano Centrale.

Everybody a mother would want her destitute son not to meet was gathered there like an unseen reception committee. A wake of human vultures, concentrated at the station by the swishing of the city. As they watched Rohan from the shadows between the columns or studied him nonchalantly over the rim of a cold, paper-cup of coffee, they instantly recognised the pickings were slim. His pockets looked empty. No bulge of tourist euros. No money belt beneath that thin shirt.

The pairs of girls with their cardboard sheets stepped back into the shadows. The man with the plastic bag of postcards lazily turned his gaze back to his magazine. The blockers and the lookouts shook their heads at the team leaders and returned their scrutinising look over Rohan's head and back to the entrances of this surreally beautiful pond of humanity. A woman with failing eyes, dressed in ragged clothing that might once have been 'traditional', in a less fortunate country, approached Rohan for a better look but, unimpressed by what she saw, she too passed him by.

Rohan noticed the people around him were wearing jackets and loose-fitting garments that, were not made of cotton but looked warm. The latent heat taken from his body to dry his shirt had left him chilled. And now the temperature was dropping. Having never experienced cold before, he was clueless how to preserve or pursue heat. Those lost souls around him were gathering in the corners, where chilling winds were excluded by the vagaries of the architecture. They were arranging their bundles of soiled belongings close to them and some were unrolling sleeping bags. These were not the pickpockets and scammers. The pickpockets all had homes to go to. These were the ones abandoned by society. The worst they would do was steal your change from the ticket machine if you were foolish, or just too slow to pick it up from the stainless-steel cups. They offered no threat to Rohan. But they had little in the way of comfort to share.

Rohan was used to sleeping on the floor. It was normal. But he found the thought of sleeping in the dust from other people's feet quite disgusting. He was spared this ordeal by finding two large, flattened cardboard boxes. He grabbed them greedily and hid himself from sight, like a crow with fresh road-kill. He tore open the boxes and lay them on the floor. Inside, they were clean, apart from a greasy stain along one of the folds. He gingerly lay down and watched his new world through carefully half-closed eyes.

Any self-importance Rohan might have felt earlier was deserting him. From his low-level vantage point he saw a middle-aged European man shamelessly wandering from one waste bin to the next, sorting through the contents. Occasionally he would pick something out that took his interest and hold it up to better study it in the yellow light from high above. After one such inspection, he bent his elbow and brought the object of interest closer to his face. Rohan thought it was for a better look. But instead of tilting his head back to peer down his nose critically, he put it into his mouth. He chewed it slowly and deliberately and with obvious pleasure.

"Mother of God, what is this place?" Rohan murmured.

In all his life he had never seen anyone so desperate that they ate from the garbage. Never. He had seen many beggars, but even they frequently had a benefactor who would give them rice and curry on a regular basis. Once, by the graveyard in Borella, Rohan had seen a smart car with blackened windows – it might even have been a Benz – slow down beside a one-legged beggar. The beggar hopped over to the car and, as the window was slowly wound down, took a neatly wrapped rice packet from the occupant. The actions were so smoothly done and without comment from either side that it was obvious this was a frequent occurrence. And Rohan was certain that this beggar, whose only possession was the dirt beneath his fingernails, would never have gone looking through waste bins for food. He would probably rather have jumped in front of a train than eat garbage.

Rohan spent a miserable night. His loneliness chilled him as much as the air. It was worst in the early hours when he was shivering so badly he thought he would die. The only time he had shivered before was from a bone-breaking dengue fever, so he assumed he had caught something and tried to prepare himself for what would inevitably follow. The old lady who had approached him earlier saw his suffering and, shuffling close, threw a grubby, threadbare towel over him. Rohan pulled it tightly around him and eventually managed to stop the chattering of his teeth. But it was impossible to sleep and, by dawn, his head ached, his throat was painfully dry and his eyes felt like they were full of sand.

He was young and the resilience that comes from being tested was nascent. If every existence has a nadir, then this was surely his. He missed his family and the easy, earthy comforts of his simple home so badly.

This was not the Italy that had been painted for him, on the luxuriantly coloured palettes of lies, by the returnees on their infrequent visits back to his village. The truth was that anyone whose family had risked everything to send them abroad owed it to those, who bore the costs of this sacrifice, to succeed. So they played the part, embellished the tiny shards of worth that pierced the glutinous monotony of their impoverished, meaningless lives, and perpetuated the myth that Rohan, his father and a thousand others, had bought into.

Rohan had added his own adolescent flavour to the dreams of others and awakened to find the reality was a nightmare. He was puzzled but for all his youth, understood that the dream had been his own. He owned it, blamed only himself and cursed his failure.

As he trudged past a waste bin, unemptied from the night before, he tried hard not to look but was unable to resist a fleeting glance. On top of the rubbish was an unused envelope in a torn cellophane wrapper. Whoever threw it there must have only wanted the card that came with it. The envelope was of a beautiful, thick, cream paper. He put it in his back pocket. He would use that for a letter to his mother and she would be impressed by its quality and show it to her friends as she went to buy the morning bread at the village shop.

Hanging from a screw in the wall outside a toilet on platform twenty-two was a green, plastic clipboard. On it was a piece of paper which showed the day divided into rows. The top row had a few ticks in boxes and then an illegible, short signature in the last box. The signature and the ticks held no interest for Rohan. The only thing he wanted was the pen tied to a string hanging from the screw. He yanked it. The pen came free and the clipboard only swung on its fastening slightly. By the time it had stopped swinging, Rohan and the pen were gone.

Money was all he could imagine as a panacea for his current woes. With money, he could buy everything he needed. Food, clothing, somewhere to stay and clean himself. They would all be available, for a price. In an unknown country where the generosity of strangers could not be relied upon, the avarice of businessmen invariably could, and it was with thoughts of obtaining money that Rohan went out into the bright morning. He sat down briefly on one of the steps until his eyes got used to the early morning sun. He took the envelope out of his pocket and, with his newly acquired pen, wrote his father's name. Then he wrote the part of the village he was from, which roughly translates as The Beach, then the name of the village and, of course, Sri Lanka. But if you or I looked at it we wouldn't have known that because Rohan wrote it in the script of his mother tongue, Sinhala.

To the untrained eye, Sinhala looks like mice and insects crawling across the page in a beautiful choreographed dance. Sinhala is a phonetic alphabet with more characters than there are cards in a deck. Each character has numerous alternative curls and crosses which the writer skilfully adds to the base letter. To see Sinhala being well written is a wonder to behold, but it gives no clues to the westerner as to its meaning. Other than the fact they both start from the left-hand side of the paper, the similarities between written Sinhala and English are precisely zero. To a Westerner, it might as well be art.

Without writing paper of a quality that would complement that of the envelope, Rohan had nothing more to write, so he carefully folded the envelope and put it back into his trouser pocket. As he did so, his fingertips felt the letter from his imaginary girlfriend. He pulled it out, screwed it into a tight ball and tossed it onto the litter-free plaza. He would take no more lies and cheating. As the sun warmed the blood in his proud Sri Lankan veins, his resolve began to return and, inside him, the Sri Lankan lion roared.

11

The run and the river bath had put Sam in such a vital mood he rode back down the hill towards the lake faster than he should. The problem with starting the day at a pace like that is that it is very difficult to reign progress back down to the more sedate sauntering which he preferred in unknown and beautiful places. His speed wasn't dangerous, and he exercised caution and observed everything. He just did it all so much quicker than usual and, on the winding road to the lake, spent most of it on the edges of his tyres. If the motorway of the previous days had left his tyres looking like those of a tentative learner, these roads were scrubbing off any corners. The rubber beyond the tread was beginning to pill up like wool on a cheap sweater. It seemed to Sam his lips were the only thing stopping his smile from tearing his face in half.

At Innsbruck, he didn't even stop. He got wobbled by a tram line he hadn't noticed because the reflection from a gold-coloured roof momentarily distracted him. The beauty of the mountains rising grandly behind the postcard Austrian city took his breath away. But today was about riding. He filled the bike with fuel when it was needed and kept on moving. He didn't feel hunger on days like this. A slug of water to keep him from getting too dry and stupid, and maybe a coffee or two was all he needed. It is conceivable that Sam and the bike swapped a few molecules with each other. The bike certainly left something of itself in him.

After leaving Innsbruck, he headed south on the E45 over a fantastical concrete bridge. A bungee jumper's paradise. And then, quite unexpectedly, he was on the Brenner Pass. Why it was unexpected he had no idea, but that really was the essence of 'unexpected'. The Brenner Pass is the busiest route across the Alps. Important since Roman times and known amongst alpine motorcyclists as a total pig. One to be avoided. It was a highway. It reminded him of being drunk: the journey there was fun but when he arrived, it was such a hollow destination. Maybe on the way back, Sam thought, he would do the Stelvio which was not that far away. He would get new rubber in Milan, find the Stelvio and then spend a day going back and forth over it. Roads that only allowed him to use the centre of his tyres were only of use for getting to places and, since it was the getting there rather than the arriving that appealed, the Brenner went right into his mental black book.

The scenery was always beautiful, but slightly shy of the perfection he had imagined it would be. Maybe the road just spoiled it. It was becoming predictably boring so, as he saw a sign for Verona ahead, he peeled off, leaving the Romeos and Juliets to play on their balconies in peace. He turned right towards Milan which, by a quick burst of mental arithmetic, he reckoned was only about one hundred and fifty kilometres away.

But it was getting late so after less than half an hour, when he saw Lake Garda to his right, he turned north and started to wander up its beautiful eastern shore. At the south end of the lake, everywhere was built-up – a wonderful mixture of ancient and modern buildings. There were odd signs that meant nothing to him and trees that stood up like lollipops. It was quiet and clean. Time had been taken to make things the way they were – like a Sunday morning version of a Cotswold village, picked up and deposited a couple of days riding closer to the equator. Sam enjoyed passing through it, but there was little opportunity for a stealth camper to make himself at home. Besides, he could see the mountains dominating the horizon to the north, and these called to him like sirens.

He took the opportunity to top up with provisions in a store that didn't know if it was a large corner shop or a small supermarket. But the store didn't care and was filled to overflowing with honest local produce in skins and rinds and jars. It smelled of the earth and olive trees and reeked of bountiful fecundity. Sam bought a bag of delights, some of which he didn't recognise but looked too interesting to leave. He would put them with the pasta he was going to cook tonight. The black haired, middle-aged signora behind the counter smiled at him as she took his euros. She gave him the gift of a smile that he would happily have travelled over the Brenner Pass a hundred times just to see. Money seemed a poor recompense for such a beautiful present. Sam tried to smile in return but, as usual, in the face of such humbling beauty, he felt paralysed and his smile came out lopsided. He turned and left quickly, catching his head on the low beam above the door to the street.

A few kilometres up the shore, the houses thinned out and the land to the right of the road became steeper as it climbed in sweeping exponential curves to the peaks far above. He took a winding single track that disappeared upwards. The abscissa was short but, boy, was that ordinate, a zigzagged road to heaven?

When he felt sufficiently alone, he pulled off the gravel-strewn road on the crest of an undulation. There were trees and rocks and the most wonderful panoramic view of the lake a man could imagine. The largest lake in Italy was spread before him in an exclusive private viewing. If the sirens came out from the woods and started pole-dancing on the trees in front of him, it couldn't have made anything any better. In fact, they just might have got in the way of the view.

Sam pulled his bike out of sight and spread the flysheet of his tent behind a large boulder. He cooked his meal in the fading evening light without a care in the world. It was a perfect place and the food, interesting. There were a couple of ingredients he really didn't know what to do with. The first was called 'O pere e 'o musso' and seemed to be chewy pieces of something dressed with olives and salt and lemon. It went in with the pasta. The second was a tub of something called Sanguinaccio. It didn't go in. The thought of eating it reminded him of something a tall American supermodel once supposedly said of Bovril.

Something along the lines of her not knowing whether to eat it or clean her shoes with it. This was not very bright as she was being paid to advertise it at the time. Anyway, it was apt. In the end, Sam emptied the chocolaty red contents of the tub into a hole he dug, then put the empty container into a paper bag in which he collected his rubbish.

Sanguinaccio? Sam suspected it was a little too foreign for him and it would be best used for fertilizing the trees of the Province of Verona from where it probably came. Earth to earth, dust to dust and all that. Just so long as it bypassed his corporeal property on the way.

It was nearly nine o'clock before the sun finally fell behind the mountains in a citrus burst of pinks and reds and fiery oranges. Not for the first time, Sam found it hard to believe he was alone to witness this magical and dramatic death of a day. It perplexed him to think there were people in all those houses by the shore below, watching the Italian equivalent of Coronation Street instead of getting their saggy rear-ends up the hill to get a life enhancing dose of the splendour of the world they lived in. Television, he thought? Satan's lantern more like. There were probably adverts being shown on it right now, extolling the virtues of Sanguinaccio.

He watched darkness descend like ink spreading on blotting paper. He listened to his own breathing as the insects of the night came out to play. For a man who was used to straight-lining emotionally, he was doing none too shabbily. More than two years without a drink and he was perfectly serene.

There was a time for Sam when contentment only came two thirds of the way down a bottle of whisky. But it was fleeting because, when he reached that level, the contentment somehow slipped from his lips and sank to the bottom of the bottle. He would chase it, but never find it. So, he would open a second bottle and recommence his pursuit of the genie of contentment, which, as every alcoholic knows, lives within the amber 'water of life' in every bottle. But that one would slip away too. And then he would sleep for two days whilst a part of him died forever and the genies would gather in his flat and broken dreams to mock him and laugh at his foolishness.

It was running that helped him cut loose from the bottle genies. He very slowly came to realise that he enjoyed his time running more than his time drinking. The two became increasingly incompatible. If he drank, he couldn't run and if he ran, he didn't want to drink quite so badly.

When the craving for alcohol came upon him, often at the strangest of times, he would put on his running shoes and head out the door. It didn't matter what time of day or night it was. It didn't matter if there was six inches of snow on the ground or it was blowing a big booming winter hoolie, he would be out the door and into his stride. The craving only ever lasted for three minutes. Once he started running and things began flowing, the desire to drink slipped away. The desire to feel the stones beneath the soles of his trainers and the muscles in his body moving freely, the way they were made to, was more powerful. So he ran until one day he told himself that he wouldn't drink again. And he hadn't so far. Part of him was frightened that if he ever stopped running he might get the craving again and not be strong enough to beat it without the help of his own momentum propelling him away from the danger.

Sam was awakened just before 6 A.M. by a gentle drizzle on his face. It was light already and, feeling like a very modern mummy in nylon, he unwrapped himself and tied one side of the fly-sheet over the handlebars and top box. He pulled the opposite side away from the bike and pinned it to the ground with aluminium pegs that spiralled round a hollow middle, like a decent corkscrew.

The fly-sheet formed a waterproof cover underneath which he could go about making his morning coffee. The ground was wet, so he took his boxers off and sat there quite happily naked. He drank his coffee where he had watched the sun go down the night before. Sam couldn't remember a time he had taken a naked coffee al fresco, but he did make a mental note that he might be enjoying it a wee bit too much. It felt, predictably, liberating.

The road beyond looked inviting and mysterious in the tripe-grey morning. It deserved to be run, so he slipped on his shoes and socks and, with barely a moment's hesitation, set off running. Naked.

Things flapped around a bit more than he was used to and the vulnerability he felt was unnerving to begin with. After a few minutes, he became more comfortable and experimented with his stride and the swinging of his arms to try and make the slap, slap of his penis on his thighs more controllable. The road continued to cross the hill in zigzags, but it seemed that the steep climbing had finished and he was running up and down topographical folds but overall, staying roughly level. The trees were thickest in the bottom of the folds and thinned out towards the tops.

It was on the fourth or fifth of these folds that he heard a bell. Then he heard more… and round the next zig the road was filled with goats. The bells were tied around their necks. The goats pushed and shoved each other as they jostled for positions in the herd, but their movement was undoubtedly towards him. This was no doubt because at the far side of the herd, driving them his way, were three goatherds. With long gnarly sticks.

They were dressed in voluminous, dirty clothes. One had dreads and a huge knitted hat. Another wore a cape that William Wallace might have used. All were carrying cans of something that looked uncannily like purple tins ('Sweet testament, Lord,' to the state they were in) and two of them had messy Rizla sausages hanging from their lips. Six-twenty in the morning on an Italian mountainside and Sam ran naked through the goats and their hippy goatherds. Not one of them registered the faintest flicker of interest. Sam laughed out loud as he passed the last of them and wondered at how fabulously wild their domestic circumstances must be.

After another ten minutes, he turned around. There was not much of a view as the drizzle had been replaced by a gentle, tumbling mist which seemed to cling to any vegetation or rock. On the way back he was looking forward to meeting the goatherds and wondered if the view of him from the back might at least elicit some kind of comment. But he never saw them again. The goats' bells had been silenced by some hippy magic.

When Sam got back to his camp the mist was lifting. He rolled the fly-sheet up after shaking as much water as he could from it and put his sleeping bag under a bungee over the top box. The wind would soon dry it out. He decided to go back down the same road and find a quiet part of the lake to go for a wash and maybe a short swim. If he felt like it, he might throw a line in.

The water was cold so his wash was thorough but brief. There was a movement in the water that caught his attention. A powerful swirl and an unhurried sweeping of the surface that only a big fish can make. He froze and concentrated on where the swirl had been. And then, as he lay floating, less than ten feet in front of him, a large trout leapt high in the air. It must have weighed three or four pounds. It looked like a salmonid but unlike anything he had seen before. It shared the colouring of a sea trout, but had the more domesticated, small-headed features of a rainbow. Maybe it was a species specific to the lake. Whatever name mankind had given the fish, it was a magical moment, to be put away with the others and used as and when needed.

The fish would be long gone by the time he got dressed, so it was pointless getting his rod. Sometimes it was better to just observe without feeling the need to collect or master things. Catching the fish would not have changed anything. He had caught thousands of fish, but this one was special. He felt tingly-happy and it was in this state of mind later that day he entered the outskirts of Milan.

12

The ride to Milan would take Sam less than two hours, pootling along almost due west, on roads that took him through a mixture of residential and agricultural areas. The houses and farm buildings were mostly single storey and the land flattened out as he left the mountains behind. Their cream and earth-coloured walls looked hot and dry in the morning sun.

The style of the buildings reminded him of ranches he had seen in old western movies. Without meaning to, he found himself trying to whistle the theme from 'The Good, the Bad and the Ugly'. Whistling in a tight-fitting motorcycle helmet can be frustrating. The exaggerated facial expressions necessary to produce the right notes were almost impossible to make and Sam sounded like somebody with a pantomime lisp trying to blow a raspberry. He resigned himself to humming the tune with his lips closed tightly. The deep resonance on the roof of his mouth made his top teeth vibrate in a way that amused him. The man who wrote the music he was rattling his teeth to had been born nearby. Maybe he too had travelled on this same road long ago?

If Sam had stopped there, even for a moment, to ponder the unfathomable interconnections and the fabulous complexity of nature and biology and human life, things would have turned out very differently. But instead, all he did was pull in for petrol. And there it was, high above the curved aluminium hood of the filling station, on a larger-than-life sign, in yellow and black and red. Luigi's fantastical, fire-breathing, six-legged dog.

The tune still playing in his head was perfect for the moment, turning the mundane into high drama. His leather trousers became chaps and imaginary spurs sparked off the concrete as he did his best John Wayne walk to the counter inside. If there had been a bucket on the floor, he would have spat into it. Sam tried to pay the man without smiling, but his carefully contrived mean stare collapsed before it was fully formed and fell into its default easy norm.

Sam pointed to the dog on a logo beside the till and asked directions for the headquarters. He was met with a predictably blank response, but the mood between them was good and they persevered in a creative session of charades, until, with an inaudible tinkle, somewhere in the background, a penny dropped.

The man behind the counter took out a map of Milan and pointed. Sam wasn't looking for anything exact at this stage. It would just be helpful to know which side of Milan he should aim for and, as luck would have it, if he turned south just before the centre, it would take him very close. The man then made things much easier for him by taking one of the corporate magazines from the counter and stabbing a nicotine-stained finger enthusiastically at a picture on the back cover. This was the new corporate headquarters or the Sede Centrale, as the petrol man kept repeating through brown teeth. It was an impressive building and one that should be easy to see when Sam got into the right neighbourhood.

Before putting on his leather gloves, he felt in the left pocket of his jacket for the olive stone. It was still there. It had nowhere better to go.

Sam turned left onto the A35. The fields became bigger, filled with early crops he didn't recognise. Tall, slender trees at the sides of the fields grew straight, untroubled by prevailing winds. The ground looked dry, but incongruously fertile. The road was quiet and the surface good. The bends were interesting without being challenging in any way. It made for relaxing riding. The tune resonating through his mind gave him all the excitement he needed.

Wah wah wah wah wah, wah-wah-wah
Wah wah wah wah wah, wah-wah-wah
Wah wah wah wah wah, wah wa wa wah
Wah wah wah wah wah, wah-wah
Mi-la-no.

And it should have been as easy as that. Except that when he came to the end of the A35 it was not what he expected Milan to look like. If Milan was all fields and agricultural buildings, then he may well be in the right place. But it was hard to imagine the world's fashionista turning up here for their annual jamboree of colourful irrelevance. Fashion week in wellies? Maybe not. He knew he was still too far from the centre. He would have admired any oil company which chose to locate its headquarters in such a bucolic setting, but it was stretching the imagination a wee bit too far.

So he headed south on a soulless motorway and took the first exit on a road that showed promise. It ran west, to another toll booth. In a car, paying a toll is simple. You wind your window down, hand the attendant your cash, he gives you your ticket and any change and on you go. Minimum fuss. Minimum delay for all concerned. On a bike, it is never so easy.

Sam stopped the bike and removed his leather gloves which he placed on the tank. Then he fumbled around in his right breast pocket for his wallet. His policy was usually just to give the attendant his highest denomination note and gratefully accept the change, knowing it would be much easier to spend. He managed all this as the first car pulled up behind him. Having put the wallet back in his pocket, he tried to quickly replace his gloves. But, after a couple of hours riding, the insides were slightly damp and he struggled to get his fingers in the correct holes. The more he struggled, the more his gloves refused to comply. Two cars.

It was no use setting off without his gloves on as there was no obvious place in sight to pull in and sort them out. Three cars.

The attendant saw Sam's dilemma and smiled.

"No problem. I motorcycle too. No rush." Sam smiled gratefully and took the gloves off to start again. The car behind tooted his horn. Four cars. The attendant started to giggle.

Sam turned around and apologetically shrugged to the driver of the car. He gesticulated to him that he was having problems with his gloves. The driver stared back evilly and blew his horn again. Sam thought the attendant was going to wet himself. He was rocking silently back and forth. Sam failed to see the joke.

Then he decided a random act of kindness was in order. He put his gloves down and took out his wallet. He told the attendant that he wanted to pay for the cars behind and put a twenty Euro note on the counter. Righteousness was obviously the perfect lubricant for wet leather because after this his gloves went on smoothly and quickly. He dropped the bike into gear and sped away. As he rode off he refused to look in his mirrors. Taking pleasure from anything he might see behind would diminish what he had just done. Like pleading for gratitude. He quickly accelerated to just above the legal limit and focused on the road ahead.

It was still incredibly dull. Concrete, mindless graffiti and flyovers the colour of old battleships. Litter discarded by passing motorists blew in eddies between the fast-moving traffic and the utilitarian concrete blocks dividing the road. There were graceless high-rise blocks of apartments like those he had seen many times beside the motorways into Glasgow. They were topped off with crude attempts at cultural iconography and were devoid of charm or character. He knew the distance from the centre that these buildings typically surrounded any major city and guessed this would be a good point to take the first road heading south.

Just as the A51 turned into the A1 his good judgment was rewarded by the sight of two likely-looking glass towers to his left. Their multi-faceted exteriors glistened like giant glass totems to the gods of mammon and lubrication. Sam smiled. He was sure he had found what he was looking for. What he hadn't expected as he turned off the A1 was that both of them belonged to the same six-legged dog company.

Sam cruised around the quiet roads surrounding the buildings. In its dull functionality the area resembled a large and unusually clean industrial estate. There were barriers across entrances and booths to pass to gain access to corporate car parks, some manned, others empty. People in suits walked purposefully on the shaded paths. The women wore high heels and sombre dark clothing. The gaiety and colour Sam would have liked were missing.

The kerbs were the biker-unfriendly type of a bygone era and the ungated drainage slits in them looked large and medieval. The tarmac roads were patched and worn, but the lawns and plants were cut back and manicured to within an inch of their lives. The buildings shone like polished gems.

The product that had spawned all this corporate excess was used in machines that almost exclusively spent their useful lives on these same roads that here looked so neglected. Sam enjoyed the irony.

By far the more interesting of the two glass temples was the smaller one. It looked incomplete. Half jungle, half Bauhaus, with the scaffolding used to erect it still in place and painted green. Sam liked it. Uncharacteristically unkempt foliage sprouted from the top and hung down the sides of the many different levels, which grew in height backwards from the single-storey entrance. The effect was pleasing enough for Sam to temporarily forgive the planners their head-splitting kerb stones.

Much as he appreciated the nod to nature of the Exploration and Production Division behemoth he realised the futility of the gesture he was planning. Whatever he gave to the suited and beautifully groomed receptionist he knew would be waiting for him behind the sliding glass doors, would be picked up suspiciously with a protective tissue and disdainfully tossed into a bin. He had a better idea.

Going the wrong way down a curved road to the entrance, he mounted the kerb onto the interlacing, boomerang-shaped stones of the pavement. His back wheel kicked out on some loose dirt which smooth, leather-soled shoes had ground to dust. He put his bike on the side stand immediately in front of the entrance and left the engine running. He was aware that at that moment unseen cameras were probably turning their lenses towards him and focusing on the uninvited visitor in the flip-front Schuberth. He was unconcerned.

He quickly reached into his jacket pocket and took out the olive stone, which by now was dusty with pocket lint. He threw it in the way squaddies hurl hand-grenades in bad B-movies. Feet planted wide apart, aiming with a gloved left hand, then twisting and quickly bending his right arm as it accelerated past his body and finally straightening it and unclenching his grip when his right hand was moving forward at its fastest.

Sam was playing a dangerous game. If armed security were present, it was at this point they would have opened fire. They would have been surprised, and ultimately severely reprimanded, when it was found that the attacker was unarmed. But subsequent CCTV footage would vindicate their actions and they would tell their grandchildren of the 'uomo folle' they once had to shoot at work. But if armed security were watching, they didn't react quickly enough. Sam launched his biological bomb into the midst of the foliage above the entrance door and was back on his bike and away on the lumpy roads before any watching uniforms had a chance to close their mouths.

Sam felt a sense of poetic retribution. It ticked lots of boxes for him.

As he rode in the direction of Milan, he thought he would break with his habit and buy a cup of coffee. He would sit at an outside table in the sunshine and watch the world go by and he would synchronise his heartbeat with the pulse of the city.

13

Rohan's rekindled energy gave him an endorphin rush which, combined with the thoughtless stupidity that an empty stomach promotes, was about to make him do something quite against his character and stunningly idiotic.

When walking through any Sri Lankan town, an act of violence never need be pre-meditated. There are always street vendors selling knives, hammers and machetes. A man sits on an upturned bucket displaying his array of lethal tools spreading across the pavement. It would be normal to see him sharpening the heavy steel blades on the concrete kerb. The majority of Sri Lankans work with their hands and these were the tools they needed to cut and chop and slit. They were never hidden under a counter for sale only to those over sixteen carrying suitable ID. If a drunken eight-year-old had the money, he could buy an axe. What he did with it was of nobody else's business. If he cut his toes off, he would hobble for the rest of his life and that was that. Because of this familiarity with working tools, most Sri Lankan eight-year-olds know how to handle a knife better than the average western teenage gangster. And anyway, if it was just violence you had in mind, most villages north of Colombo had an army deserter or two who would sell you a hand-grenade for the price of a bottle of beer. Fortunately, though, the use of hand-grenades tended to be monopolised by the needy few who had political ambitions.

So it frustrated Rohan that after wandering around for ten minutes he had seen nothing more intimidating to steal than a stirato. Then he saw a butcher's shop. It was nothing like the meat stalls at home, but where there was meat to cut, there were knives. The butchers in Sri Lanka had long, heavy knives with blades that were razor sharp. For a working man, having a knife that was not sharp was the same as having a pen without ink. Pointless.

Rohan had no intention of using the knife he would steal, but he hoped anyone who saw it would be frightened enough to do as he asked.

The window in the meat shop was clean and the men inside wore white coats, unsoiled with the dried blood from the work of the day before. The produce was stacked behind a glass counter in large cuts on shiny metal trays. Many of the joints were tied up with string or stuffed in white net bags. All Rohan had eyes for was the twelve-inch paring knife that was lying beside something that might have come from a pig. The knife and the meat were on a white, plastic cutting block behind the counter.

The men were stacking the produce under the worktop then going back through an open door behind them to a store room. They would load up their trays and carry them into the shop. Rohan hovered nonchalantly outside the door. He watched everything with an intent sharpened by cunning and desperation. When, for a second, both men were in the back room together, he rushed in and grabbed the knife. With his right thumb hooked into the front pocket of his trousers he casually pressed the blade to his body, hidden behind his forearm. It would not fall and, despite its size, it remained unseen to all but the most observant passers-by. He was out of the shop in less than four seconds. He forced himself to walk casually away. Any remorse he might have felt for stealing was compensated for by the enormous thrill of something at last going right. It gave him a sense of power and confidence which he was going to need for what he was about to do next.

Robbing shops was something that he didn't want to play a big part in his future. Ideally, he would rob one and that would be it. He would hopefully get enough to set himself up on a more conventional career path. Early in the morning, a baker was not an option. He might manage to steal the float from the till and a bite for breakfast but he would have to do the same again tomorrow – and the day after that. He needed somewhere that had a lot of cash or stock which was valuable and easy to carry. Cash was always going to be a problem in the morning and if he waited until the evening, when the tills were full, he was not sure he would still have the resolve to go through with it. It needed to be something of high value which could easily be sold.

To any Sri Lankan villager, gold was the status symbol of choice. The amount of gold a madam wore, was a visible measure of her wealth. Most fishermen didn't have bank accounts. They had gold. It was easy to hide when the relatives were coming and as liquid as cash. Gold was the answer to the question Rohan was asking himself.

Eventually, he wandered into what looked like a wealthy neighbourhood. The buildings were four or five floors high and the streets tidy and clean. Tram lines ran along the wider avenues and overhead was a latticework of cables and wires. Cars and scooters were parked side by side. The road surface was a mixture of tarmac and ancient cobbles which gave a clue to their antiquity. The shops were minimalist, almost Spartan in appearance. Nothing to upset the ambience of affluence.

Despite this being new to Rohan, he had seen enough of Milan to know this was the honeypot. Any jewellery shop here would not be selling yellow-coloured plastic. Being Sri Lankan, he knew that gem stones could be worth more than gold. He had heard stories that some gems were even more valuable than Sri Lanka's famous blue sapphires.

He turned into a wider street. There were tram lines on either side laid into the large stone cobbles. The top floors of the buildings on the opposite side of the road were lit by the morning sun as it progressed slowly upwards. Down the street to his left there were fewer sunshades which he had noticed the better shops always had above their windows. The people he saw there were walking purposefully and not ambling in the way that idle shoppers do. So he turned to his right.

A bright shaft of sunlight beamed diagonally across the road, having had an unobstructed path down some unseen side street parallel to the one he had just emerged from. It shone upon the white bars of a pedestrian crossing, guiding his eyes across the road to where it fell on the corner of a building, illuminating it from the top floor to the street. The stones glowed with an amber warmth. At street level was a large window of thick protective glass. The sun was still low enough to shine into the window under the canopy of the shade which cast an umbra in a thin grinning arc. And what was in the window sparkled. He had found his jewellers.

Carefully, he approached on his side of the road, the knife still pressed against his body. As he crossed the street, following the path of the sun, he could see another similar-sized window around the corner. Next to this window was a large iron gate up a single stone step. The gate, which nestled in a wide and elaborately carved archway, was open. The space above the gate was filled with extravagant ironwork which resembled a sandakada pahana, a Buddhist moonstone. This was a blessing in disguise for, although Rohan was a Catholic, he knew and respected the sacred importance of the moonstone which symbolised the cycle of Saṃsāra or the beginning-less cycle of birth, life and death. Beyond the archway was another glass door which led directly into the jeweller's shop. It too was open. The shop faced a small piazza in the middle of which were two stone stairways which descended out of sight. People climbed up from whatever was below and blinked in the morning brightness. Some were carrying bags with names on them he recognised from the T-shirts the beach boys in his village wore.

Rohan knew he could run faster than most. As a boy, he had won many events at school sports days and was always the one chosen to run for the batsman in the Sunday afternoon Elle matches. He looked further down the road to make sure he would be able to lose himself down the side streets which criss-crossed the area. As he entered the jewellers, it struck him how similar it was to the butchers'. Two men in suits were busy carrying trays of precious metals and gems from a strong room at the back of the shop and putting them on glass shelves under the protective cover of the transparent counter. There was no better time to have entered. And, these two men, dressed immaculately in dark suits with white shirts and sombre silk ties, like the butchers, had no blood on their clothing. Not yet anyway.

Judging by the alarmed expressions which spread like a sudden disease across their faces, Rohan was not the kind of customer they were used to welcoming. When he quickly hooked his thumb behind the hilt of the knife and turned his wrist simultaneously down and outwards bringing the blade of the knife suddenly into view, both men froze.

Everyone freezes in a situation like this, just for a moment, as the flood of fear knocks the other senses into the background. Everyone, that is, except for children brought up in a war zone and those rare individuals trained in the darker arts of mortal combat. The two jewellers fell into neither of these categories, so, like the rest of us would, they froze. Their eyes widened and their mouths opened involuntarily. The smaller of the two was nearest to Rohan and in less time than it took for the dangling wristband of his expensive watch to stop swinging, Rohan was upon him. He spun the man round sending the trays he was carrying spilling to the floor. The jewellery scattered noisily over the polished marble, but the knife was against the man's neck. Rohan pressed the flat side of the blade in hard. A minor adjustment of its angle gave a cruel hint of what it was capable of. The other man put the trays he was carrying down on the counter and raised both arms in the air, as if the knife Rohan held was a loaded revolver. The little camera in the ceiling recorded it all without curiosity or comment.

Rohan nodded his head in the direction of the trays on the table and said one of the few words in English that he knew.

"Bag."

The man evidently understood and quickly took a dark brown bag with white string handles out from behind the counter. His eyes never left the knife and he moved steadily and, despite the circumstances, with patience. He put the trays in the bag and, when Rohan motioned to the jewellery on the floor, got down on his knees and carefully started to gather the precious spillage. It was the urgency in Rohan's voice rather than any understanding of what "ikmanthe" meant, that urged the prostrate jeweller to complete his task with haste.

The jeweller with the knife at his neck had begun to perspire with the gushing intensity of a menopausal hot flush. His neck became greasy and slippery. Rohan felt revolted as the little man's sweat oozed through his fingers, which were shaking so much he was frightened of losing his grip on the knife. The quantity of jewellery on the floor had reached the point where the law of diminishing returns applied. Rohan knew this was the moment he had to grab the bag and run. It was a calculated decision and, once he had made it, he acted swiftly and what would later be described as 'brutally'. He threw the sweaty man from him and raised his hand holding the knife at the same time. Although it was never his intention, in the blur of momentum as the man spun away from his grasp, the blade severed a large part of his left ear. He let out a high-pitched shriek as he fell to the floor, holding his hands to his face. Blood flowed through his trembling white fingers.

Rohan saw none of this. He crossed the shop floor in two bounds and grabbed the brown bag where the second jeweller had dropped it as he cowered against the wall. On the man's face Rohan saw a look of terror that he hated himself for. But he was smart enough to know that now was not the time to struggle with emotions. Now was the time to run like a mad dog. He could regret what he had done at leisure and take his time to make things right with his conscience and his God.

He dropped the knife in the doorway. His forward momentum sent it clattering out onto the piazza where it noisily drew the attention of several morning shoppers. The blood, the large bag and the speed with which he was leaving an exclusive jewellery shop made it obvious that a robbery had just taken place.

The air filled with cries, whose volume rose dramatically when someone rushed into the jeweller's shop and let out a horrified scream. But nobody wanted to play the hero and Rohan ran unhindered. He instantly regretted his lack of forward planning, but the reassuring weight of what was in the bag briefly vindicated his impulsiveness. For the want of anywhere else to go he ran across the piazza and down a sunlit road on the opposite side. He knocked over two bicycles that were leaning against a metal frame and nearly lost his balance, but his speed and the flood of natural chemicals rushing through his bloodstream helped him stay on his feet. He sped down the centre of the road away from the shoppers and pedestrians who had all now stopped to see what the commotion was about.

The cries increased and were taken up by those further down the street so that he found himself running into a cacophony of accusation. One man in a uniform at the door of a particularly large shop stepped into the road as if to block his path, but Rohan screamed at him and stuck out his bloodied forearm and the man backed off just enough for him to leap onto the bonnet of a parked car on his left and continue his flight down the pavement. Shoppers pressed themselves tightly to the wall as he fled past. He was aware of the sound of engines starting behind him. Small two-strokes. The sort used in Italian scooters.

The high buildings on either side closed in on him forming a blurred tunnel. He heard the blood pounding through his veins. There was no time to think... and he didn't need to. He was unaware of his feet hitting the floor and felt like he was flying. Compared to the ambling pedestrians, he was, but not to the gathering hoard of scooters which were rapidly catching up. There were six of them. The scooter riders had their lights on and blew their horns. They screamed at Rohan and, just as a snowball rolling down a hillside gathers snow, they gathered a wild, unruly mob which stuck to them as they passed. The volume and mass of the mob grew, baying for the body fluids of the young man clutching the bag of stolen jewels. Rohan disappeared around the corner and into a narrower side road.

When the mob reached the corner, Rohan was gone. He had turned right and then left onto a larger road. If he was breathing, he never noticed. Escape was all he could think of and the only way he knew how to do that was to run and turn and run and turn. For a short while it seemed to be working. At the end of each alley there were two choices, left or right. At crossroads, there were three. The opportunities for escape multiplied at each intersection and the number in the mob following each possible path reduced correspondingly.

The baying must have been exhausting because, as the chance of a bloodletting appeared to lessen, some of the mob got bored and resumed their journeys. A few continued, convinced they were on the right route and that Rohan was just ahead of them, maybe around the next corner. The scooter boys were covering a lot of ground. They all had mobile phones and organised a thorough search of the area in a fraction of the time it would take the authorities to do so.

Central Milan is a maze to those not intimate with its convoluted twists and turns. Rohan did a couple more left turns then right ones and escaped his pursuers largely by returning close to the place where his escape started from. He approached it from a different direction, so there were no familiar landmarks. But his heart missed a beat when he saw ahead of him the name of the jewellery shop written in gold letters on a brown sign. The name and the colour matched exactly the one on the bag he had under his arm.

By now the Polizia di Stato had arrived and two men in orange overalls were guiding the man with the severed ear into the side door of a white van. The van had bright orange stripes down the side of it which matched the paramedics' clothing. They were the only ones at the scene who appeared calm. The police were running in and out of the jewellery shop and barking instructions into handsets in their cars. There were six policemen in sight and three police cars parked at unlikely angles where they had come to sudden stops on the piazza. For Italians, they surprisingly missed out on looking cool by a country mile. They marshalled the crowd back to a respectable distance, one or two of whom involuntarily raised hands to their mouths as the bloodied shop assistant, supported on either side by the men in orange, dripped some of his blood onto the stone floor beside the white van.

Rohan too was shocked at the sight of so much blood and wondered how it could have happened. Only now did he understand that the blood on his arm must in some way be connected to that which the jeweller was so copiously losing. He stopped, open-mouthed, at the sight of what he had done. His breathing was so loud and laboured that people turned to face him and began to stare. Understanding came slowly to most but almost instantly to the one-eared jeweller. His face lost what little colour remained and his eyes opened wide. He grew tall out of his injured stoop and wordlessly raised his right arm and, with the ghostliest of bony fingers, pointed steadily and silently at Rohan. Blood drooled in a long coagulating line from his wrist.

Rohan accepted the crimson accusation of guilt and ran. This time he was not flowing. He was no longer on automatic. This time every step was an agony and every breath a rasping blast in his tortured lungs. He felt he was running through something hot and sharp and much heavier than air. But he had to run. He had to continue when it hurt the most. The Polizia quickly ran to their blue and white cars. The sirens started immediately.

The police cars were rapidly closing the gap that he was paying such a painful price to create. He turned right down a side street. The street was just like others he had run down in the last few minutes. Tall buildings, cars parked at one side, a mixture of smaller shops and anonymous-looking offices. There were a few pedestrians, but Rohan was not worried about them. He knew they would move. At the bottom of the street was a crossroads. He could see it ahead, brightly lit by the sun. He felt shackled as the police cars turned into the street he was on. At the crossroads ahead two scooters passed from left to right at speed. The pillion on the first one glanced quickly up and down the side streets as they passed.

Rohan heard the rubber being scrubbed off the small scooter tyres as the rider applied the brakes hard. The second scooter added to the sound of tyres on a hot road when an excess of friction is added to the mix. He heard the engines rev and then, almost at once, the two scooters came back into sight and raced directly towards him.

He was sandwiched between the authorities and the scooters. His only choice was to turn left down his last possible escape route. It was a passageway where shadows lay thick on the ground. The cars could not follow but the handlebars of the scooters were no wider than the shoulders of a man. They would quickly bear down on him. The floor-level grills and empty barred windows offered him no alternative but to keep running. He saw parked cars brightly lit ahead at the side of what must be a bigger road. People were briefly visible as they passed the end of the alley. Italian pedestrians going about their Italian business, unaware of the drama that was about to erupt onto the pavement.

If they had listened carefully they would have heard the scooters rapidly closing on a desperate man running for his life towards them. Maybe they were distracted by the sound of sirens somewhere on the other side of the block. Sounds which were growing in volume and urgency as their echoes bounced between the buildings. It was a sound that would distract most people. Certainly, it momentarily distracted a solo motorcyclist in a flip-front Schuberth helmet.

Rohan only just made it into the sunlight ahead of the scooters. He burst out of the darkness and, without pause, threw himself between the two cars parked directly in front of him. The cars were beside a busy main road that ran around the centre of Milan. The motorcyclist who hit him didn't even have time to touch his brakes.

14

He was turning right, then left on a whim and deliberately losing himself on roads of quarried setts. He was revelling in the joy and chaos of the city, drinking in its atmosphere through his travel-stained pores. He was doing what no car driver could ever dream of and celebrating the freedom of riding a motorbike. He emerged from a labyrinth of smaller lanes onto a busier main road and adjusted his speed accordingly, accelerating out of his foggy romanticism and looking ahead for a street café. There was an unholy racket going on somewhere as sirens cut the air with acoustic reflections that were disconcerting to his rural ears. He was keeping more than a door's width away from the parked cars when a blur from his right caught his attention. His eyes moved but his head had no time to follow when the sound of a meeting between machinery and human flesh rose over that of the sirens. The splintering violence that followed, as machine and bone gouged grooves in the unyielding surface of the road, would be long remembered by all who heard it. As the bitumen absorbed the momentum of bike, rider and pedestrian, all three came to an ugly and brutal stop. The air fell silent, as if humanity was holding its breath.

Sam was the only one to move. Fluids leaked from both the bike and the pedestrian and spread across the road at a roughly equal rate. One was yellow, the other red. Sam was still functioning. His body was bruised and his clothing torn, but all his limbs moved in the ways they were meant to. His left shoulder had taken the impact on the road and he was lucky nothing was broken. The armour in his jacket had done its job. His arm felt numb and his thigh felt hot. He was aware that his breathing was unusually fast, but he knew he was not seriously hurt.

The pedestrian looked to be a young Asian man. His eyes were open and he seemed conscious. A bag he had been carrying had been thrown into the middle of the road and its contents were spread in a wide glittering arc. People rushed forwards. It was the sight of the jewels and not the blood that kept them from coming too close. Sam was the first to get to the young man. His experience was limited to a casual interest in first aid and a few 'First On The Scene' bike accident training days, but he instinctively took two deep breaths to try and calm himself. He recognised classic primary, secondary and tertiary injuries to what he now saw was just a boy.

There was a long bone fracture to the left leg caused by the impact of the front wheel. The jagged end of the femur had torn a hole in the boy's trousers. Blood was spilling from this wound but was mostly being absorbed by his clothing. As his left leg had been shattered, the boy's body had twisted from the impact and the right handlebar and brake lever had made a long open gash level with his diaphragm. The way the blood was frothing from this wound seemed to indicate lung damage. The boy was breathing faintly and began to move his arms slightly. What concerned Sam most was the injury where the boy's head had been slammed down onto the road. Blood was spreading rapidly from the back of it.

Sam knelt beside the boy and realised he was way out of his depth. He had dealt with gravel rash and even the odd broken bone, but this was a situation beyond anything an evening class could cover. He knew the boy was not going to survive unless help arrived immediately. He could see some of the onlookers already on their mobile phones so he tried to comfort the boy as best he could. Under the circumstances it wasn't much more than gently touching the boy's forehead and making noises of the 'there-there' type. He knew this was inept and inadequate, but he had nothing more to offer.

He was frightened to lift the boy's head in case its contents were left on the road. So he continued with his stroking and soothing and waited for professional help to arrive. With a staggering effort, the boy slowly reached his hand into his back trouser pocket and slid out a folded piece of paper. He tried to say something, but it was inaudible. As Sam leaned closer, the boy pressed the paper into Sam's blood-soaked hand. At that instant, the boy and Sam both knew something was ending. The boy's eyes glazed and the life in them died. Sam groaned and collapsed backwards.

If there had been a machine there that measured the vital signs of life it would have shown the boy was not yet dead. His heart continued to beat and his chest gently rose and fell. Death did not happen suddenly like turning out a light, it left like a reluctant party guest, waving over its shoulder all the way down the road. The boy's body had been damaged beyond repair, but Sam recognised that, even in death, something about the boy had not been broken.

As human beings, we are all broken. Everyone everywhere is. As a species, we break easily. But for most, brokenness is a rite of passage, a journey through which we must travel. Eventually we see a glimmer of light shining through the cracks. There is a Japanese art of repairing broken pottery called Kintsukuroi. The pieces of the pottery are repaired with gold and, when complete, it is more beautiful for having been broken. At the end of their journey, broken people are like that.

But for a few, the ones Sam thought of as being broken, the walls their fragile egos build around themselves to stop the pain getting in only serve to prevent it from leaving. These are the ones with no future and no present, just an ugly past. And, for some of them, life runs out before the healing is complete and only then, crushed and defeated, does their loneliness die with them.

It is all about love, really. The broken no longer have the ability to love fully. And in this dying boy, through his fear and shattered bones, Sam sensed a capacity for love that shocked him.

The police arrived and the crowd closed in to satisfy their morbid curiosity. A small man in a suit climbed hurriedly out of the back of one of the first police cars to arrive. The officers went immediately to the boy. The man in the suit went to the jewels scattered on the road and began to collect them and place them tenderly in his jacket pockets. His relief was palpable to anyone who cared to look. The police gently helped Sam sit down in the back of one of the cars. Sam left the door open. The world was closing in on him too much to think of shutting it. He needed fresh air and the whole of Milan didn't have enough of it.

Nobody else touched the boy. The pool of his blood had stopped growing and was thickening on the hot tarmac. Just meat and bones. A suitable epitaph for mankind. When the paramedics arrived, they quickly established the boy was dead and a sheet was draped without ceremony over the shell of his body. After a change of latex gloves, the men in orange suits turned their attention to Sam. They wanted to check him out thoroughly, but he would have none of it. He shrugged off their perfunctory attention more vehemently than he intended. They understood and diplomatically backed off. One of them had a few words with the policeman who seemed to be in charge and satisfied him that Sam was probably OK.

Another policeman was talking to the small man in the suit, whose designer pockets were now bulging. When his pockets were full, he had taken out a blue and gold silk handkerchief to gather together what jewels his pockets couldn't hold. When he knotted it, he reminded Sam of Dick Whittington. At one point in their conversation the little man shuddered and looked up. The policeman pointed to Sam and the little man nodded in approval and immediately came over. He bent down and leaned into the police car, "Grazie, Signore. Grazie. Grazie, Signore." His sincerity was alarming.

Sam looked back at the man apologetically. He did not understand what he was being thanked for and decided he did not want the little man's thanks anyway. When Sam shrugged, the man pointed to the lifeless body of the boy and again repeated, "Grazie, Signore." Sam closed the door and decided to let the world swallow him if it wanted to.

Later, at the police station when events had been explained to him by a female officer, Sam felt sick. Sick at what had happened, sick at what he had seen and sick at the thought he had been responsible for the boy's death. He was sickened too, on a different level, at having been on the receiving end of the gratitude of the little man, who he now understood was the owner of the jewellery shop.

The female officer brought Sam a coffee. Small and black and strong. When he hesitated, she nodded encouragement for him to drink it. It was very good, but not the one he had imagined less than an hour before. But it did the trick and brought some of the situation into a hazy focus. He asked the officer for another. She smiled and left the room. It was then, as he began to relax, that he noticed, for the first time since it was placed there, the slip of paper in the slowly unclenching fist of his left hand. The blood had dried and stuck the paper to his palm. When he opened his hand, it remained there like a persistent memory. He peeled it off and unfolded it to see it was an envelope. A good quality one of thick cream paper. There were smudges of dried blood, some of which had soaked right through, and a few distinct bloody fingerprints on the back. It had been carefully folded down the middle and was clean enough on the address side to read the script

The writing meant nothing to Sam. It appeared to be carefully written but was not recognisable as anything he had seen before. The fact that it was written on an envelope made him assume it was a name and address. The policewoman came back with his second coffee. He quietly put the envelope in the pocket recently vacated by the errant olive stone. If it could talk, what stories that pocket could tell.

15

After the second coffee, Sam wasn't left alone. It became obvious that he was being monitored, more than likely for his own good. Accordingly, he acted as normally as he knew how. The female officer had gone off duty and been replaced by two friendly young men. One of them spoke good English and the other smiled and made a few notes. It was clear he was not going to be charged with anything. In fact, it appeared that he was held in high esteem for neutralising a violent criminal with no further casualties. The paperwork was going to be minimal for such a traumatic event and that pleased everyone.

There was a knock on the door and, without waiting for an answer, the jeweller entered. He wore a fresh suit with teardrop-shaped button holes. The first buttons of his cuffs were undone. The pockets of this suit were empty and he looked calm and well-groomed. He had showered and oiled his dark, thinning hair. He took hold of Sam's right hand with both of his own and shook it with the grip of a jellyfish. Sam looked at him with suspicion. There was nothing suspicious, however, about his gratitude towards Sam. His sincerity, again, was obvious.

The handshake went on for too long but eventually Sam succeeded in extracting himself from the cloying grasp. The jeweller withdrew a white envelope from the breast pocket of his suit. He offered it to Sam with a slight bow of his head. Sam guessed it was money and put his hand up in an adamant gesture of refusal. The jeweller took this as the act of a truly modest man and redoubled his platitudes until he was grovelling.

"No," said Sam, becoming increasingly uncomfortable. The jeweller made his skin crawl. He felt he was sinking into a pit and desperately wanted the man to go. But the jeweller was not going anywhere until he had completed his task. The policemen looked on with a casual indifference but when Sam thought he recognised an echo of his own emotions in the downturned corners of the mouth of one of the officers, he looked pleadingly at him for help. The officer raised his eyebrows and nodded slowly to Sam then rapidly jerked his face in the shape of a tick towards the door. Sam understood that the officer wanted him to take the envelope and the jeweller would then leave. In the absence of any other, this sounded like the best plan. He forced himself to smile as he accepted the envelope. He took it with both hands, leaving nothing to shake, and nodded his thanks to the grateful jeweller.

Despite what Sam thought, the jeweller was a civil man. In handing over the reward, he was satisfying a moral obligation. He was the fourth generation in a dynasty of jewellers who had founded their family business on hard work and a strong tradition in civic engagement. A belief in generalised reciprocity was part of his being. To not reward Sam would have been a mark of dishonour. Once his honour was intact, he backed out of the door, repeating his thanks and, with a final thin-lipped grin he was gone. Sam gave an audible sigh but when he shook his head and nodded towards the door in a clumsy attempt at bonding, the officers ignored him.

Sam gave them his passport details together with other personal information. They asked him where he was staying and he told them he was camping. This was met by expressions of cultural incomprehension. They suggested a hotel nearby, but he refused. They eventually told him of a campsite on the other side of the city and said they would take him there.

His bike, or rather the various parts of it, had been brought to the police station and he was able to give it a thorough look over. It was not pretty. To say the bike was totally in pieces would have been an exaggeration. But if she had been an old lady, her body would have been mostly intact, but her wig, teeth, pearl necklace and most of her clothing would have been shredded and piled beside her leaking corpse.

Sam was shocked. Where was the soul of the machine he had appreciated for so long? Are we all just meat and bones beneath our pretentious finery? Stripped of the sculpted fairings and burnished alloys, his bike was a naked, mangled, ugly and surprisingly rusty piece of German engineering. The shock was not so much seeing it like this, but more because he had no feeling for it whatsoever. What he saw in front of him and what he had been riding earlier that day were not connected. One was beauty, efficiency and power and the other was broken scrap. Sam felt no sadness to see his bike like this because it was not his bike.

The left-hand upper and lower fairings were shattered and lying beside the machine. The front and rear indicators were missing and torn wires from the loom hung loose like brightly-coloured friendship bracelets woven by an idiot. The bike itself was leaning against the wall with the relatively undamaged right-hand side hidden from sight. The handlebar had a jaunty angle to it and the clutch lever was broken. The left-side mirror was gone. The generator cover was broken and it was from this that fluids were leaking onto the concrete floor of the police yard. The rear foot peg was missing together with a piece of the sub frame. And if there was ever any doubt that this was an insurance write-off, the damage to the exhaust made sure of it.

His bike was five years old and even the parts for the quick catalogue of destruction he had already noted would come to more than its value. Once labour was included for putting it all together, and after the painstaking job of fishing the bits of the engine cover out from the heart of the motor, the repair bill would be more than double the bike's value. More importantly, it would never be the same bike again. The confidence and trust that is built up over a period of long ownership and a meticulous maintenance schedule, once lost, are never fully regained. Better to start anew.

16

S am removed the soft panniers and the contents of the broken top box. His fishing rod was undamaged, as was his tent. It was more than he could easily carry, so the officers helped him. Between them they placed everything in the trunk of a police car. With no sirens sounding, nor tyres squealing, the driver, with remarkable restraint, turned right out of the police station and drove back through the centre of Milan.

Sam wanted a drink. He deliberately distracted himself by considering what a whimsical and ephemeral emotion pride in ownership was. He asked himself if we ever really own anything and concluded that we probably didn't. The policemen kept looking around and checking him. They were worried that the knock he had taken was only now having an effect. But Sam smiled wearily at them to put their minds at ease. As they were well overdue for lunch, their minds were easily put at ease.

He thought about the future and how he was leaning towards a mindful minimalism. He was slowly working out that possessions were an irrelevance. Then it dawned on him that minds could be every bit as cluttered as a spare room and maybe a cerebral cleanout would be just as cathartic as hauling domestic detritus to the dump. If that was the case, then first on his mental hit-list should be the bureaucracy necessary for ownership of so many things. It was a means by which other people exerted their power over his life. He needed to remove it to free his mind and simplify his life. *Simplify, simplify, simplify.* It became obvious to him that there really was no other way.

Sam had always been diligent in maintaining the paperwork relating to the ownership and use of his motorbike. But now he saw bureaucracy as a contraflow of unwanted printed words coming towards him and hard-earned printed money moving away. The paper traffic on both sides of the central barrier was heavy. The whole charade was a shackle on his liberty. He was certain that doing away with it would mean living parts of his life outside the law, but he revelled in keeping under the radar (this morning being the exception) and, if he tried hard to make himself less visible, he was sure he could.

He remembered something by the French writer, Antoine de Saint-Exupery, about perfection not being achieved when there was nothing more to add, but rather when there was nothing left to take away. That struck a chord – and it was a stonking F5 power-chord. The urge for a drink had passed and he had never felt less broken in his life.

As Sam came out of his new-found reverie, they arrived at the campsite. One of the officers spoke with a man at the gate who glanced sympathetically at him and raised the yellow barrier for the car to pass. Sam looked around and the dullness of what he saw reminded him of the Neil Innes song which contains the line about having '... as much imagination as a caravan site.'

The police car pulled up between a large blue family tent and a modern motorhome. The motorhome had a satellite TV dish on the roof and a coiled cable coming from a recessed socket in its side, like an umbilical cord connecting it to the pulsing heartbeat of a civilisation Sam didn't want to be a part of any more.

The driver looked at Sam for approval. Sam shook his head silently and pointed to the far end of the campsite, which was still unpopulated. It was early in the season. There were trees and hedges that his small tent could be hidden behind and that suited him. Sam needed to be alone. He thanked the policemen mechanically. He understood that he would be required to attend the police station later and they would come to pick him up. They looked concerned as they left.

He pitched the tent as quickly as his practised hands could and as far away from anyone as it was possible to be. As soon as the last guy-line was tight, he retreated inside like a whelk withdrawing into its shell. He zipped the flimsy nylon door closed, sealing out the world, and sat cross-legged, quite still, in the centre of his space. His remaining belongings were lined up in front of him. He closed his eyes and went to a place of nothing. As thoughts and emotions came, he let them go and eventually retreated, as close as he was able, to a place of infinite possibilities. A place without desire or prejudice. A place from where he could see everything.

He sat like that for the rest of the afternoon. When he opened his eyes, it was dark. He needed food and coffee but above all else he needed to reconnect with the world. To reconnect with it on his terms. His mind was clear now. As he walked out of the campsite, he was aware that eyes from the darkness were watching him. The background hum from the rest of the world silenced momentarily as he passed through its gaze. He was grateful for this bubble of silence and wore it like a coat of invincibility. The watching eyes meant nothing.

He found a café about half a kilometre away. It was busy with locals at that happy time of day when the crowd was a mixture of those coming down from a hard-working day and those building up for a night out on the town. Their joie de vivre was wonderfully intoxicating. Sam found a tall, heavy stool at the bar and ordered a coffee. The man next to him had a simple wooden board covered with a colourful selection of meats and cheese. He was enjoying them with a bottle of dark red wine and half a loaf of coarse, white bread. As the waiter brought his coffee, Sam pointed to the platter and asked for the same.

"Salumi e formaggio?"

Sam nodded. When it arrived, he ordered two more of the small strong coffees and a glass of water. He took out the envelope the dead boy had given to him. The bloody fingerprints were now dried completely, brown and dirty. A scab of the boy's blood flaked off and fell onto a piece of soft, white cheese, destroying, in an instant, his appetite. He paid the waiter as soon as he could attract his attention, gave a generous tip, drained his coffee and water and stood up to leave.

By the door were two coloured men. Sam had little experience in identifying people of different races. The dead boy had looked Asian, and Sam had to start somewhere. These two men were as good a starting point as any. He walked up to them slowly. His over-exaggerated casual approach attracted their attention. He was not flowing with the motion of the café. He carefully tried to cover the worst of the bloodstains with his fingers and held out the envelope for the men to read.

In the only language he knew, he asked simply if the men could read the writing. Their blank faces told him that they were as unfamiliar with the script as he was. Before leaving, he asked them which country they were from so he could tick it off his list.

"Italy," they both replied indignantly, before the smaller of the two dismissively waved him away with the back of his hand. The men carried on with their conversation as if the interruption had never happened and Sam knew the interview was over.

He quietly walked back to his tent, sealed himself in his hermetic nylon world and tried to sleep. It didn't come easily.

The guilt, remorse, fear and despair he might have expected to be suffering from, were reasonably easy for him to deal with. Sam had enough life in him to know he had done nothing wrong, so guilt was really a non-starter. He could have wallowed in feelings which might easily be labelled as guilt, but he knew that would have been lazy. Happiness, and therefore satisfaction, could only be achieved by making the right choices in life. In killing the boy, Sam knew there had been no choice for him to make. He had been presented with an eventuality and how he felt about it depended not on how it had happened, but on how he responded to it. He had no control over what the police decided to do to him so any emotions about it, one way or another, were pointless.

All this he could easily rationalise. But there was still a yawning emptiness. A numbness that came not from the physical impact his body had suffered but from a source he could not yet identify. A run would be his best chance of finding an answer.

When the morning eventually came, he knew the dullness in his head was a state of mind and tried unsuccessfully to shrug it off. He made a coffee and drank it joylessly. The grass on the campsite was short and free of litter. The gravel roads and paths were raked smooth. Everywhere was orderly, but around the perimeter of the site the grass was longer, and a track of bare earth had been worn by joggers and dog walkers. It was around this that Sam decided to run. He ran barefoot. He wanted to connect with the world again but he found in trying to, it disappeared.

The dullness in his head was the first thing to go. It was replaced with a runner's void that left no space for emotions. He ran for over an hour until his feet were dark with the earth. And when he stopped he knew that any clarity and peace of mind would only come from what he decided to do next. The money he had been given, the reward, was the disturbing factor. It was this that turned him from an observer into a participant and he was unsure of what the right thing to do was.

He showered and cleaned his teeth in a stone-built toilet block. A warm shower washed any remaining torpor away and he emerged, if not a new man, then a very much refreshed one. He changed a sock, zipped his tent door closed and headed back into Milan. The railway station should be a good place to start.

He was directed to a bus where a fellow passenger, with good English, told him where to get off and where he could find the tram which would complete his journey. The station looked grand and the sky was vast and blue behind it, reminding him of the big skies of Caithness. The station was the centre of humanity of the type that Sam needed to find. He looked for anyone of colour. The people he approached were polite, but nonplussed. A shrug of the shoulders was as much as he got.

A small group of young men, with a girl, sat outside a coffee bar inside the station. They were immaculately groomed, hair combed and clothing neat and purposeful. The girl was attractive, quite dark and had a small gold ring through her nose. One of the boys wore Italian loafers with no socks. They were probably in their early twenties, maybe a little younger.

Sam wasted no time ordering coffee, but immediately approached the group with the envelope held in his outstretched arm. The youths remained relaxed, but curious, as Sam explained in slow English that he wanted to know what language the script on the envelope was written in. Instead of the shrugs he was expecting, he was confused by a short sideways wobble of the head and a smile from the boy nearest to him which told him that he had recognised what he saw.

"What is it?" asked the girl in English. She snatched the envelope from the boy then opened her fingers in alarm as she saw the dried brown stains. She held it between her thumb and second finger and bent her other fingers as far away from the paper as she could. Her hand made that shape you do when you want to throw a shadow like a rabbit from a lamp onto a nearby wall. Her fingers were slender and beautiful, and she made the gesture look like part of a dance.

"It is Sinhala. We are Tamils from Sri Lanka. Ravi can speak Sinhala, but the stupid boy cannot read it," she teased, pointing at the boy she had taken the envelope from. Then her face lit up.

"Wait a minute, Sir."

She took out a mobile phone from her jacket pocket and photographed the envelope. She pressed a few buttons, put the phone down on the table in front of her and returned her gaze to Sam.

"Where did you get it from?"

While Sam was thinking how best to answer her, the phone rang.

"Hi Suren. Yes, yes. Centrale. Si."

Suren, which Sam heard as Soo-rain, sounded as if it described a particularly soft, morning mist tumbling down a Highland glen. The rest of the conversation was less poetic and totally incomprehensible. The girl looked at him with a steady and confident gaze which made him feel that he was being described. He straightened up self-consciously. Despite her conversation being on a phone, the girl did that same slight wobble with her head as the boy. Finally, she said "Ciao," and ended the call. She stared meaningfully into Sam's eyes, but remained silent. Sam began to feel uncomfortable as two of the boys began to speak to each other quietly. The phone pinged, and the girl picked it up and read the message.

"Do you have a pen?"

Now it was Sam's turn to shrug. One of the boys handed a pen to the girl who passed it to Sam together with his envelope. She placed the phone on the table for him to read its message. The screen was black, apart from an orange box which had white text written in it.

WM Laxman Perera

Wella Mawatha

Thalagamma

Sri Lanka

Sam wrote this down on the back of the dead boy's envelope. He thanked the girl sincerely and then backed away as quickly as he could to avoid the questions he knew she was preparing to ask him.

"Sri Lanka," Sam said to himself as he walked towards the big blue sky outside.

It was late afternoon when he returned to the campsite. He called at the café he had visited the night before. It was quieter now, and the waiter eyed him suspiciously as he sat on the same stool. He repeated his order from the night before and momentarily regretted not having at least tried to eat around the scab on his previous visit. He savoured the continental atmosphere filling the café with unfamiliar smells and textures. The quality of the sunlight through the windows was different to what he was used to. It was whiter and harder. The dust caught in the shafts of sunlight scarcely moved. A passing waiter disturbed them only slightly. Sam sat contemplating nothing whatsoever, but deliberately cleared his mind in anticipation of having to shortly make a serious decision.

In the corner of the room, beside a door to the toilet, was a table on which were leaflets for various local attractions. Probably for the benefit of the tourists from the campsite. After turning a few over and then carefully replacing them, he found what he was looking for. The A5 flyer was stiff. Almost, but not quite, card. Purple and, uniquely amongst the ones Sam had checked so far, blank on the back. Sam caught the eye of a waiter and did a scribbling motion in the air with his right hand. The waiter understood and brought Sam a ball-point pen. It had the name of the cafe on it in gold letters. He drained his espresso and stared at the blank side of the leaflet. He divided the paper in two with a line that went down the middle. At the top of the left-hand column he wrote 'Carry on' and at the top of the right-hand column, 'Go back'. He stared intently at the paper as he ate from the wooden board, paying no regard to what he was picking up. He chewed slowly, never looking from the paper.

Eventually, the first thing he wrote under the words 'Carry on' was, 'Give money to boy's family.' He moved his attention over to the empty right hand column and stared at it for five full minutes. When he finally wrote a single word, he inhaled long and audibly. The word he had written in the right-hand column was, 'Why?'

It was then that Sam realised it was really a simple choice. He could continue, in the left-hand column at least, adding reasons, but he understood that it would just be an exercise in filling blank paper. Those two simple statements, 'Give money to boy's family,' and 'Why?' were all the justification he needed to continue his journey with enthusiasm and single-minded determination.

Sam knew the money was not his. He had never wanted it and felt contaminated with it in his pocket. But once the idea of handing it to the dead boy's family occurred, it gave him a purpose, the virtue of which at least went some way to making the lucre slightly less filthy.

He was fifty-six years old, lived on his own, had nobody depending upon him and had enjoyed the last few days on the road as much as any time in his recent past. He was free. As free as he had ever been in his life. The understanding suddenly came to him that freedom was only freedom when it comes with a sense of purpose. Without that, freedom was like having the shackles removed but the cell door still locked.

It didn't matter to Sam whether what now drove him on could be realised in five days or five years. The important thing was that it guided his next step. It gave him the justification to strive for a new horizon. And a life without striving was one filled with terminal boredom. Boredom frightened Sam more than anything on earth. It was a black hole in his psyche. One which he had skirted around the perimeter of on a couple of occasions. When the yawning abyss came too close, he panicked and raced from the edge of it with frenzied bouts of chaotic activity which only stopped once he had reached the relative safety of the adjacent tectonic plate in his psyche. Living in the moment was fine, but it was so much easier to appreciate the present when he knew what direction the future lay in.

Sam picked up the pen and wrote in large capital letters along the bottom of the paper the words, 'CONTINUE THE ADVENTURE.'

He folded the paper carefully, creasing it emphatically by pulling it slowly between the wooden table-top and his fingernail. As precisely as he could, he tore the paper down the fold. There was no further need for the reasoning once the action was decided. He read the words again on the piece he kept, mouthing them silently.

He paid the waiter and put the purple paper into an inner pocket of his leather wallet. The instruction manual for his future was safe there for the time being.

He had to call back at the campsite on his way to Sri Lanka.

17

As Sam approached his tent, it was obvious that things were not as he had left them. The zipped door was hanging open and his running shoes and towel were lying on the grass. The laces of the shoes were still tied together. They looked sad and dirty and worn out. Inside the tent, what remained of his possessions had been carelessly thrown around.

His tools were gone, as was his stove. His sleeping bag lay in a corner along with a few of his clothes. Anything that was apparently of value had gone. They left his coffee. His passport and any other document that the world used to label him were gone. None of this mattered. His life would be simpler without the distraction of the clutter. An aesthetic outlook to life suited his new purpose well and he viewed the robbery and vandalism more as a helpful push in the direction he was going than the catastrophe you or I might have done. He felt no anguish or bitterness. But he did wish they hadn't taken his fishing rod.

Sam spent a short while gathering a few things from what the tea-drinkers had left. This didn't amount to much. The coffee, his running shoes and sleeping bag. The soft panniers were still on the floor where his visitors had emptied them out then thrown them aside. He stuffed what remained inside them. His coffee mug was still there, together with his old, dented, aluminium saucepan. So that was OK. He would fashion a hobo stove as soon as he found an old tin can and a couple of metal skewers.

Sam felt he should probably know how much money the envelope contained. Reluctantly, he took it out and tore open the sealed flap. The wad of new notes was thick. On one side of them was a beautiful, three-arched bridge, like something a horse and carriage might be seen riding over. On the other was a rather pointless-looking grand archway. What both sides had in common, other than their mossy, undernourished colour, was the number one, closely followed by two zeros. One hundred Euro notes. Sam spread them out and counted them. When he was less than halfway through the stack he guessed that there were fifty. Five thousand Euros in new hundred Euro notes. Not a five-hundred Euro "Bin Laden" to be seen, but rather, the highly valued and highly exchangeable crisp hundreds.

The tarpaulin was missing and Sam guessed the thieves had probably used it to cart away their booty. He paused for a moment. There was a multitool in a brown leather sheath which he usually carried with him, either on his belt or in a jacket pocket. He remembered that last night, he had put it in a pocket which was sewn into the inner tent. He sometimes kept things that he wanted close to hand there, often a small torch or insect repellent. The pocket was behind where the sleeping bag was lying. His guests hadn't noticed it. Sam smiled as he opened the blade.

The tent was of no interest to him now, where he was heading was warmer and he wanted to travel as lightly as possible. But the sewn-in ground sheet would be useful. It was light and waterproof. He stuck the blade through the green rip-stop fabric and guided it neatly from one corner to the next. The material cut with the pleasing sound of a keen blade doing what it does best.

He took the sheet outside, pulled out four of the steel tent pegs and folded the groundsheet neatly around them. He placed it in one of the panniers and pulled the fastening strap tight. He slung the bags over his left shoulder and was shocked by how light they were. His imagination and this meagre collection of belongings were all he had to get him over the next eight thousand kilometres. He walked out of the campsite gate like a cowboy whose horse had been ridden into the ground and died. And, in some ways, maybe he was.

It was early evening and the journey towards his future began with the sun sinking low to his right. There was nothing he wanted to look back at. The bones of a plan were coming together in such a connected way that he felt they had been doing so all his life. Travelling light was no longer a choice, it was a necessity. He would use throw-away bikes. Bikes bought in car parks and on farms. Bikes whose only paperwork was the small amount of cash used to buy them. He would head in the direction of Sri Lanka via farm tracks and back roads. He would cross borders where there were no people. He would be as free to head south as a migrating bird. And Malta was not on his route so avoiding avian exterminators should be possible.

Sam felt liberated by poverty. He had nothing worth stealing and so nothing to protect. OK, in fairness he had the five thousand Euros which he had to be careful with, and a credit card in his wallet, but as far as material possessions went, there was nothing to envy. He wore no outward signs of affluence and his clothes would quickly become the colour of the countryside he was travelling through. He would wear the muted shades of poverty and dirt and become invisible. His beard would grow to disguise his features and his complexion would change with the season. He would be Siddhartha on a moped.

Although his school atlas had disappeared, Sam knew his best bet was to head back east towards Venice and that, if he stuck to countries ending in 'ia,' he would eventually get to Turkey. He had often heard that Istanbul was the gateway to Asia, so it made sense to head there. It would be something over fifteen hundred kilometres. The priority now was to get out of town then find somewhere to sleep. He could start looking for his first 'paperless' bike in the morning.

It was only after walking ten kilometres that the buildings started to become smaller and the window baskets of flowers, most of which were already in bloom, became less frequent. The flowers, together with the tall trees in the centre of the road, had given a relaxed and civilised feel. People lived in the city but wanted something of the country around them. Sam appreciated that. But the commercial area he was now entering was clinically devoid of foliage and decoration. Only occasional vacant sites between the buildings had their own vegetation and wildlife, which went a small way to balance the harmony between man and nature.

Sam bought some simple provisions and a bottle of water. He had also picked up a large, empty can outside the back door of a small restaurant. He rinsed it out under a tap in the yard and put it in one of his panniers. He imagined looking like a hobo might be the perfect disguise for some parts of the journey ahead, but in the suburbs of Milan, less so. He needed a bike quickly. On a bike, he would look the part. The saddle bags would take on relevance.

A motorbike shop caught his eye. The place was closed for the night and the windows shuttered with substantial metal grills. But he could see through them and, beyond the Ducati streetfighters and Japanese plastic rockets, was a collection of scooters. Vespas, mostly, which were the right sort of species. But these shiny new models were not what Sam was looking for. If they had what he needed, it would be at the back, behind the locked gate to the workshop, out of sight of customers and passers-by. It was certainly worth a try. And on the opposite side of the road was just enough nature for him to disappear into for the night. He would be less than a hundred metres from the main road but hidden. Very few people lived in this area. Why would they? The roadside plots were given over to commerce which, after nightfall, were empty. The lights went out and they ceased to exist until people came back to work in the morning. This had happened to many of the city centres Sam knew as a young man. The streets where families used to live had been replaced by smoked glass and stainless steel which buzzed with an economic hum and the smell of fresh coffee during the day. At night, they became as cold and pointless as an empty crypt. But, tonight at least, Sam would be bringing life to this corner of the commercial desert.

He found a quiet patch amongst the untendered shrubs and bushes. He was well hidden but nonetheless set up the groundsheet to make an additional barrier between himself and the road. Any flame from the stove he was about to make would be invisible from the road. He had never used a tin can stove before and was unsure how it would perform.

He tied the groundsheet between two small trees and then bent the bottom side of it back along the grass to give him something dry to sleep on. It was like the backdrop photographers use when they want the background to blend seamlessly into the floor. He imagined Henri Cartier-Bresson setting up his Leica rangefinder to capture the craggy black and white nuances on the face of this Milanese tramp.

With the multi-tool, Sam cut out a door at the base of the can, large enough to fit his fist through. The top had already been removed by the restaurateurs. Just above the bottom rim he stuck his blade through and twisted it. He repeated this every inch so that there were fourteen triangular-shaped holes, each big enough to put the end of his little finger through, running around the base from one side of the door to the other. These would let the air flow freely to feed the fire. The door was for the wood, twigs and leaves that would be the fuel. He notched the open top of the can so that three of the tent pegs could rest across the opening above the flames. On these would sit his battered aluminium pan.

In theory, it was a practical and inexpensive way of heating water or cooking food. It cost nothing and there was almost always something lying around that could be burned. In practice, it turned out to be better than he could have hoped for. The first attempt to get a fire going failed but, after Sam had cut the door a little larger and faced the opening into the direction of the gentle evening breeze, the stove worked well and boiled the water in his pan in just over five minutes. His Chinese stove would had taken around half this time, but what life-changing things could he have done with the two and a half minutes it would have saved?

He reckoned it was time well spent watching the flames burst into life and grow. There were not many better ways to spend a couple of minutes than watching a homemade fire and getting lost in the beauty and purity of the yellow-tipped fingers of flame. And all the while, the water for a fresh coffee was coming to the boil. It was like watching a pint of Guinness being poured, slowly, deliberately. The anticipation was a valuable part of the experience. Without that it would just be a stout.

Sam slept well, unencumbered by any subtle niggles from being in possession of valuable items in a potentially vulnerable situation. Nobody robs a tramp. In the early morning he even managed a decent run, and that felt good. He ran down paths and roads, past empty parks with narrow cycle lanes. The architecture was sterile, lacking anything of the appeal of the nearby city. High-rise buildings with narrow slits for windows looked like crude copies of medieval fortifications. He saw no archers behind the curtains.

The only thing that pulled him up short was the rattling, chopping call of a woodpecker. It took him completely by surprise. Tak-tak-tak-tak-tak-tak. At odds with the chirpy background banter of the garden birds. Tak-tak-tak-tak-tak-tak. Sam looked carefully in the direction of the call. He knew woodpeckers were shy birds and often moved around to the side of a tree trunk, away from passers-by, playing a game of hide and seek. Patience was usually rewarded with at least a glimpse as they crept round from the blind side. So he leaned against a tree and waited, gazing up at the panoply of trees that made a formal perimeter windbreak to a park.

After a minute, he saw the bird, hopping around the trunk into view, pecking tentatively here and there for insects or other things that took its interest. It looked like a Greater Spotted, a bird that he had heard several times on Skye, but only ever once seen. A car drove past. Sam thought how close the driver had come to seeing something special.

There was nowhere to wash, so he would try to find somewhere later in the day to take a swim and maybe rinse a T-shirt. There was no rush. It was still too early for the people from the bike shop to have arrived, so he made another coffee. He left just enough water in the last bottle to clean his teeth with and rinse his mouth. His body might smell, but there was no need to have coffee breath, because this morning he might have some negotiating to do.

At 8:30AM he saw two young men arrive on foot at the bike shop. They opened the steel gate and entered the showroom from a door in the yard. Lights came on and the shutters were lifted. Then a bike arrived and parked in the yard. The rider entered the lit showroom and unlocked the front door. He turned an oily-fingered sign around which read, 'Aperto'. Aperto sounded good to Sam.

He wanted access to the yard, to see what basket cases lay rotting there. The shiny Italian monsters at the front were not the kind of transport a man with no paperwork needed. Three steps into the yard were enough for Sam to identify the sort of thing he was looking for. It was a small Vespa of uncertain but considerable age. Originally, it had been white, but rust and time had won an epic struggle and the white remained only in vestiges of tired paint here and there. The plastic double seat had been torn and taped. The front tyre had some tread but was deflated and old chains from bigger and faster machines had been hung carelessly over the slim, flat handlebars which lacked such modern frivolities as mirrors.

Trying to disguise his enthusiasm, Sam sauntered over to the bike. The simplicity of it was overwhelming and had a beauty that could only be appreciated by someone who had seen enough summers to be unimpressed by bling. If the engine ran, didn't leak oil and the brakes stopped it, Sam wanted it. Other things were details that could be duct-taped together or WD-40'd loose.

The man who had changed the door sign was the first to notice Sam and he walked out to greet him. He was smiling but didn't speak. No doubt he was forming an opinion of the bedraggled stranger poking around in the scrapheap.

Without the gift of a common language, Sam shook the young man's hand then arched his eyebrows and twisted an air-throttle. Adding clarification to the mime, he gave a spittle-spraying imitation of what he imagined a scooter engine should sound like. Then he shrugged his shoulders and rubbed his thumb against his curved index finger in an expression that left the bike shop man in no doubt of the question.

The man was surprised that anyone could be interested in the Vespa, which had lain untouched since before he had started work there. It was a feature of the yard, like a sculpture or a fountain in the entrance to a grand hotel. Nobody really noticed it any more. It was slowly dissolving and melting into the fabric of Milan.

Another man was called over and a conversation took place. When the exchange was finished, the mechanic took the Vespa by the handlebars and dragged it sideways out into the main part of the yard. He threw the old bike chains against the wall and, with a creak like a small vault being opened, pushed the scooter off its centre stand and wheeled it towards an empty service bay. The scooter was dwarfed by the racks of high-tech tools and diagnostic equipment, but the mechanic began his rudimentary inspection showing no signs of ridicule or offence. He removed the side panels and the seat. There was a hook to hang a shopping bag from, a feature that must have been lost to the creative genius of Pierre Terblanche. A shopping hook? What a fabulous idea. Sam's imagined hanging his running shoes from it.

Heaved up on its centre stand, the mechanic gingerly kicked the engine over. And it moved. Freely. That was a good sign. Satisfied that there was at least a possibility of resurrecting the ancient scooter, he systematically went through the essentials. After an hour and a half of pampering, a new battery was fitted and some fresh petrol administered to the patient with as much care as if it had been life-giving fluid from a saline drip. And the mechanic kicked her over. Nothing.

Kick.

Nothing.

Kick.

Cough.

Kick.

Bigger cough.

Kick.

Then she fired up. Just like that. The grand old dame was brought back to life. She smoked like a trooper, then wheezed on and settled to a racing tick-over. The mechanic did some adjustments, the tick-over became steady and the smoke reduced to something acceptable for a bike of its age. Indicators were barely invented when this bike was born. None of the lights worked. Bulbs were changed and wires reconnected, the side panel, then the seat were replaced, the soggy tyres were inflated and, after two hours, the Vespa was good to go.

It was a rare situation where everyone was a winner. The owner of the shop, because he had sold some junk from his yard, the mechanic, because he took pride in the resurrection and enjoyed playing with a bike that could be fixed with only spanners and ingenuity, and Sam because he had just got what seemed to be a perfectly acceptable form of transport for one hundred and fifty euros. It was, however, a surprise to the shop owner and the mechanic when Sam paid the money and rode the bike out of the gates and onto the road. They had expected a minimal conversation about paperwork and documentation. Sam's reluctance to enter a dialogue about it was fine by them. They just shook their heads, laughed out loud and went back to work. Sam thought if everyone journeyed through life leaving the people they came across as happy, the world would be a better place. He was also wise enough to know that scenes of happiness should be left quickly before anything went belly up. Just like telling a joke well, timing was important

The bike handled well enough through the trees to where Sam had stored his belongings. He had anticipated the small wheels would feel awkward over the rough ground, but the Vespa was so light that it was no issue and the bike seemed as happy on the dirt as on the road.

Piaggio, who made and owned the Vespa brand, had origins in the aeronautical industry. Clues to this could be seen in the beautifully spare and streamlined shape of the bike. It was pared down to a minimum. There was no fuss. The bike was made before the word bling was coined and before engineering complexities became the norm. It was beautiful both in its lines and its uncluttered simplicity.

This same simplicity made fastening on his possessions extremely difficult. Apart from the wonderful shopping hook, there was nothing. The job was only made easier when he found a wire supermarket basket discarded nearby. With a minimum of fuss, he found a way to gaffer-tape it to the back of the double seat. Later he would try and fashion some metal brackets. But for now, he needed to get moving – and gaffer tape was one of man's best inventions when it came to making do.

Somewhere on his journey he was sure to come across a rural blacksmith who was used to repairing farm machinery and improvising where necessary. To such a person, making a bracket for the basket would be the sort of thing they could do in their sleep. Something uncomplicated and fabricated in mild steel so that any Tom, Dick or Abdullah could weld it when it eventually broke.

And so, remembering where the sun had risen, Sam set off in a south-easterly direction for Sri Lanka.

18

It was just after 10 A.M. when Laxman returned home. He had been at sea since the early hours of the morning, pulling in by hand the baited long-lines he had set the day before. The fishing lines were made of a monofilament fluorocarbon, stronger than old-fashioned nylon. It had a harder surface, so was harder for large fish to bite through. The snoods were tied onto the long-line every two fathoms, or bamba, as Laxman called them in Sinhala. At the end of each snood was a barbed hook almost two inches long.

In the hours before dark, Laxman and his crewman would sit on the beach beside their boat and bait each of the one thousand hooks. They used strips of cuttlefish or small fish, depending on whatever was plentiful that day. The cuttlefish were easy and the hook was repeatedly pushed through the creamy, firm flesh, then twisted and pushed back from the other direction until the strip curled up and around the shaft of the hook. The fish required more skill to bait correctly. It was a skill every Sri Lankan boy who lived near a beach had gained by the time they were six years old. The hook would be turned into the fish near the base of the tail on the ventral side. The fish would then be gently contorted so that the hook was threaded through its body and the point would come out below its gills. It was then worked up the hook so that the shaft was hidden inside the fish and only the line itself came out near the tail.

The long-line was carefully coiled inside a large, open, wooden box and the hooked bait fish hung over the inner lip of the top of the box sequentially so that when the line was being shot, the fish could be thrown off in turn and the long line run out freely. Each end of the line was buoyed with a polystyrene float and a couple of empty plastic bottles. Twenty-five kilometres out to sea, close to the second coral reef, was where the best catch was to be found. At a depth of twenty to thirty metres, the baited hooks would attract the brightly coloured inhabitants of the reef, collectively known as gal malu, or stone fish. Mostly Laxman caught mullet or small stingrays. There were always other exotic fish that added value and variety to his catch. Occasionally there was a decent sized shark. But the thrashing hammerheads with the girth of a lazy man were long gone. Very rarely, Laxman would land a yellowfin tuna. When he did, he would get drunk with his crewman and the money they got for the fish would be enough to buy rice for his family for a month and a new school bag for his daughter.

Today there were no tuna or sharks, but there was a reasonable catch of mullet. The fish-buyers descended on any boat just in from the sea like crows around a dead dog. Within minutes, the entire catch was sold. Almost fifty kilos. It was not great, but it meant he and his crew got a wage and their families could eat today. They would be able to afford vegetables to go with their rice and fish and the children would have small pots of rubberised yoghurt to finish with. Laxman would only need to buy one pot of yoghurt today because his son was in Italy.

May was the hottest time of the year and today the heat was enough to drain the strength from any man, even one as strong as Laxman. There was no escaping it. Air conditioning was a thing people in Colombo had. People who went to work in suits and pointed shoes and sat behind desks stamping bits of paper with rubber chocks to show their importance. There was not even a fan in Laxman's house.

After bathing at the well in his garden, his wife would feed him a solid village breakfast, hot with fiery chillies. Then he would lay down on the polished concrete floor in the coolest part of the house and sleep for four or five hours until his daughter came back from school. Her school dress was white and her long, oiled hair was tied in two neat plaits with red ribbons at the ends. Laxman would sit in front of his house repairing lines or making nets whilst his daughter did her homework. Late in the afternoon, he would walk back to the beach and bait the hooks.

None of the fishermen wore watches. None of them divided their days into numbers. It was divided pragmatically into tasks and every day the sequence of their work was the same. It was not 4:00 P.M. to the fishermen, it was time to bait the hooks. Similarly, nobody set an alarm clock to wake at 1:30 A.M. They just knew when they had to meet at the boat to go to sea. Nobody was ever late, unless they had died. They were hard-working, disciplined men who knew the responsibilities they had to feed their families. Instead of a welfare state, there was a community spirit, just as there once used to be wherever human beings called home. But here, it was still strong and, if a family had disaster descend upon them, everyone in the village would help. If someone had money and it was needed elsewhere, they would give it. The women would cook an extra meal and send a plate of food, covered with newspaper, for fear that jealous eyes would poison it, to those who were hungry.

There was a simplicity to life as a fisherman. It was difficult and dangerous, but what was expected of a man was clearly defined. Imagination was not necessary. Their hands were hard and their hearts were big. Until their sons grew into men and could in turn provide for them, apart from Sundays, there was not a break in this daily routine. Holidays, like presents at Christmas, were a western invention. Laxman was a man, and therefore work was an accepted fact of life. He was contemptuous of any boys who chose not to go to sea and tried to scam a living getting tattoos and pestering the occasional tourist. In Laxman's mind they were not men. But, like all the fishermen, he did admire the youngsters who found jobs in Colombo. Maybe driving for a rich businessman or working as a peon in a private company. Some youngsters even got enough of an education to work as teachers away from the Western Province. They were the rare ones. If a boy without a university education wanted another life, the only respectable one on offer was to be found abroad. And, of all the far away countries he had heard of, Italy was the best.

Laxman believed that in Italy, Sri Lankans were respected and given trusted positions, which paid ten times what they could expect to earn at home. He knew that because, when village boys returned, as men, after three or four years abroad, they wore expensive clothes and jewellery. They hired cars for the month or two that they stayed. They drank arrack freely and ate at Chinese restaurants. Life for them was good and they told stories of the money and girls and adventure back in Italy. As word spread amongst those young enough to still have choices, their desire to get to Italy grew. Huge financial sacrifices were made by parents and extended families to get fraudulent sponsorship and a ticket to this European El Dorado.

Loan sharks would lend money to families desperate to secure a wealthy future for their sons or daughters. Interest was charged at four percent a month and the family house would be taken as security.

The sum borrowed could be as much as five times what an average fisherman would earn in a decent year. They believed a good job in Italy could pay that back easily.

But the stories were all lies and the reality was that the Sri Lankans abroad mostly worked as cleaners or housemaids. They often lived as many as six to a room and ate boiled rice with whatever they could find or steal to add to the pot. They sent what they could spare back to their families to try and service the growing debt. But it was rarely enough. In time, the property would be taken and the family remaining in Sri Lanka forced to live on the charity of friends and neighbours until they could scrape enough together to build a shack near the beach. Often, the interest payable on the original loan had built up so much the property alone would not clear all the debts, so they would lose their home and still be impossibly in debt to the money-lenders. At times like these it took a strong man to resist the urge to drink pesticide or engine oil. Only with death would the debt be cancelled.

But Laxman was a fisherman and therefore naturally optimistic. If ever a fisherman lost his optimism he would never put to sea and his family would starve. The old men who spent their days on the beach, waiting for the boats to come back, only ever told stories of the good days and the big fish they had caught. They had forgotten the endless days of nothing when the sea was so rough it would toss their boats right back onto the beach. Or the days when their children went to school hungry and painted the ends of their white socks black to disguise the holes in their shoes. Only an optimist could live such a life. A pessimist would drink the oil.

So this morning, as Laxman wearily walked the path back to his house, carrying two good-sized fish and four hundred rupees tucked in the top of his sarong, he knew that his son would do well and it was only a question of time before the money started flowing back to Sri Lanka. When it did, Laxman could relax and his daughter would have a pretty dress and a bicycle. His wife could have a new sari from Colombo and he might even buy a three-wheeler to take her to the Sunday market for her shopping. The fisherman allowed himself a small and secretive smile.

19

I stanbul was now the focus of Sam's attention. The bridge over the Bosphorus was the gateway to Asia and Sri Lanka. There is a motorway that goes almost directly from Milan to Istanbul. The total distance is only one and a half times that from Land's End to John O'Groats. On a good road, it is just about doable in twenty-four hours. For Sam, that was not an option. To fly under the radar on his undocumented Vespa meant that he covered almost twice this distance and took just under three weeks.

Once he had navigated around the top of the Adriatic Sea, he stuck largely to the coast. When he saw signs of affluence and tourism ahead, he turned inland and bypassed any urban sprawls. He learned to measure affluence in many ways, but most reliable amongst them was the number of people, excluding police officers, who wore sunglasses. If it got to more than three or four out of ten, then he knew it was time to turn left. Conversely, the more rural and backward an area, the higher the incidence of policemen wearing shades would be. When it got to point where seven or eight officers out of ten were wearing sunglasses, he knew he was heading in the right direction, wherever that might be.

On occasions, the side roads lead nowhere, so he would turn around and retrace his steps, then turn right and start a bigger arc around a no-go zone of affluence. As he left Italy behind, the affluent areas became scarcer and he felt confident riding through all but the busiest towns. Tourism seemed to be restricted to strictly defined areas which were easily avoided. He preferred the company of farmers. Where there was agriculture, there was hospitable indifference and invisibility in full view. He wore the dust of the road like a Venetian mask and became whatever he needed to be. It was a perfect disguise.

He slept under bridges or behind empty buildings. There was space enough in the open scenery for him to blend into it unseen. He was travelling slowly enough to feel the change in temperature with the passing days and only felt a chill when, after nine days, he climbed through forests into a mountainous region. The night-time temperature fell to around ten degrees Celsius and he needed all the warmth his sleeping bag could offer him. On mornings, he ran wherever he could. Not too far, because of the danger of not finding his camp again since the features of the landscape were unfamiliar to him. Wild boar roamed the forests and he was disturbed more than once in the dark by something large and curious sniffling around him.

After crossing the mountainous area, Sam took a chunk of the southerly out of his direction and headed more to the rising sun. He occasionally referred to a new atlas, he had picked up from a village store, to get general directions. He read it without noticing the names of countries or cities. Names were irrelevant. He had no idea what country he was in or what the next one would be. It didn't matter. The roads and paths he used were there long before the man-made borders that soiled the pages of his atlas. Topography dictated where his route lay, not the ephemeral politics of men and women who would never go there.

The people who lived their lives on such routes tended to live apart from the bigger society. They were strong and self-sufficient. They were helpful and courteous to strangers and never asked too many questions.

The opportunities to speak with people were few and, when he did, the most common question, if one were asked at all was, 'Are you hungry?' Sam couldn't be certain that this was what was being asked, but he wanted it to be. It fitted the way he was beginning to see the world. Race, religion, wealth and marital status were of far less concern to these people than the simple question, is there food in your stomach? How much simpler and more beautiful could civilisation get? Favours were not sought or banked away for later use. Generosity was spontaneous and sincere.

As Sam assessed his life so far, whizzing down a rutted mountain path, the Vespa singing sweetly and the wind blowing cool and fresh on his face, this bit of it truly was the donkey's bollocks. Contentment spread out from him like blood from fresh road kill. It was impossible to live this way and not leak happiness and joy. He tried to imagine a world where everyone felt this way. And as he did so he got closer to Istanbul – the crux move.

Whenever Sam had been around climbers, they had talked endlessly about routes and rocks and splattered their conversation with technical jargon which baffled the non-climbers around them. Sam had picked up some of it through conversational osmosis. The bits he enjoyed most were when they talked about the crux move on any particular route. They waxed lyrical about the challenge this presented and then about the audacity of the move they had completed to overcome it. Sam felt it was a bit like all defining moments in life. He knew that when all was going well and he was in the flow, crux moves were never so 'cruxy'. He breezed past them with the same ease with which he would avoid wet leaves on the road ahead. But on those occasions when things were not going well, one small thing could begin a descent into a mosh-pit of events that resulted in disaster. After a life in business, Sam had learned to look out for these signs and had developed a sensitive radar that would alert him when an imminent trap event came over the horizon. But since he was feeling so good, he dared to hope his crux, Istanbul, would be a doddle.

He knew that in any city divided by a strait there would be commuters who needed to cross the water. In fact, over 300,000 people took the dozens of ferries across the Bosphorus every working day. What he feared was that, in a city as congested as Istanbul, these passengers would never take their vehicles and, if the ferries were all passengers-only, that would leave one of the bridges as the only possible route to Asia. He was worried about traffic restrictions and aware that any minor confrontation with the authorities would necessitate him having to show some documentation. Such a meeting was best avoided.

The Bosphorus is the strait that joins the Black Sea, to the north, with the Sea of Marmara, to the south. Below the jellyfish-shaped Sea of Marmara is another natural strait that connects the Sea of Marmara to the Aegean Sea. This is the iconic Dardanelles, or Hellespont. Sam knew this to be the venue for an annual swim by hundreds, who braved the waters and swam from Europe to Asia, emulating the feat of Lord Byron, who was the first non-mythological being to swim the strait, two hundred years before. If it was swimmable by a man with a bad leg, Sam reckoned he could work out a way to get his Vespa across.

Consequently, he gave Istanbul a body swerve and turned right. The northern bank of the Dardanelles was perfect for Sam. The roads were small, but good by the standards he had become used to. The area along the shore was sparsely populated and became greener and postcard-perfect as he approached Eceabat. There were pine forests and beautiful beaches. There were also the bones of over a hundred thousand soldiers buried in the soil. This was the peninsula where the Battle of Gallipoli was fought in World War I and he passed numerous memorials. He slept out of sight from the road, behind a concrete bunker on one of the beaches. He cooked a breakfast of eggs, which he ate with bread and coffee, whilst wistfully gazing on the sun rising over the gentle hills. It seemed rude to not be silent and contemplative in an area soaked in so much blood. When he ran along the pebbled beach, he did so as quietly as he possibly could. After a dip in the sea, he was ready to press on.

At one point, he saw the remains of trenches dug by warriors from another era. He stopped his bike beside them and walked for a while amongst the labyrinth of earth corridors. Mature pine trees grew in abundance where once fallen soldiers had lain. They gave a cooling shade to the land, but only added to the melancholy that was beginning to descend upon him. He had to leave. It was impossible to shoulder the burden of mistakes made by an earlier generation without the black dog nipping at his heels. His mood had changed completely and would only be relieved by hitting the road again.

It was mid-morning when he reached the ferry terminal at Kilitbahir and he was relieved to see a small RoRo ferry that could easily have been ex Cal-Mac. The loading area was next to a huge heart-shaped fortress and was busy with cars being lined up and passengers gathering for the next ferry which was just about to arrive.

Sam was shown to a small area to the right of the cars on which four other motorbikes and their riders were waiting. Two had the look of seasoned adventurers and rode GS1200's with Stuttgart plates. Their fabric suits were dusty and expensive, and their bikes bristled with technology which would no doubt speed them to their destination with a minimum of inconvenience to any village they passed through. The other two seemed to be locals. They had dark skins and black hair. One was a youngster in his early twenties and the other an old man of indeterminate age with deep lines etched in his face. Both smoked fat, unfiltered cigarettes. Neither of them wore helmets. The old man had the stature and gait of a man accustomed to manual labour. Sam had seen similar, well-used muscular bodies on some of the old-time crofters on Skye.

He parked his bike next to the Turks. The German tourists ignored him, but the older local gave him the faintest nod from under his thick eyebrows. This minor acknowledgement gave Sam such a glow of satisfaction that it blew the war-horror blues away. Whether the Germans ignored him because they believed he was a local or because he wasn't riding a BMW made no difference. He revelled in their aloof distain and knew he had gone a step further towards blending in.

The young man rode an ancient Honda step-through and the old man a Kanuni. Sam knew little about the Kanuni brand except that it was Turkish and had taken on MZ when the former East German 'People's Factory' had gone into financial meltdown. Sam had a high regard for the much maligned MZs, ever since being humbled by one along the Loch Lomond road many years ago. The bike had probably not been worth more than a fiver, but had left him in cloud of blue, two-stroke smoke and, despite his best efforts, he had been unable to catch up. The fact that the MZ's engine sounded like a bag of spanners made no difference. They sounded like that fresh from the factory. No-frills, economy biking.

Sam guessed if the two Germans were foolish enough to ride without their helmets they would be stopped by a well-fed policeman, probably wearing shades, within half a kilometre. In Turkey, it is illegal to ride a bike without a helmet, but the locals do it all the time. The reasoning is simple. Why would the police stop a helmetless local when they knew the rider had no money to pay the fine? Much easier to stop a tourist, whose pockets would be bulging with Euros.

The ferry beached on the wide, concrete ramp with a grinding metallic screech, the same as Sam had heard a hundred times whilst waiting for the Loch Dunvegan in Kyleakin. Once the cars and a new tourist bus had driven off, the bikes were loaded first and directed to a small hatched area to the right of the ramp at the far end of the boat. There was plenty of room for all five of them. The Germans led, and the locals followed. Sam took his time.

The Germans blipped their engines. One of them stood on the foot pegs and manoeuvred on board as if the ramp was a formidable obstacle in the Scottish Six Day Trials. The older man sat on his bike and pushed forwards with one firm kick. The momentum took the bike over the lip of the ramp and, as he accelerated down the slope, he gently pushed the bike into gear and the 90cc engine quietly fired into life. Everything was done with a practiced economy of effort. Nothing about it was unnecessary or for the entertainment of anyone watching. Sam watched in admiration at the poetry of the man's movement. He parked the Vespa next to the blue Kanuni.

The old man walked to the railings and lit up another cigarette. The Germans locked their bikes, chained their helmets to the frames and set off to the open upper deck to get the best views. Sam walked around the Kanuni. In such company, the Vespa had a certain panache and style. The Kanuni had a plastic box tied to the frame where there was once a pillion seat. The box was empty, apart from some dried straw, and it bore the dirt and scratches of animal inhabitants at some time in the recent past. It wore heavy-duty saddle bags, hand-sewn from a canvas tarpaulin. Crudely cut leather straps passed under the box and joined the two bags together. It was simple, but born out of necessity, and Sam knew it would work. There was nothing from the Wunderlich catalogue about the bike.

On noticing Sam's interest in his bike, the old man slowly came to join him. He returned the compliment by walking around the Vespa. In the short time Sam had owned it, he had customised it into a functional working a machine. Like the Kanuni, it was practical and devoid of the unnecessary.

The wire supermarket basket Sam had fitted in Milan, had been replaced by a sturdy wooden box with a well-fitting lid. The two men started walking around the parked bikes as if in a strange mating ritual. There was no communication, other than the occasional nod of approval.

The old man stopped first and looked up at Sam, gazing directly into his eyes. He was assessing the man, not the bike. He must have liked what he saw because he reached over and took the key from his bike's ignition switch and held it up in the air between them in a clear gesture of invitation. Even so, it took a moment for Sam to understand what the old man was proposing. If he was right, the man was offering to swap bikes. It took less than a heartbeat for Sam to realise that this would be perfect for both of them. The old man got a relatively exotic, slightly bigger, entirely practical machine and Sam got local agricultural transport with Turkish plates, the identifying marks of which said 'anonymous'.

The ferry took fifteen minutes to cross from Kilitbahir to Canakkale and in that time the deal had been struck and the possessions of each had been transferred and packed onto their new machines. Not one word had been spoken. Documents were neither asked for nor expected. The only contact either man had with a society that neither felt members of, was a minimal use of the infrastructure it conveniently provided. Otherwise, they lived their lives untroubled by the bureaucratic legalities that tied most of humanity to its geographical, political and financial pillars. To Sam, being paper-free was a liberating discovery. To the new owner of the Vespa, a consequence of poverty.

The Kanuni stalled as Sam tried to emulate the old man's effortless bump start. He smiled as he pushed the bike up the concrete ramp into the province of Canakkale. It was a wonderful thought that he was now on the same continent as Sri Lanka and he could ride to within fifty kilometres of the Sri Lankan coast. Fifty kilometres. That was the distance between Portree and the Skye Bridge.

The route there would be over ten thousand kilometres, or forty days at two hundred and fifty kilometres a day. How long it took him, though, was irrelevant. The only thing waiting for him was the unenviable task of telling a mother and father that he had killed their son and then giving them the money. Sam couldn't decide if it was kinder to get there quickly and put an end to their worries or take as long as possible and spare them that dark truth.

Ten thousand kilometres is a good journey but, whilst kilometres are precisely defined, a journey is an subjective thing. The Iron Butt Association of hard-arsed motorcyclists has a minimum entry requirement of having ridden a thousand miles in less than twenty-four hours. And that entry route is only the 'Saddle Sore' one. The 'Bun Burner' entry requires fifteen hundred miles in twenty-four to thirty-six hours. Canakkale to the Palk Straits, which separate India from Sri Lanka, could be done by a committed Iron Butt aficionado in less than a week. OK, Sam acknowledged to himself, the roads he would face were likely to be less than perfect, but it put things nicely in perspective.

Sam had a rule of thumb when it came to sports, or feats of endurance; if an Olympic athlete could do something in x minutes or jump y metres, Sam reckoned he was doing well if he could cover the same distance in $2x$ minutes or jump $1/2$ y metres. So, if a world class athlete could do a marathon in just over two hours then Sam was happy if he were able to finish it in just over four. Using the Iron Butt benchmark, fourteen days to Sri Lanka, was clearly impossible, but allowing for the handicaps of the roads, the very underpowered bike he was riding and the necessity to avoid customs officials at all costs, he reckoned forty days was about right. It occurred to him that his life was a constant assessment of back-of-the-beer-mat calculations like this. He enjoyed them enormously but sometimes wondered if contentment would only ever be achieved when such calculations were no longer necessary.

20

It took him longer than forty days, but after a while he stopped counting. If it took him the rest of his life, then that would be just fine. Travelling at Kanuni speeds, the globe opened before him one day at a time. It felt like he was on a giant treadmill and was simply staying still whilst the world revolved slowly beneath him. Mountain ranges were visible long before he got there. He learned to anticipate them by subtle differences in the atmosphere. Deserts didn't suddenly appear before him, the land gradually changed. When things started to look too dry or formidable, he would turn right and drop further south. If the way then proved too difficult, he would backtrack, on one occasion for a couple of days, and try another route south.

If there was a deity, or a very high-flying bird, looking down on him his path on this earth would look as random as the dried silver trail a snail leaves when crossing a dirt path. When the sun rises, footpaths all over the world are covered in these chaotic, ghostly tracks of slime. If the snail avoids being crushed, then somehow, it always gets where it wants to. The detail is chaotic, but the progress is directional, and so it was with Sam.

On the second day from the coast, the road began to climb up to the Anatolian Plateau, a vast and varied semi-arid landscape pierced by volcanic peaks. The roads looked new and the traffic on them light. Sam preferred the tracks and paths that criss-crossed the arable landscape. Wheat was predominant in the larger fields, but crops of lentils and chick-peas broke the monotony.

Closer to the villages the fields were small and irregular and worked by the villagers who owned them. They tilled the dry soil with care and made full use of the little land they owned. Infused with a politically correct western sensitivity, Sam disliked the word 'peasant'. It sounded condescending. But 'peasant farming' described perfectly what he saw.

He stopped to admire the efforts of a family working their plot and ate some bread and fruit he had bought in the last village.

The crop they were working on stood on thin stems about a metre high and had hairy leaves which were long and indented. The flowering season was clearly over and the few petals that remained were white, turning to violet at the claws. Large bulbous capsules on top of the fibrous pedicels were still green.

Three small children in colourful loose clothing were walking carefully between the broadcast crop, extracting weeds, and laughing.

Turkey has a history of growing poppy in the area for many hundreds of years. Poppies are used for food, fuel and fodder. And opium.

And of course, it was an industry that was not immune from world politics. With a shock, Sam realised he was looking at a field of opium poppies.

The poppy seeds, spread thickly on his bread, should have been a clue.

The USA forced Turkey to ban poppy production entirely – too many Vietnam vets had become fond of it. But by 1974 the clever Turks had persuaded the Americans to help them develop poppy growing into a licit industry. The void created by the termination of Turkey's illicit supply had already been filled by Afghanistan anyway.

Sam spent a night in the open beside a frighteningly dead looking inland Salt Lake. The shore was crispy with white crystals which were up to ten centimetres deep beside the still water. Other than the crops growing on the lake's western shore, the only other signs of industry were low tech salt collection centres and it was beside an unmanned one of these that he rolled a sheet out to sleep on.

He was grateful for his supply of bottled water because as he looked around to the crystalline horizon, there was not a drop of water to drink.

His only company that night was a flamboyance of flamingos which maintained a flatulent merp mehep merp mehep as they continued their noisy nocturnal feeding until dawn.

In his salty dreams he was the Ancient Mariner and the flamingos were albatross tormenting him with their beauty.

Occasionally he would go all day without speaking to another human being. Petrol and basic food items could usually be bought with cash and gestures. Conversation became like frilly ribbons on a birthday present for a thirty-year-old; superficially attractive, but unnecessary. His thoughts were loud enough to fill any void left by the absence of small talk. Sam believed smiles were more meaningful than words most of the time and he gave away smiles easily and frequently. And, for the most part, they were returned.

Sleeping out became easier as the density of human beings decreased. It was the week after the summer solstice and daytime temperatures were formidably hot. If he kept moving, the breeze was generally enough to make it bearable, but ensuring he had a constant and plentiful supply of drinking water became a major concern. Through abuse, and several purges, his stomach became immune to the various bugs that Asia seemed to be gifting him and most water became potable.

He was strict about ensuring he had enough to eat but was relaxed about what exactly it was and how frequent his meals were. He would gather food from beside the road where possible and supplement his forages with cuts of meat, vegetables or pulses local to the region. The road-kill got bigger and, once, he took a strip of meat off a camel.

The animal was warm when he found it. Whether this was because of what remained of its own body heat or the intense heat radiated from the dusty road was a moot point. But there were no flies around the eviscerated contents of its abdomen which had projected out over the road like red and yellow toothpaste squeezed violently from a giant tube.

Its forelegs were shattered, and its head almost detached near the base of its neck. The loser is an unequal battle of momentum. One natural and yielding, the other not, and bigger. But, in this instance the loser happened to be edible.

Sam started at the single hump. He had heard the flesh from there was the most prized, but when he finally managed to push the blade of his knife through the tough tightly-grained hide, the meat that was exposed was more fat than flesh. The silky white fat lay in thick sheets like blubbery lasagne. He found it fascinating but unappetising so continued the cut down and backwards, cutting deeper as the incision started to gape. When he found the spine, the flesh immediately above it, the loin, was lean and dark red like grass-fed beef. He took only as much as he would be able to eat and was unsure who to thank, the camel or the lorry driver.

His morning runs were still an important part of his daily regime, although his trainers were nearing the end of their useful life. A replacement pair was so fanciful he wasted no time thinking about it. When he ran, Sam overpronated. This was not a major problem, but it meant that the insides of his shoes wore out more than they would in someone with normal pronation. The idea came to him to give his shoes a new lease of life by wearing the left shoe on his right foot and the right on his left. He just did it, and it felt no different.

He had become darker and leaner. His muscles were clearly visible beneath his leathery, browned skin. His body had become purposeful through use and frugality. The sun and wind that had started to bleach the ends of his hair had dried and aged his face drastically. This was more than compensated for by the indefatigable vitality that glowed from his body. If he had bothered to time his morning runs, he would have found that he was running faster and using less energy to do so than at any time in his life.

His physical changes were matched by the differences in his attitude. He embraced simplicity and, in doing so in a practiced and disciplined way, the richness of life began to reveal itself to him. He took pleasure and satisfaction in tiny details before moving on to the next horizon. Sam was a man at peace in a way he never had been before. Things about his past life that had troubled him seemed laughably insignificant. He could take more joy now in the gift of half a cabbage than anything he could think of from his former life.

The humans he did meet were unfailingly generous and gently courteous. There were no outward signs of affluence or ostentation anywhere and, significantly, Sam thought, there were no obvious signs of brokenness. If he were to be picked up at this moment and dropped in Somerled Square in the centre of Portree, people would look at him as if he was seriously and irrevocably damaged. Maybe Sam too would look at the new him and cross the street. But he had never felt better in his life. With a shudder, he wondered how many broken people felt the same. Maybe we are all less than perfect in somebody else's reality? It occurred to him that judging another human being might well be the height of arrogance and reflect more about the nature of the observer than the observed. Sam found a tree and pulled in under its welcome shade. It was too heavy a question to continue with unconsidered.

If he crossed any borders, he was unaware of them although at one point the road signs become unintelligible. The script reminded him of the traces raindrops made on a windscreen in a wild storm. They tailed off in the general direction of somewhere else, like an English alphabet that just couldn't be bothered.

Shortly after the signs changed he became aware of a curious habit people had of refusing to take money for the goods he was buying. At first, he took their generosity at face value but always, on his insistence, the money was, eventually, grudgingly, taken. It was normal to go through this pantomime of offer and refusal for three rounds before the money was reluctantly accepted.

"I cannot take your money. What I have given you is worthless," was a common line when he tried to pay.

Worthless? It is four litres of petrol, thought Sam.

What Sam was learning about, of course, was Iran's complex rules of etiquette embodied in *taarof*, a beautifully subtle ballet of communication, where raising another's status at the expense of your own is the honourable goal. When both sides are practicing taarof, they achieve equality and the gum which keeps society stable is spread that little bit further.

Politeness and honour are essential parts of everyday life. Outrageous generosity seemed to come as naturally as breathing to almost everyone he met. Sam wondered about the tensions that this must create in the psyche of individuals living in such a hierarchical society. He would have loved to get a glimpse behind the locked doors to see the contradiction that he felt must exist between the two worlds. But he was content to pass on through Iran imagining what international negotiations could be like if only the incumbents of the White House truly embraced the Persian poetry that is taarof.

The main obstacles to his progress were natural ones and he found that, with practice, they could often be anticipated. In the isolated areas labour was often itinerant, following work with the seasons. These workers had their own well-travelled routes, used by their people for generations. They eschewed the busier roads and preferred their own pragmatic paths, which were usually punctuated by remote villages. Sam used these, often travelling with other migrants and occasionally in the opposite direction to a steady trickle of humanity. No questions were ever asked because little curiosity was ever raised. Sam had perfected the art of disguise. He adopted local clothing whenever he noticed his own to be at odds with what others were wearing. Often this change would require nothing more than new headwear and a different length of shirt. He grew a beard and hid behind it. With neglect, it achieved a uniformity with those of his migrant peers.

The Kanuni died outside a small village in the middle of a staggering mountainous area which Iran seemed to be made almost exclusively of. Sam had discarded the Turkish plates when people he passed started to stare at them. Without them, the bike was once again anonymous enough to go unnoticed. He pushed it for six kilometres in a heat that almost sapped his will to live. The thick dust on his arms and chest greedily soaked up the sweat that dripped from his face. When he found a shack with rusting bikes stacked against the wall, he leaned the Kanuni against them, knowing it would be used for parts by the grateful mechanic who lived there. It had served him well. The next bike, which he bought from the mechanic for the price of a fish and chip supper, didn't. It was a dog. It lasted two frustrating days, during which he barely covered fifteen kilometres. After having a local spanner-man spend the best part of a morning trying to fix it, Sam decided to leave it and negotiated for a similar-looking 'Heinz' bike. In years gone by, Heinz, most famous for their baked beans, used to have the words '57 Varieties' as part of their logo. This bike had been cannibalised from an untold number of donor machines, so Sam christened her 'The Heinz' and, after filling her with petrol from a glass soda bottle, rode her away, leaving the smiling mechanic with a handful of cash.

Naturally, a bike of such humble pedigree came with no documents and no plates. Sam managed as far as the next village before finding another mechanic who could change the rear wheel bearing and fit stiffer shocks on the back. The old ones were shot and the rear wheel slewed around on its axle like a drunk on ice skates. After an oil top-up and general tightening of cables and bolts, The Heinz was ready to ride forth in all its multifaceted pride and glory.

With a GS, riders often talk about the bike being more than the sum of its components, as if there is some special and unforeseen magic conjured up by the juxtaposition of seemingly ordinary bike parts. Well, the Heinz was no GS but at least it felt solid and purposeful. It had been born, brought up and abused in the rugged terrain around it and the various parts had proved themselves and outlived the bikes they had come from. Maybe there was a bit of pedigree there after all. Sam liked to think so.

Two weeks later, after almost fifteen hundred kilometres of trouble-free riding in some of the driest, hottest and most inhospitable terrain Sam had ever seen, he rechristened it 'The Heinz GS'. It had proved to be a phenomenal little machine. At its heart was probably a Honda 125 single, or a pretty good copy of one. There were few other clues to its origins and it didn't matter one iota. Sam put petrol in it and it went until the petrol ran out. He had never owned a less demanding machine and the sheer audacity of it gave it a grin factor of at least eight out of ten which was up there in the giddy, delirious heights. Ten was necessarily unachievable and nine was reserved for something very special that may or may not come along once in a man's lifetime. If ever there was a keeper, this was it.

It was stolen, on the outskirts of a vast city Sam had been unable to avoid. A large green road sign told him the city was Karachi.

Why anyone would want to steal the Heinz GS was astounding. Sam would have put money on it having a better chance of dissolving overnight than of being stolen. But it was gone, probably to be disassembled and used to bring life to various other machines, rather like an organ donor. Sam hoped it found a use. And thus, the cycle of death and rebirth continued. Very Buddhist, in a mechanical sort of way.

21

Now he was stuck, somewhere in the vast slums and suburbs, with only the clothes he wore and a long-handled canvas bag of possessions hanging over his shoulder. If this was what a low ebb felt like, he realised he was invincible. There was nothing more he needed. Anything else would be window dressing. Milan seemed a lifetime ago and he felt that everything that came before was only preparation for this moment.

There had been a rumbling of thunder for the last few nights and occasionally distant horizons demanded his attention as suddenly they were brought to life by sharp and violent flashes of lightning. But until now it had been dry. The air crackled at night, but the dust still lay thick on the ground and swirled in diffuse curls around his feet as he walked. The atmosphere might be getting heavier, but the landscape was as dry as psoriasis.

The first fat drops of rain came from nowhere. One moment the sky was clear, the next it was black and foreboding. Sam had seen Hebridean downpours where the rain comes in from the sea horizontally with a gust that blasts you in the face and drives the icy needles deep into your pores. If Skegness truly was bracing, a deluge in the islands could probably bring life to the dead.

But this was different. It was warm. The first drops sizzled on the baking tarmac. After that the volume of water coming down was unlike anything Sam had seen and quickly turned every surface into running water which did the gravity dance. Footpaths quickly became rivers.

Traffic stopped. Motorcyclists rode their bikes into covered shop fronts and people ran for shelter wherever it could be found. Many made futile attempts to cover the tops of their heads with newspapers or plastic bags. Umbrellas appeared from nowhere like giant broken spiders devouring the heads of the people below them. Humanity was disappearing from the scene with a speed learned from practice.

Only Sam stood in the middle of the road with his arms outstretched and his face turned up to the black sky. He closed his eyes to protect them from the rods of rain that soaked him through in less than five seconds. There was not a single person who saw Sam, laughing at the sky, who didn't think he was deranged. Sam revelled in the childish simplicity of getting soaked to the skin. The dust was sluiced from the blackened creases in his forehead and the grime on the back of his neck was blasted away. He felt born again.

The rain lasted for just over thirty minutes. And for the first ten, Sam didn't move. Only when he was in danger of being washed away with the force of water rushing down the street did he carefully climb three rough concrete steps to shelter under the tin roof at the front of a shop. The shop sold fruit and vegetables, displayed in wooden boxes and on dirty brown gunny bags laid out on the ground.

People gave him space and stared at him. To Sam, it was a strange sensation. In the west, people are careful about staring. If somebody catches you looking at them, out of politeness, you look away, only bringing your gaze back when you are almost certain they will be looking somewhere else. Here it was different. People stared not just into his eyes, but at every inch of the space he was taking up. They devoured him in an ocular barrage. There was no shame or threat, just a natural curiosity that needed to be satisfied.

When the rain stopped, Sam and the rest of humanity resurfaced and went on their various ways. The gaudy, blinged-up buses were the first to brave the flooded streets and they pushed a bow wave in front of them with careless disregard for other road users. The water was over their headlights in places, but their ancient Leyland engines went on without missing a beat. Motorcyclists pushed their bikes through water that covered the wheels. Three-wheeler drivers brave enough to attempt crossing the deluge were constantly in danger of floating away. A cart passed him, being drawn by a donkey. Any semblance of order on the roads was forgotten in a crazy, Brownian dance. And over everything, the water flowed. The only constant in a chaotic scene.

The higher ground would be cleansed at the expense of the lower. Debris and detritus swirled in the chocolate-brown waters. When it was gone, there would be some seriously unpleasant shovelling to be done by those, topographically speaking, at the bottom of society. But this was the beginning of the monsoons. Nothing would be properly dry for another two months.

As the water subsided, Sam could see the damage done to the infrastructure that people drove, rode and walked on. Weaknesses had been found out and exploited. Some of the pavements had disappeared and some roads, by western standards at least, were left unusable. But nothing was unusable in Karachi. New obstacles were just tackled more aggressively than before.

A quick assessment of the situation made Sam realise that biking through this was probably not the best idea and made any lingering regrets about losing the Heinz GS easier to deal with. So he wrung his clothes out as best he could then gingerly got back into them to dry them with his body heat. It was one thing wearing wet clothes, but putting on wet clothes, like sitting on a warm toilet seat, was something that always made him shudder. It wasn't right.

He decided that in order to pass through the vast, soaking city as quickly as possible it would be best to use public transport. And the most anonymous way to move around would be to use a bus. But he had no local currency. A search for a currency exchange centre would be worse than useless, so he did the next best thing and found a place that served as a bus station.

It was a quagmire. The buses were lined up beside an open-sided building with a tin roof. The building was in the middle of a field of sticky, red mud and glutinous puddles. It was impossible to walk to it without getting clarted to the knees. There were no suits here. This was a bus station that served a poor local community and they bore the stains on their shalwars with a dignified indifference. There was a gaggle of auto rickshaw drivers brooding malevolently on the fringe of the muddy apron, waiting to pick up hires from the bus stand. Sam knew that these men needed a special resilience to survive. They eked out a living wherever they saw an opportunity and, being rickshaw drivers, they saw more opportunities than most. If they couldn't change a few Euros, they were certain to know someone who could.

As Sam approached, they bristled to an affected, nonchalant attention. Assuming Sam wanted a hire, and the pecking order having been established, one of the men stepped forward. He stared at Sam without expression, waiting for instructions. When Sam spoke English, the man's demeanour changed instantly to one of exuberant warmth. It was his chance to grandstand to his peers. His English was perfect and Sam was stunned to hear that he spoke it with a broad Yorkshire accent.

It turned out he had been a taxi driver in Batley for over fifteen years and had only recently returned to his native Karachi. In his time as a Tyke, he had worked hard and saved enough to support his extended family in Pakistan. But the time had come when he wanted to return to his wife and three boys, to oversee their education and subsequent marriages. He had enough to get by but paid the daily bills with what he earned from the rickshaw.

Changing the Euros was easily done and, although Sam was unsure of the exchange rate, he felt certain that what he had been given was more than fair. It was good to trust people, thought Sam. If the rate had been verging on criminal, it would have made very little difference to what was in his pocket. He chose to think of the rate as good and his day was better for it. Not for the first time, he reminded himself that, whilst he was unable to change the circumstances he found himself in, he was always at liberty to decide how he reacted to them.

The rickshaw driver, who was called Shafiq, wouldn't hear of Sam getting a bus into the city. He insisted on taking him there. Two of the other drivers came along for the ride. It was a joyful three-wheeler that took the men to a sprawling covered market of lanes selling spices and small caged birds. The men were tall and fair skinned and looked comfortably familiar. At Shafiq's insistence, Sam bought a new ash-grey shalwar kameez and a dark, itchy waistcoat with a turned-up collar. It had useful pockets and far too many buttons. To complete his authentic look, he bought a pair of sturdy, leather, open-toed sandals with pieces of tyres for soles. To say that Sam was indistinguishable from everyone else would be pushing it, but he was close enough for jazz. And, for Sam, that would do.

Whilst the other two men stopped for a plain tea at a street vendor, Shafiq took Sam aside and asked what his plans were. He omitted certain details, but Shafiq was made to understand that he wanted to press on into India and then finally to Sri Lanka. When it became obvious that Sam had no documentation, Shafiq's concern was palpable. He explained that the Indo-Pakistan border was one of the most secure in the world and anybody seen trying to cross through prohibited areas would most likely be shot – probably by soldiers from both sides. Many had tried and, although there were a few heroic tales of occasional successes, most recently in a ridiculous Bollywood film, the reality was that death was almost unavoidable.

Until now, Sam had exhibited a justifiable and enviably relaxed attitude to the laws and etiquettes of international travel but being shot at was not high on his wish list. He knew Shafiq's concerns were genuine. If it had been easy to do, an enterprising man like Shafiq would know a way to do it. He explained that the international border between the two countries, including the feared Line of Control, was built by the Indians. It consisted of two floodlit, electrified, razor wire fences, separated by a patch of ground which was one of the most heavily land-mined in the world. With money, though, false documents could be bought, and crossing the border might be possible. Probably by using the Lahore to Delhi bus.

If a British passport could be found, it was highly unlikely he would raise any eyebrows at the border. But the only significant amount of money Sam had were the Euros thrust upon him in Milan and he would rather chance the landmines than spend a cent of that. Sam and Shafiq went to join the others for a cup of tea. There was never a question about sugar – it was just added. In large quantities.

Shafiq continued to impress upon Sam the futility of chancing an attempt at the border. To each of Sam's "What ifs?" Shafiq said simply, "You will die." The finality of the answer hit Sam hard. Questions about boats, buses, trains and even tunnels were all met with the same morbid response. For the first time on his journey, the next step seemed dangerous and, quite possibly, stupid.

In truth, there had been no real danger to what he had done so far. Sure, he had winged it by the seat of his pants, but any life-threatening moments, if they existed, had passed him by without him being aware of them. His guile and caution had steered him clear of unwanted attention. But the Pakistan-India border was a game-changer. He was fanciful enough to think that if it were possible he would be able to do it. But he was pragmatic enough to realise that he wasn't Jason Bourne and any bullets heading in his direction would tend to hurt a lot more than those in Hollywood blockbusters. He should try hard to keep as much space as possible between himself and any rapidly moving projectiles. The thought of landmines just gave him the willies.

Sam spent that night with Shafiq and his family. They sat down to eat around a *dastarkhan*, a tablecloth which defined the eating area, which Shafiq's wife spread on the floor. The meal was a fragrant mixture of goat stew and lentils with pickles and yoghurt which they ate with sesame-covered naans that Shafiq had bought from a baker on the way home. They formed a circle and ate from two large bowls in the centre of the dastarkhan. Sam was observant enough to follow the others and remove his shoes before sitting down and to use only his right hand to eat with.

Shafiq's wife spoke only Urdu, but the eldest boy had a good grasp of schoolboy English. He believed that Sam and his father had been friends in England and nothing Sam could say would convince him otherwise. In the end, he gave up trying and, when the boy asked Sam if the taxi his father drove had been a Benz, Sam just smiled, patted the boy's head and said, "Yes, son, a Benz." And, as easy as that, everybody was happy with their own version of reality. Sam slept on the floor with Shafiq and the eldest boy. There were no beds, just plastic woven mats that were rolled out after the room had been diligently swept. Shafiq's wife slept in a side room with the two youngest boys.

At some point in the night the rain started again and hammered on the tin roof. It sounded like Amebix, were playing next door, but Shafiq and the boy slept soundly through it. By morning, the rain had eased slightly and Shafiq's wife appeared before first light and busied herself in the kitchen.

When Sam relieved himself at the spotless squatting toilet he tried to be as quiet as possible. Having lived on his own for so long such subtlety did not come easily. A small hand appeared under the rough planks of the toilet door and carefully placed a new toilet roll, wrapped in tissue paper, on the floor. The hand didn't linger. It withdrew like it had touched a live wire. Sam was as grateful for that as he was for the toilet paper. There are certain things that a man like Sam felt he needed to do with a degree of privacy – and attempting a silent, stealth-approach to a squatting pan experience was one of them.

Outside the toilet was a plastic showerhead coming from the concrete wall which surrounded the small yard. There was a large block of bright yellow soap that looked like it had been cut by hand from something bigger. It smelt of disinfectant and Sam decided it would do fine. He carefully hung his shalwar and kameez up on a nail hammered into the wall and stood under the showerhead as he turned a stop-cock on.

The water was cold. Wonderfully so, and Sam lathered up a storm with the soap. He kept his underwear on as he was unsure about who might wander past. But he made sure that every inch of his skin was scrubbed clean. As he finished, a hand popped round from the side of the toilet, waving a freshly-laundered, dark blue towel. The hand moved the folded towel around to attract Sam's attention. Sam grinned and stepped forward to take it and whispered his thanks to the owner of the tiny hand. This time the hand did a thumbs-up before disappearing. The roof of the yard was open to the sky and now the rain started again. Sam quickly dried himself, wrung out his underwear and put on his shalwar kameez.

When he returned to the sleeping area, breakfast was ready and once again the family gathered together to enjoy spicy omelettes with chunks of warm bread and a saucepan of tea. They followed this with fresh mangoes, which Shafiq's wife expertly peeled and prepared. At the end of the meal, there was a hint of moistness around Sam's eyes as he looked at these wonderful people. Even before he stood up, though, Sam realised he would have to leave immediately. His memories here were too beautiful to risk staying longer. He decided to get the cash to pay for the documents needed to get to India.

Shafiq was relieved to hear of Sam's change of mind and put himself at Sam's disposal for the rest of the day. It was agreed that Sam needed a passport. Although it would have been entirely possible to go to the British Consulate as himself and claim that his documents had been stolen, it would put him back on the radar and Sam was quite certain that it would take a lot more than the rest of the day for the bureaucrats to get their fingers out and produce a replacement. What Sam needed was something quicker. Quicker meant shady. Something slightly Bournesque. Shafiq, unsurprisingly, knew no diplomats but, when it came to underworld dealings, he was a networker extraordinaire.

The two of them went in Shafiq's three-wheeler to a shopping complex in one of the suburbs. The air was a bruised grey and any scent of the sea on the wind was disguised by the multifarious smells of a city of almost ten million people. The complex was a rectangular affair, three floors high. In its centre was a large open area with a market for fresh produce. The vendors squatted on hessian sacks and advertised their wares at full cry.

On the ground floor, brightly coloured shops faced the central area, their goods spilling onto the busy walkways. The first floor was a similar arrangement with a wide walkway at the edge of which was a concrete wall topped with stainless-steel railings. Groups of men chatted and leaned on the railing, looking out onto the free enterprise below.

The third floor looked to be almost deserted. The shops, if there were any, were dull by comparison and any gaudy advertising was absent. Occasionally, men in white shirts and ties could be seen walking quickly from one door to another. Shafiq and Sam climbed the narrow concrete stairs to the third floor. The noise below seemed distant the moment they stepped out from the stairwell and turned left onto the walkway. An old man in a dark worsted suit brushed past them without a glance. His black leather shoes were old and dusty. Sam saw serious-looking men and high stacks of bundled paperwork behind each of the open doors they passed. Wherever they had come to, it certainly wasn't the Comedy Writers' Guild.

Shafiq paused outside the door of the last office before the walkway turned right down the next side of the building. Sam wondered if it was by chance that this was the furthest office from the stairwell. As he entered, he almost hit his head on a three-wheeler's wing mirror, fixed to a metal plate and screwed to the top of the door frame. As Sam looked down the row of doors, he noticed that every office had a similar mirror arrangement. He wondered how he could have walked down the row of offices without noticing something as odd as that.

Inside was a large desk. Numerous grey metal filing cabinets corralled the room. There was a heavy brown curtain, drawn across an opening, beside the desk in the corner furthest from the door. Dusty bundles of paper were piled high on top of the filing cabinets. Everything spoke of age and dust and a dark stillness. It smelled vaguely of cats. Behind the battered wooden desk sat a small, severe man. His thinning hair was unnaturally black and oiled back over his bony scalp. His skin was particularly fair. On Skye his complexion would have been described as 'peely-wally,' though in Karachi, it made him look distinguished. He looked up at the two men as if the effort might break him.

"Hello, Uncle," said Shafiq.

The thin-lipped old man nodded wordlessly towards the two tubular steel office chairs at the other side of the desk. Shafiq pulled one back, scraping it on the cement floor, and beckoned Sam to sit. He coughed briefly by way of small talk and said, "Passport."

That was it. "Passport." Nothing else.

The old man did a peculiar movement with his head. First, he looked up and straight ahead to the left of Sam's head. Then, without moving his head he moved his eyes up and further to the left. He repeated this as if he was watching an imaginary tennis match where the player to his right had sliced the ball high. Sam smiled as he understood that the first glance was checking one walkway. The second was to check the mirror above the door so he could see the walkway from the stairwell.

Satisfied with what he saw, Uncle said, "Where?"

"England." An infinitesimal raising of the old man's eyebrows may or may not have occurred. In the long silence that followed Sam wondered if the old man had died, but Shafiq said nothing and so he too remained quiet.

The rain started again. Within a moment, the broken ends of the plastic downpipes from the roof above were running heavy with water. The noise of the vendors below running for cover was lost in the deluge. Sam didn't understand what followed. He was sure that, if necessary, the uncle could speak English, probably in a clipped home-counties accent. But it was all good. At several points in his monologue, the old man stopped and looked directly at Sam. Then, before dragging his eyes away, he would resume talking to Shafiq.

Shafiq suddenly stood up and thanked the old man, making his way backwards to the door. Sam too expressed his gratitude, though for what, he wasn't yet sure. Outside Shafiq put his arm on Sam's shoulder.

"He likes you."

"Really?"

"We need to get passport photographs and you need to get some money for Uncle."

"How long will it take, Shafiq?"

"Uncle said an English passport is not as easy as some and will take quite a while."

Sam felt his soul take a lurch toward his shoes. "How long, Shafiq?"

"He is very sorry, but he cannot finish it before three o'clock."

"Today?" asked Sam in a voice that was too high pitched to be taken seriously.

"Of course today."

"How much?"

"The normal price is three lakh of rupees, but Uncle says he will do it for you for one and a half lakh. Because he likes you."

"Shafiq, what is a lakh?"

"Ah, a lakh is one hundred thousand."

"So, how much is one hundred and fifty thousand rupees?"

"Just over a thousand quid."

This presented Sam with an immediate problem. He supposed a thousand pounds was not over the top for a fake passport produced within the day, but it was more than he could withdraw on his credit card. There was only one way to do it.

"Have you got some photo ID, Shafiq?"

"Er, yes."

"I'll need to borrow your phone for a UK call. What's your full name?"

"OK, no worries mate," said Shafiq, reverting to a Yorkshire dialect. "Shafiq Ali."

Sam dialled an international number, which was answered in the Bank of Scotland on Somerled Square in Portree. Dianna was the manager and she and Sam had a bit of history. Not much, but enough that Sam trusted her implicitly. She had agreed that if she ever received a call like this from him she would do what he asked. The only condition she insisted upon was that, being the manager at the Bank of Scotland, she wanted to be above any fingers of suspicion that might be pointed in her direction if things ever went pear-shaped. To this end she insisted that Sam open an account at the Royal Bank of Scotland, down Wentworth Street and around the corner. Dianna had no access to the information in this account which suited her fine. What she did have was a book of signed cheques Sam had left with her almost two years ago. He had been a boy-scout. He had been prepared. It was a 'no-cost' financial bail-out if ever he needed one. She had never had a reason to use it until now. She listened carefully to what Sam said. When the call was over, she put on her coat and walked through the rain blowing down from Ben Tianavaig and hugged the leeward side of the street, past the chemist, to avoid the worst of the weather. Dianna didn't enjoy the luxury of warm rain that Sam did.

Within fifteen minutes, Shafiq's phone alerted him that a message had been received. Shafiq passed the phone to Sam, who read the text, smiled and told Shafiq they had to go to Areeba Heaven on Quaid Avenue and that he would need some photo ID. They reached Quaid Avenue in just over twenty minutes. In a city with a population twice as big as Scotland, it would have been reasonable to expect the journey to take much longer.

Sam saw the MoneyGram sign in the window of a dirty commercial building. Banks shared the street frontage with fishmongers. A broken barbed wire fence bordered an empty lot. Everything looked damp and sad with the recent rain. Two dogs were fighting with a bedraggled audience of canine supporters. Shafiq parked the three-wheeler on broken paving stones at the side of the road. There were few other vehicles around and the wet streets reflected the concrete buildings and grey sky. The place had the empty, achingly desolate feel about it that only a severe downpour in a poor urban environment can achieve.

At the desk, Sam showed Shafiq an eight-digit reference number which he in turn wrote down for the MoneyGram teller. With a minimum of formality and a brief examination of Shafiq's CNID, money was counted and put into an envelope which was handed to him and which he immediately passed to Sam.

"Let's go and get some clothes and photos."

"Clothes? What is wrong with these?" asked Sam waving his hand at himself, like a small child protesting his innocence.

"You, my friend, are once again going to be an Englishman. Right now, you look like a Paki."

"Fair enough," said Sam, unable to see a flaw in Shafiq's logic.

They went to a small clothing supplier, indistinguishable from dozens of others that lined both sides of the street. Cheap jackets and waistcoats were hung on plastic coat hangers from strings stretched the length of the shop. After a friendly greeting, the tailor took a tape from his neck and, without any hesitation, bent down and took Sam's waist measurement. It was a good job he started with the waist because the next measurement was more intimate.

Sam looked up quizzically at Shafiq.

"Levi's," said Shafiq by way of an explanation. "Made to measure."

A couple of casual, long-sleeved shirts were offered, together with various western-looking items of underwear. When the shopkeeper put two pairs of beige socks on top of the growing pile, Sam insisted, in a very matter of fact way that brooked no argument, that he was staying barefoot in his tyre-soled sandals. Both the shopkeeper and Shafiq shrugged and the socks were removed from the pile. Sam was encouraged to wear one of the shirts and, by the time he had finished buttoning it up, a pair of jeans that could passably have been taken as 501s were handed to him. Although he was never in doubt they would, they fitted perfectly. Once the sandals were added to the mix, Sam looked like the seasoned western traveller he was supposed to be. The cost was less than drinks for two in the Portree Hotel.

The passport photo studio was up a narrow flight of steps above a regular photo shop which seemed to specialize in huge glossy wedding pictures. All the women were beautiful and the men were dressed as princes. Upstairs was less regal. Shafiq spoke briefly in Urdu to the photographer who pressed his hands together and nodded sagely. He sat Sam down on a rickety black stool and selected a scrappy white back-cloth which he hung with plastic clothes pegs from a string. The camera was a Canon EOS 5D with a very smart EF-L lens, way beyond anything Sam could afford. Before using it, the photographer took a plastic jar from behind a desk together with a bristle paintbrush and began dusting Sam's face with talcum powder. Sam began to protest, but Shafiq held up a hand and told Sam firmly this had to be done.

The four identical pictures, when they came, made Sam look pasty and drained of emotion and character. He was slightly horrified by what he saw.

"Good," said Shafiq, holding them up to a light bulb. "Very good."

"Really?"

"Oh, yes, these are what we need. Now, my good man, we are going to get your hair cut. It is necessary."

The hairdresser was on the second floor of the uncle's shopping complex. There were three chairs for customers. One was an old dentist's chair with the stuffing coming out of the arms and seat. The other two were tubular steel office chairs and one had a plank resting on the two arms for children to sit on. Sam was waved ceremoniously to the dentist's chair. The barber pressed the electric foot controls with a flourish to bring Sam to the position he wanted. A position that had more to do with making the hairdresser's job easier than anything related to Sam's comfort. The cut didn't take long and Sam saw the floor fill up with his brown hair which was bleached at the ends by the sun. It looked at odds with all the black cuttings spread thickly on the floor.

Almost always, Pakistani men take pride in their appearance and very rarely had Sam seen a man who looked like he needed a haircut. Most of them seemed to be able to grow thick, black beards almost without trying. With their beards, a few enjoyed some high-maintenance liberties, but their hair was always traditional and immaculate. During Sam's cut, several men came into the salon to admire themselves in the grubby mirror that ran the length of the wall in front of the chairs. They would reach onto the melamine work unit to pick up a dirty comb to add the finishing touches to their princely perfection. Then they would walk out. Nobody minded.

Sam had to admit the cut he was given suited him. And once the soggy talcum powder was scraped out, with a tissue, from the lines in his face he looked quite distinguished. Distinguished and maybe a little athletic. He was pleased with the results. After a few finishing touches with a deft snip here and there, Sam leaned forward for the barber to remove the nylon cape that had been fastened tightly around his neck. The barber pushed him firmly back in his seat and reached for a chunky bottle with a turquoise and gold label and a heavy glass stopper. He splashed a good dose of the contents into his right cupped palm and began vigorously rubbing it into Sam's scalp. The indescribably relaxing head massage that followed lasted longer than the cut had done and sank Sam into a dream-like state. Too suddenly, the massage ended with a flourish and a snap of the barber's fingers as he pulled his hands away from the back of Sam's neck. It was an unnecessary signal that the session was over. Sam ran his fingers through his hair to achieve the desired effect. He had very rarely looked so good.

"Wow, you don't get that in Batley."

"You do if you know where to go," said Shafiq with a smile.

The uncle looked approvingly, first at the photos and then at Sam. "The difference is plausible." His English was perfect.

Sam began to say, "I don't understand…" But the uncle had already lost interest in him and it was left to Shafiq to explain there needed to be a credible difference between his appearance now and the photo on the passport. If they looked as if they had been taken on the same day, suspicions would be raised. Sam understood that the talc had given him a complexion more suitable for a UK climate. Very clever.

The uncle reached out and struck a brass, dimpled bell on the corner of his desk. Then, without looking, he held out the photographs towards the curtain. A large hand of clumsy proportions reached around from behind the curtain to take the photographs. The owner of the hand was never visible, other than from his fingers up to his elbow. But from that alone, Sam knew that it belonged to a powerful man of formidable presence.

Uncle now turned his attention fully on Sam. After doing the tennis match thing with his head, he held out his right hand. His palm was gently open and facing upwards as he traced his thumb repeatedly over the tips of his fingers in a universal gesture that signified it was pay time. Sam took the envelope from inside his waistcoat and counted out one hundred and fifty thousand rupees in new five thousand rupees notes. After a quick check again at what was happening outside, Uncle took the notes from Sam's hand and, like the good magician he was, made them disappear in an instant.

"Come back in an hour."

22

It was now almost two months since her son had left for Italy and Shani knew something was wrong. If you had held up a map of the world, Shani could not tell you which continent Italy was on. All she knew was that it was a long way from home. A long way from where she could dote on her only son and wrap him in the protective pillows of her powerful love. She prayed every day, at home and at the church. She was resigned to something bad having happened, but with the naïve optimism of uncomplicated love, she yearned for good news. And if Rassika ever mentioned her brother or the fact it had been a long time since he left, Shani would find something to throw and chase her out of the house.

Laxman kept quiet. But he spent long hours at sea troubled by his thoughts. Rohan had never been away from the family before and he knew his son would do whatever was necessary to get a message home to his mother. He would be frightened what his father would do to him if he didn't. Something was not right, but Laxman would rather die than admit it to anyone, least of all his wife. The atmosphere in the home was heavy with words and fears that were never spoken. Laxman slept at the beach with some of the other fishermen more often than he came home.

Shani found a comfort in prayers that was beyond Laxman's understanding. As a fisherman, he took his comforts from wherever he could, but mostly these were based on going to sea with a well-serviced engine, plenty of fuel and water, tangle-free lines and a crew he knew and trusted. God just couldn't come close to these pillars of his faith when the weather turned bad.

Rohan had gone from his life. One day he had been there and the next he was gone. And since then there had been nothing. The pride and elation had long since disappeared. Calls to the man in Colombo were pointless. Four days after Rohan had left for the airport Laxman had tried his number, but it was a dead line. Every day since, Laxman had quietly called the same number, always with the same result.

When there was a problem in his life, Laxman sorted it, without fail. This self-reliance was born of spending so much time at sea. If he didn't sort out problems when they occurred, nobody else would. This gave him a profound confidence in his ability to live his ordinary life on his own terms. Partly this was where his trouble with the church stemmed from. It offered nothing tangible. Nothing he could fix a broken engine with. So, over the years, Laxman and his church had drifted apart. When he and his crew set out to sea, once they had crossed the breaking surf, he would turn his boat towards the small fishermen's church on the beach. This was for the benefit of his crewman, who remained devout. Laxman used the moments his crewman offered prayers to his God to change the fuel line from the petrol used to start the outboard to the much cheaper kerosene on which it ran.

Where Rohan had been in Laxman's life, there was an empty space. A heavy, malignant void which left no clues as to what had happened to the boy. What he found hardest to deal with was his own impotence. His utter helplessness twisted his fear into anger – at Shani, at the villagers and at anything that crossed his horizon. He knew he was wrong to take it out on others, especially his wife, but he had no other way of dealing with the questions which tore him apart.

Surprisingly, Laxman didn't turn to drink. All too often he had seen his friends and neighbours try to bring some calm to their lives by taking kasippu. But it only ever ended in misery, for themselves and everyone around them. The empty bottles that littered their neglected homes, stood as silent witnesses when the drinkers' livers exploded.

And they died in the night in a frothing mess of blood and vomit that thickened to crimson jelly before the first light of dawn.

Laxman didn't want that. Mostly because he didn't want the drink to soften his anger, not even for a second. If he could help his son at all, he believed it was only his anger that could galvanise him to do so. Without a vent, this anger fermented silently inside him.

23

It was almost four o'clock by the time Sam received his new passport, complete with a current Indian visa which was valid for six months from a date three weeks ago. It was authorised for multiple entries.

After a nervous couple of minutes examining the big man's work, Sam could see no flaws. Nothing caught his eye as being unusual, and he was very good at details. Slipped between the back pages was a ticket for the Lahore to Delhi bus. It was scheduled to leave somewhere called Gulberg lll in Lahore at 6 A.M. the day after tomorrow. Lahore was over a thousand kilometres away, but Sam guessed that Shafiq and the uncle had already thought about that. These guys were good at being bad. They turned it into an art form. If there was a Turner Prize for unscrupulous efficiency, they could be sure to be short-listed.

The bus from Karachi to Lahore left in seven hours' time and would take just over twenty-one hours. The cost was three thousand rupees. Sam knew the tourists spent almost twice as much on the Citylink from Inverness to Portree, a journey of around three hours.

Riding through the choking evening streets, packed with weary commuters, Shafiq still had time to take Sam home, where they enjoyed a last leisurely meal with his family. Then it was back out onto the streets to whisk his visitor off to the bus station. At least it wasn't raining. As they parted, Sam reached into his bag and took out the MoneyGram envelope, still thick with cash.

"For the boys' school fees."

Shafiq looked wide-eyed at Sam. Despite his years in Yorkshire, his culture prevented him from insulting Sam by saying, "Thank you." Instead, he grasped Sam in a lung-squeezing bear hug. The wonder in Shafiq's eyes was all the thanks Sam needed.

As they parted, Shafiq called back to Sam and told him to swing his arms confidently as he crossed the line of control. Perplexed, Sam stored the instruction away for later. And then Shafiq was gone. Sam had thirty minutes to wait until the departure of his bus. He spent a few minutes buying bottles of water and some fruit, unsure of what arrangements the bus had for stopping to refresh passengers. Then he took his seat on an unexpectedly comfortable single-decker with a uniformed driver and attendant. There was a large TV screen mounted above the driver which was already showing a pop-art-coloured Asian film complete with fabulous dance routines and an indecent number of costume changes. It was enjoyable pap but Sam wondered if he had the constitution for over twenty hours of it.

The bus pulled out onto the late-night roads on time. Men stood around in small groups on street corners, dressed in flowing white robes and elaborate headwear. Very soon they were travelling on a large urban road and, as they picked up speed, they passed numerous tankers and small lorries.

Instructions came over a loudspeaker to fasten seatbelts. Apparently, it was the law in Pakistan. Evidently, it was also the custom here, as elsewhere, to ignore the law. On this occasion, blending in was not what Sam was about. He was a well-travelled British tourist. He had decided to pitch his new persona as 'confident, but out of his depth'. So he smiled a lot and fastened his seatbelt tightly. His fellow passengers mostly ignored him and, one by one, began to nod off. After about forty minutes, the gentle motion of the bus sent Sam to sleep as well. He was vaguely aware, at some point in the night, of the bus stopping and some of the men getting off to stretch their legs and urinate at the side of the road.

Sam woke as the sun began to rise. It was a strange dawn with no clear focus. A uniform, diffuse, pale orange crept upwards and onto the surface of the world. This slowly turned to pink and then yellow and the day was finally born. The land was mostly scrub, with a few palm trees looking desolate and misplaced. There were no road markings. The imaginary boundaries that separated the carriageways were open to negotiation and, from what Sam could see, momentum was a good point to negotiate from. The verges were rubble that transitioned gradually into the surrounding scrubland.

They pulled in at an open truck stop called the Rose Bar-BQ, where the buildings were made from an attractive, earthy red brick. The ambitions of the owners lay beyond the single storey that had so far been completed and an ugly, raw, concrete frame for further floors stood above the brickwork, like rust-stained ribs of a long-dead boat. Men stood outside smoking like it was an Olympic event. It was as if each had been contracted at birth to smoke his own weight in cigarettes before the results of his efforts finally killed him.

They set off again through a barren, lunar landscape. Men rode bicycles in the middle of nowhere. It was areas similar to this that Sam had come through just a week before. He knew there would be a labyrinth of small tracks out of sight of the main road, known only to the locals. They passed cattle, grazing on whatever they could find, and shanty towns which abounded with goats and poverty. Eventually, industrial hell-holes replaced the hovels, but still the cattle found places to graze. Camels and donkeys drew rusted steel carts with bald lorry tyres on shaking wheels. As the day was beginning to end, they drove through vast plantations of mango trees. The fading light gave a beauty to the pastoral scene that Sam suspected full daylight would cruelly strip away.

An hour before they reached the sprawling mess of Lahore, darkness fell. The steaming industry was beautified by twinkling lights reflected on ground-water. The reflections didn't discriminate between cesspits and sweet water springs. The evening roads were crowded with lorries carrying their goods piled high in what looked like benders, once favoured by new-age travellers. And why not?

Lahore has a population about half of that of Karachi. But when the rains come in July, it typically receives eight inches of rain in the month. Karachi might expect that much in a year. The elevation is quite small, but the average July temperature is around forty-two degrees centigrade, ten degrees hotter than the coastal town of Karachi.

The moment Sam stepped off the bus and away from the throat-parching air-conditioning, he was acutely aware of this difference. Any thoughts he might have harboured about sleeping out in a park or hanging around the bus terminal quickly went out of the window. He needed to find some accommodation. The bus for Delhi departed from a terminal in Gulberg lll, five kilometres from the Main Ferozepur Road Station he was at. Since it seemed to have worked for him so far, he asked the driver of a three-wheeler to take him to the Gulberg lll bus terminal. He wanted to get an idea of where he needed to check in at 4 A.M. the following morning.

After giving the terminal a quick once-over, the driver took him to a local eating place. He was hungry for a real meal and the thought of cooking up on a hobo stove neither appealed nor fitted the image he was trying to portray. He ended up at the Yasir Broast, a short walk from the terminal. It reminded Sam of an upmarket version of the Karachi Social Club in Bradford. He ordered a Mutton Karahi and a steaming plate of chapattis. Maybe this was not wise when he was about to undertake a serious bus journey of several hours and was unsure of on-board toilet arrangements. But he reckoned that over the last three months he had exposed his body to an unimaginable array of bugs that would probably have finished him off back on Skye. And he was still here, and fitter than ever, so he took the chance. And what a delicious chance it turned out to be. Not better than the Karachi, but different. Maybe it was the smells and sounds of authenticity that filled the air. Or maybe it was the fact that the customers here were not mostly made up of police officers from the Karachi Social Club's neighbouring Trafalgar House station. It didn't matter. He enjoyed the food enormously and the impeccably-groomed young men who ate with him treated him with polite indifference.

When he mopped the last drop of spicy gravy up with the last piece of chapatti, it was already late and there were less than six hours until he had to check in. It seemed pointless finding a hotel when there were any number of small tea shops and eateries that showed no sign of closing. He would find somewhere quiet, ensconce himself at a corner table and watch the night-time world go by.

His stomach had that happy, tight feeling he had not enjoyed for a long time. He undid the top button on his new made-to-measures and loosened his belt.

The hours passed quickly until 3 A.M., when he decided to stretch his legs before checking in for the bus. He started walking briskly and even tried running in his tyre sandals. But he felt stiff and awkward and, when he noticed that his running on the dead-of-night streets was causing momentary alarm in the people he passed, he stopped and satisfied himself with an amble. Sam had walked through many streets at ungodly hours and often seen people wearing a soft-focused bruised look, indulging in depraved activities that the dark seemed to excuse. But he had never before witnessed the serene dignity of the night-walkers that he did here. Maybe it was alcohol, or rather the absence of it, that made the difference, but there was no sense of threat, which disappointed him slightly. There was none of the dark-side tingle that gave life an edge. It was more like strolling through an outdoor kindergarten. With the lights out.

By 4 A.M. there were a handful of people waiting at the terminal for the Delhi bus. Sam joined them in a haphazard and ever-changing queue. It was obvious that British queuing etiquette didn't apply. When in Rome, thought Sam, and unsuccessfully attempted to maintain his position.

After checking documents and weighing baggage, and the subsequent resolution of the inevitable arguments, the bus left with a police escort, five minutes after its scheduled departure time of 6 A.M.

The vehicle was a comfortable, air-conditioned Volvo. Only twenty-eight of the forty-two seats were taken, which surprised Sam. Everyone was filmed getting on board and, although the atmosphere amongst the passengers appeared relaxed, there was a forced, unnatural dimension to it. Some ate spicy mixes from newspaper packets as they listened to Asian music, but Sam sensed a fear, which only grew as they neared the border. The entire journey would last about eight hours and included four stops, the first being the Wagah Gate.

Because it was early morning when they got to the gate, there was none of the choreographed absurdity and mock-aggression that accompanied the gate's nightly high-kicking closure. The fan-tailed bonnets and pompous uniforms of the pantomime performers were nowhere to be seen. In their place were serious and purposeful-looking soldiers, on both sides, whose demeanour spoke not of theatre, but of ruthless and clinical efficiency. Sam suspected they were there in the shadows even when the crowd-pleasing show started two hours before dusk. The paramilitary Pakistani Punjab Rangers looked like they were dressed by Marks and Spencer and then given a French beret.

All the passengers disembarked as they approached Indian Customs. Here the screening was much stricter and the unloaded baggage was carefully checked with dogs and electronic devices. When it was Sam's turn to present his documents, he remembered Shafiq's advice, which for the first time made sense. He swung his arms confidently as he walked towards the officer. Any apprehension Sam might have had about entering a country with fake documents was quickly dispersed by the sudden change in attitude of the customs officer. Where previously he had glared with intimidating hatred at each of the passengers in turn and gone through their paperwork like a monkey looking for nits, when it came to Sam, he beamed widely. The ends of his luxuriant moustache stretched and rose like the wings of a bird about to take off.

Sam was a tourist and, as such, deserved to be welcomed to India. There was no reason for a tourist to use an illegal passport. And the visa? Well, all he had needed to do was to apply for it. They exchanged pleasantries and talked briefly about cricket and the merits of the current English team. Sam knew nothing about cricket and all he could think of to say was, "Mike Brearley." It worked. His passport was stamped and the officer's face resumed its twisted look of loathing as he prepared himself to terrify the next in line.

On the bus the relief was both palpable and contagious. Passengers spoke to their neighbours with an enthusiasm that fear had previously robbed them of. Sweets were passed around and a song started spontaneously. Sam smiled to himself as a glow of warmth spread down the aisle. He had been more curious than afraid to see how the border crossing went. From the moment he had checked his new passport he had never doubted that it would be successful. But for some of the others, the consequences of things going badly could have been life-changing. It made little difference if they had been guilty of any wrongdoing or not. In a situation where there is nothing to differentiate accusation from guilt, they were right to be scared. It was a fear that the diligently scrutinising authorities on both sides ruthlessly exploited. The crossing wasn't designed to be easy and the only strategy for those being manipulated was to try and keep their heads down. Sam was not entitled to be part of this crowd. His strategy had to be different. Swinging his arms had not just been a physical thing, it was an attitude.

As tiredness robbed the singers of their voices, and Sam of his vicarious joy, most people took the opportunity to catch up on missed sleep. His final thought before he joined them was that India was the last country he would have to cross before he reached Sri Lanka. This neither pleased nor displeased him. He was beginning to understand that his destination would constantly change and that he would never reach it until he was able to lay aside the load on his spirit. He slept and dreamed he was a black man, running towards the horizon.

At each stop they were given light meals and refreshments. So, when they arrived in Delhi at two-thirty in the afternoon, Sam was well fed and raring to go. After Karachi and Lahore he yearned for open countryside and the tranquillity that a rural lifestyle brings. With only his carry-on bag to weigh him down, he left the rest of the passengers struggling with their heavy bundles and suitcases. A myriad of blue-coated porters carried them effortlessly on their heads. Their backs ramrod, sergeant-major straight.

24

He soon found himself wandering in awe around Connaught Place, a Lutyens masterpiece of British Palladian grandeur. Once the headquarters of the British Raj, it was now home to the largest financial and administrative centre in India. Sri Lanka was just over three thousand kilometres away. It was time for him to become Mr Anonymous again, a feat that became harder the further he left European features and skin tones behind.

A bike seemed like it would hit the spot for what was to follow, but he knew the sort of bike he wanted would not be found in the slick cosmopolitan walkways of Connaught Place.

In an effort to curb New Delhi's chronic air pollution, the iconic Indian and Harley Davidson-powered Phatphatiyas had been swept off the streets some years before. It was a shame, because Sam would have quite liked to ride one of those monsters south.

He followed the crowd down to the underground Palika Bazaar and bought himself some authentic Indian wear. His Levi's were too uncomfortable for Delhi. The temperature was hovering around thirty-six degrees centigrade.

Having changed what was left of his Pakistani rupees and got just over half the number of Indian ones, he bought himself a couple of earth-coloured kurtas and a shalwar. It was very like the outfit he had been persuaded to jettison in Karachi. It struck him as ironic that he had been forced to dress as a westerner to travel between two neighbouring Asian countries and reinforced his belief that people are, by and large, the same everywhere and borders are just bollocks.

Feeling free and flowing in his new country clothing, Sam caught the attention of a passing green and yellow three-wheeler and instructed the driver to take him south. There was a moment of incomprehension on the driver's face and Sam could see he was mentally running through the suburbs of New Delhi searching for anything that might sound like 'south.' Sam clarified his request and the three-wheeler whizzed off in the general direction of Sri Lanka. They passed a golf club, where Sam was sure he saw peacocks parading around the greens. It was so beautifully manicured it made him briefly think about taking up golf. The utilitarian functionality of the Defence and New Friends Colony housing complexes he passed, reminded him of Milton Keynes and, made him feel sad for the people who had to live there.

After more than an hour, when they stopped for fuel, Sam realised the three-wheeler driver was, geographically speaking, well out of his comfort zone. They were close to a heavily wooded area, so he paid the driver twice what he was asked and let the man go home. The parkland looked inviting. The air was breathable and there were birds noisily flitting between the trees. Sam knew this was going to be his home tonight. He crossed a busy road and bought some provisions that would make his night more comfortable. He entered the park through a red-brick arch, past the locked DDA office carrying bottled water, some mangoes, grapes and a small loaf of crusty white bread from the small supermarket. He still had the groundsheet, cut from his tent, folded in the bottom of his bag. That was all the bedding he needed. Children were playing in a bright plastic play area and people were jogging and cycling and parading their dogs.

As Sam went deeper into the park, the trees became denser and resembled a jungle from an old Tarzan film. It was still an hour before dark, but he felt the need for a rest. Not a physical rest – he was fit for anything – more a recharging of something deep within him that felt depleted. People couldn't do that for him and neither could food, a soft bed or a hot shower. Being surrounded by nature was the adaptor required to charge the needs of his soul. That was the main reason he loved Skye so much. His house was only a shelter and a place where people sent bills to. His real home, the place that made him grateful for life, was amongst the hills and lochs. He needed a dose of that now, and this park was probably the nearest thing to it he was going to find so close to Delhi. Away from the visitor attractions, the park was surprisingly quiet. It was easy to vanish into the densest part of the jungle.

It was the smell that first alerted him to the fact that the large tree he had chosen to sleep under might not be the best place to rest. The smell came from the ground but, apart from the luxuriant growth of grass and small shrubs, there was no obvious source. It was an acrid, animal smell, pungent and sharp. The sort that leaves a bitter, face-curling taste at the back of the mouth. When at last it occurred to him that it might have been dropped from above, and he looked up, the fruit bat colony covering every branch of the enormous tree, collectively decided it was the right moment to leave its roosting place and begin its nightly search for food. It is not uncommon for flying animals to purge their bowels immediately after taking off. It seemed to Sam that most of the many thousand bats, which simultaneously took off, decided to use him as target practice. He quickly moved on and discarded his bat-splashed shirt.

The second tree he chose was surrounded by small blue-green bushes covered with an abundance of tiny, white, waxy flowers. A fragrance of jasmine filled the evening with a sweet intensity that nullified the last remnants of the essence-of-bat in his nostrils. He stopped to smell the flowers. His spiritual recharging had begun.

The night-time temperature in Delhi at this time of year doesn't drop below thirty degrees centigrade. It was too hot to cover himself and the mosquitos took full advantage of any exposed skin. He didn't mind the bites so much as the incessant buzzing as they closed in on the sides of his face. He quickly learned that swatting them in the dark was futile – and for every one that he killed, there were two to take its place. 'Which is worse,' he wondered, 'the tropical mosquito or the Highland midge?' It was impossible to quantify but it took his mind temporarily off the buzzing in his ears. There were stories that the Scots used to kill the hapless English by staking them out, naked, overnight in the long grass. Having experienced midges, whilst fishing on remote hill-lochs, in numbers so vast that he couldn't help but breathe them in, he could believe it. Unless you were unfortunate enough to catch malaria, it seemed unlikely that death by mosquitos was common so, on balance, he decided to award the bad-ass gold medal to the midges. Nonetheless, he pulled a T-shirt over his head and rolled the sleeves of his new kurta down over his bare arms. The barn owls, made fat by the rodents of the city, played games in the trees overhead and punctuated his sleep with their screeches. A porcupine ran by him in the early hours, bristling at the human intruder.

Such was the wonderful sense of jungle remoteness he felt, it would not have surprised him to see a leopard walk by. It was, in fact, only as recently as the 1970s that the city's leopard population began its rapid decline as the natural corridors for wildlife began to disappear. Since then, Delhi and its suburbs had become a vast wildlife sanctuary for a species far more dangerous and territorial than the leopard. Homo sapiens. But other than Sam there were none of them in the park, so he managed to get some sleep.

He awoke at around 5 A.M. and found what he was looking for. A park of such vibrant splendour would need some significant irrigation for the hot dry summer months, and irrigation usually meant standpipes. He stripped off and took an extraordinary amount of delight in scrubbing his body with a bunched-up handful of coarse leaves and as much cool water as he could use. It was still dark, and here he was getting a naked wash in a jungle. What hotel could match that for such a magnificent start to the day?

He peeled a palm frond off a young tree and pulled it tightly across his back before drawing it up and down. The leaf acted like a flexible blade and scraped the water from his body. A short, naked run would have been perfect, but he fought the urge because he was not sure he would be able to find his clothes again.

Outside the park, Sam was surprised to see the number of people already around, even though it was still before 6 A.M. There were two sources of light in the sky as he walked down the road; one, a broad pale-yellow glow from the city behind him and the other a smaller, barely discernible soft pink of the sun rising on his left. That meant he was facing Sri Lanka so he boldly stepped forward. When a bus, looking like it had been designed by a six-year old with a ruler, pulled up beside a shelter, he joined the small group of people who had been waiting. It was standing room only, but that was fine. When it was his turn to pay, having noticed what others were paying, he offered the conductor a purple note with a picture of Mahatma Gandhi on it. The conductor said something to Sam, to which he readily agreed with a smile. By reply, the conductor gave him a ticket and a few coins, then squeezed past him.

The bus eventually reached a station and the last remaining passengers got off. Sam, who had only just found a seat, stood up, slung his bag over his shoulder and alighted with a youthful skip in his step. From his window he had seen signs for a wildlife sanctuary and one for a Leprosy Colony.

The bus terminal was in the middle of a wasteland of sterile housing projects which were of little use to him in 'bike-search' mode. He turned left off the main road onto a smaller street that looked like it might lead somewhere more promising. After a couple of kilometres, it was still a monotonous residential area that showed no signs of ending. He decided to retrace his steps to the main road. There was a well-established dirt walkway, so he crossed the road and walked with the traffic. He hadn't gone far when a black Ambassador pulled up beside him and, through the open passenger window, the elderly gentleman behind the wheel asked if he could be of any assistance.

Sam bent down to reply. The smell of mothballs and cigarette smoke was overpowering, but the man, in a cream linen suit, was smiling. His thin, white hair was long and swept back. His brown-toothed smile was infectious and the creases around his eyes were made by a lifetime of looking on the bright side of things. He was clearly a glass-half-full sort of chap and Sam instantly warmed to him. After explaining what it was he was looking for, the old gent invited Sam to, "Hop in", and said that he knew a place where they might be able to help. They drove back to the main road and turned south.

There were patches of vegetation now between the houses and crops began to appear in some of them. This was looking more promising. After fifteen minutes, when the houses had ended, and agriculture had securely gained ascendency, they turned right into a small town. Sam had rarely had such an intense, probing, enlightening and thoroughly enjoyable conversation in his life. The old boy just didn't do small talk. He displayed a powerful intellect and a keen curiosity Sam found as delightful as it was refreshing. They parried with language on subjects as diverse as chemistry and philosophy. Feeling a warm and quickly familiar ease, Sam told the old man he was going to Sri Lanka. He received an admirably impartial, potted, version of the on-going civil war there. The brutality of the struggle for an independent state by the Liberation Tigers of Tamil Elam was made clear to him. The old man took his left hand off the wheel and touched Sam's shoulder gently as he made him promise to take care.

He was the antidote for anyone who felt that their culture was crumbling under the weight of ignorance and apathy.

Sam gently prodded for a hint of what, he was sure, would have been an extraordinary life. But with a giggle, the old man deflected Sam's questions with some of his own. In the end, in an attempt to shut Sam up and move on to something that interested him, he sketched in a few details.

After explaining the fundamentals of Newcomb's Problem to Sam, and demanding an answer, he hastily confessed to being an Emeritus Professor of Architecture and a former head of the department at Cambridge. Earlier in his career he had lectured at Calcutta University where he had inspired a national resurgence of interest in Vastu Shastra, the ancient traditional Hindu system of architecture.

All this information was given without intonation or punctuation. The only part where he momentarily hesitated was when he had said 'Vastu Shastra.' At that point he looked directly at Sam for a flicker of recognition. When he saw none, he quickly returned to Newcomb and pressed Sam for an answer.

Questions were more than a conversational lubricant to the old man. He genuinely sought answers and in Sam he had found a man whose opinions might amuse and even enlighten him.

But before Sam could reply, they pulled into a rust-coloured engineering workshop. Two men were at work turning machine parts on ancient English lathes. Others were filing and cutting T-bars on floor-mounted reciprocating saws. One was bending stainless steel pipes and sparks, from unseen machines, were flying in several places. This was a busy workshop and Sam saw immediately that everything was being done purposefully, without sloth or waste. This is what he remembered industry to be like in the UK in the days when Britain made things for the rest of the world. Now, the expertise and a willingness to get dirty hands had all been exported to the other side of the globe. Sam was grateful there were places like this still around, where a man could do skilled work with his hands to support his family. A man with work like that can take pride in what he does and could enjoy a satisfaction that would never be understood by a banker or city executive earning a hundred times more.

The old gentleman walked past all the manufacturing and into a small office at the back of the workshop where he was loudly greeted by a man in immaculate blue overalls seated behind a metal desk. They shook hands fondly, neither being in a hurry to remove his from the others' grasp. Sam waited outside and absorbed as much of the atmosphere of industry as he could. Eventually, the man in overalls walked to the door and opened it for the old gentleman who introduced Sam to the owner of the workshop.

"You need a motorcycle?" asked the man in overalls.

Neither of these guys beat about the bush, thought Sam, relishing their directness. He entertained the thought that this is what people could be like if televisions were banned.

"Yes," said Sam, not wanting to spoil this beautiful economy of words.

"Enfield?"

"Perfect."

A hefty chain and well-oiled lock were removed from doors clad with rusting sheets of corrugated iron, pop-riveted onto steel frames. As the doors were heaved ajar, Mr Overalls reached in and flicked on an unseen switch. Four dusty fluorescent tubes fought their way to life with a crackle and a pop that sounded more like a breakfast cereal than modern illumination.

Sam stopped breathing momentarily as the light revealed a staggering collection of two-wheeled history. Most private museums would have been proud to claim bikes such as these. There were three rows of machines leaned closely together – maybe a dozen bikes in each row. Some covered with grey, coarsely-woven cotton, others not. Sam could see a plethora of BSAs including the polished chrome tank and long vertical cylinder of a Gold Star. The beautiful, aggressive lines of a Norton Manx, looking like something that Thor might ride as he levelled mountains with his hammer. At least four Triumphs, one of which he immediately recognised as a pre-unit Bonneville. It was light blue and immaculate but looked devoid of character in such exalted company. There was a silver fishtail exhaust on a dark and exotic Velocette, which from the hump on the seat, Sam guess to be a Thruxton. And, as if as a joke, the horizontally opposed, hollow framed greenness of a Douglas Dragonfly.

What lay under the covers, he could only imagine.

The five bikes on the left-hand side of the front row were all Enfields. All ex-military machines, and with nothing obvious to differentiate them. The workshop owner appreciated Sam's awe and clapped him on the back. Then he went to the Enfield at the end of the row and wheeled it out into the morning sun. He clapped his hands twice to attract the attention of one of his workers. No more instruction was needed. The worker appeared twenty seconds later with a fully charged battery, which he fitted beside the regulation tool kit.

Everything happened so quickly that Sam was unprepared when the workshop owner indicated with a simple sweep of his hand that Sam should try it for size. When Sam was sitting on it grinning his approval, he was handed a key and invited to start it. Eventually he found the ignition switch, and clumsily tried to find top dead centre. He kicked the engine over with a futile aggression. The owner and the old gentlemen laughed fit to wet themselves.

At last Sam had to admit defeat and join them in their exuberant and contagious mirth. The old man stepped forward and, doing everything slowly and deliberately in an unpatronizing but didactic manner, turned the ignition switch, the petrol and the choke on. He paused to make certain that Sam had taken all this in. When Sam nodded, he continued. He pulled the decompression lever in, kicked the engine over until the ammeter needle swung over to the left, released the decompression lever and then, almost effortlessly, kicked the army-green beast into life.

The reward for his effort was a sound that was music to all their ears – the glorious throb of a four-stroke single, designed in England and built in India. This was a 1959, Indian Enfield Bullet 350. One of the first made entirely in India from tooling supplied by the British factory in Redditch. Until 1962, a few of the parts were still made in the UK and shipped to the Indian factory. This was one of these mixed-race machines. 'Made like a gun, goes like a bullet'.

Sam pulled the decompression lever to stop the engine and then tried repeating what he had seen. Like the old gentleman, Sam started it first time and let out a very un-Indian whoop of joy.

"Is this fit for purpose?"

"Oh, it is perfect, but I – "

He was cut short by the old gentleman. "To the office, Mr Sam."

Sam followed in their wake. Three plain teas were waiting for them on the corner of the office table. Each was in a glass cup with a white, upturned saucer on top. Sam knew each would have enough sugar in it to give the most popular drink on earth a run for its money. But hey-ho, when in India, and all that. From a filing cabinet, Mr Overalls took out a brown card file with the details of the bike hand-written in beautiful, flowing, black ink on its cover. Inside was a file of papers relating to the bike and its known history.

The bike had been bought from the Indian Army by the old gentleman, along with four others, in 1965. They were the start of a collection the two friends had been building ever since. The bikes were totally original and fastidiously maintained. Every so often, the two of them would choose a bike and take off wherever their whims took them. There was nothing in the collection that was too precious to ride. They shared the philosophy that bikes were there to be ridden and, although they might be beautiful pieces of engineering, true pleasure could only be found by firing one up and doing on it what it was made to do. The old gentleman handed the documents to Sam.

"Enjoy it."

"But I – "

"We are pleased to give you the bike. We have enough to keep us going." And at that they both started chuckling again.

"Really?"

"We cannot think of anyone who would get more pleasure out of the bike than you, Mr Sam. When you get where you are going, or decide you have had enough of it, would you kindly do us one small favour?"

"Of course."

"Find someone else who will get as much enjoyment as you have had out of it and pass it on to them."

"With the same request," added the old gentleman. "All the documents are here, including the ownership book, although it probably makes no sense to go through any formalities. If the police stop you and the paperwork is not correct, it can usually be 'corrected' for a couple of hundred rupees. If anything gets serious, refer them to us."

"Delighted to have met you, Mr Sam. Now, go. You have a journey waiting for you," said the man in overalls.

The tank was topped up with fresh petrol and a battered old white helmet found. Sam was waved out of the gates by two of the most wonderful, generous gentlemen that he had ever met.

How less broken is it possible to be? thought Sam. Maybe part of the secret of happiness is uncomplicated generosity? Whatever it was, these two friends had found it.

There were two hard, green panniers on the bike, but Sam didn't have enough belongings to fill one of them. All he had was a couple of changes of clothing, his threadbare running kit and the groundsheet together with half a beach towel and a toilet kit minimal enough to impress a pole-sitting hermit. The few bits of paper he still possessed and the money for the Sri Lankan boy's family were in a home-made money belt fastened tightly around his waist. His coffee was finished. What he had in place of all the bits and pieces, previously indispensable, was a desire for nothing and a huge ability to improvise. And, together, they would keep him well supplied and took up very little space.

In his haste to leave, Sam regretted he had not had a peek under the covers to see what gems had been hidden from sight. It amused him to imagine that there might be a Rudge or a Panther or, just possibly, a Brough Superior. Sam thought of the old gentleman racing through India in his linen suit in the same way that another gentleman Brough Superior rider, Lawrence of Arabia, once did to Clouds Hill.

He treated himself to a folding road map of India and sat down on a pile of bricks beside the road under a large tamarind tree. The dried pods crunched under his feet. Sri Lanka lay almost due south. Sam reckoned he could make his way down the centre of the country. That way took him through Agra, which was a big plus. The alternative meant swinging out to the west coast and following it round to the bottom of the country. This way would take him through Goa, and as every sweet, pretty, country, acid house Alabama 3 fan knows, you don't go to Goa. Little man.

Due south it was, then.

Navigation should be easy. All he had to do was make sure the sun was on his left on a morning and on his right throughout the afternoon. Eventually, he would find the ocean and, if he had worked it out correctly, once he got there, the next land mass due south would be Antarctica. That very nearly blew his mind, but Agra seemed a good target for today.

The road between Delhi and Agra was well used by tourists. Air-conditioned buses thundered past. The pale European pensioners inside looked down their long, red-veined noses at the red-earthed world beneath them. Sam saw a wake of vultures devouring the carcass of a newly dead cow. He stopped to watch them reduce it to a skeleton in less than an hour. Sitting there as a grisly voyeur, Sam began to appreciate the important part vultures played in this ecosystem. They were a true dead-end for pathogens. If it were not for the vultures, their role would be taken by less efficient dogs and rats, which were, biologically speaking, little more than mobile incubators. Living, breathing dirty bombs for everything from rabies to bubonic plague. Vultures were avian recyclers of carrion without comparison in the natural world and the people of the sub-continent owed them a huge vote of thanks.

Sam felt hungry. Because of the tourists, there were plenty of small places to pull in and eat at. He chose one the coaches ignored, but which was well patronised by Indians. The food was prepared and served on a simple mobile stall by an energetic young man dripping in sweat from his exertions. At the centre of his table was a shallow steel wok, a metre in diameter. He turned the food over with a large metal spatula, giving it an appetising, oily, golden glow. Travellers were milling around in no discernible queue, waving money in the air to attract the cook's attention. Everyone demanded their food at once.

The smell of cooking onions and spices filled the air and teased the crowd, who salivated with a Pavlovian sense of anticipation. When the food at one side of the wok achieved the optimum golden hue, he would serve small portions, which he put into paper bags made from old magazine pages carefully glued together. A dash of yoghurt would be spooned into one small plastic bag and bright red chutney into another. Together, they were handed over to an outstretched hand from which the waiting money was taken. The cook's partner was dealing with drinks. She had a table laden with fruit, most of which Sam didn't recognise. There were plastic buckets filled with luminous liquids covering the rest of the table. Large blocks of ice bobbed around the surface of the garishly-coloured juices. She ladled the drinks out with a plastic jug into waxed paper cups that bore the name of *that* fizzy drink. Sam smiled and waved a note at the cook.

He took his food and waited in vain for any change. When it was obvious that none was coming, he collected a pale orange sharbat from the lady and went to find somewhere to eat. Most diners had brought their own blankets and plates. They spread the blankets on the ground and sat together, cross-legged, around their makeshift picnic. Sam remembered the groundsheet in his pannier and, feeling pleased with himself, spread it on the ground beside his bike. In lieu of a plate, he took a sheet of newspaper from the food stall and spread his aloo chaat, chickpeas, yoghurt and chutney carefully out on last week's copy of the Amar Ujala.

The food was good. The potatoes were suffused with cardamom and turmeric with fresh coriander sprinkled on top. The drink had a medicinal taste unlike anything he had ever tried. Any health-giving qualities of the fruit had been negated by the addition of vast amounts of sugar. The boys in Atlanta would have been proud. If they were ever to consider franchising this sharbat, they would need to recalibrate the bliss point, because this lady had taken the dissolved sugar content into uncharted territory. Sam enjoyed the food but tipped the drink onto the earth beside his groundsheet. Small black ants appeared almost instantly and attacked the pithy remains of the drink. Nature really does have recycling sorted out.

On completing their meals, his fellow diners would remove their plates, which they would wash with water from large plastic bottles, and then pull their blankets out from whatever remained on them with a Tommy Cooper-like flourish. The debris from the meal was discarded where it fell. Paper, cups, plastic, uneaten food – everything. No eyebrows were raised. It was just the way it was. It wouldn't be the last time Sam looked at Asia and wondered if the people here had a genetic defect that made litter invisible to them.

What Sam didn't know was that the lady who made the drinks would periodically leave her table and sweep all the debris, with a grass broom, into a large heap, which she would then diligently incinerate. In an area where refuse collection is unheard of, this was a well-practised and pragmatic alternative. It might be more enjoyable to have a picnic just after a sweeping session rather than before it, but if litter is invisible to you it matters little anyway.

Physically incapable of throwing his rubbish on the ground, Sam screwed it all up and stuffed it into the empty paper cup, then looked around in vain for somewhere to dispose of it. Unable to see anything resembling a rubbish bin, he put it into the empty pannier on his bike. Eyebrows were raised.

Sam wondered if it was ever possible to fully integrate into a foreign culture, or are we always destined to be hostage to the morality of our upbringing?

25

Shani was preparing vegetables for the midday meal. She squatted on the floor and held the wooden handle of a large, upturned knife between her toes. There was a clean sack spread on the floor under the blade onto which the slices of vegetables would fall when she pushed them with a long, smooth slicing movement along the cutting edge. To a westerner, working like that would be torture. To a Sri Lankan housewife, it was just how it was. The kitchen was outside the back of the house. A simple space with a polished cement floor and bare brick walls. The ceiling was made of overlapping woven coconut leaves which did a good job of keeping the monsoon rains out. Being a fisherman, Laxman had made sure the knots tying the leaves together were tight and secure.

A bell from a bicycle sounded at the front of the house. Shani's heart missed a beat. She dropped the bitter gourd and the knife and ran around the outside of the house at a speed that was less than dignified for a woman of her age. The postman stood astride the crossbar of his ancient Raleigh, idly thumbing through a bundle of envelopes. Shani approached him at a more respectable speed, smoothing out her lungi. He held out a pale blue envelope. The edges were bordered with red and blue chevrons. There was a stamp which she did not recognise and an address which read...

WM Laxman Perera
Wella Mawatha
Thalagamma
Sri Lanka

Only 'Sri Lanka' was written in English. The rest was in Sinhala, a script Shani had been familiar with all her life. Her hands trembled as she lay the envelope down on the centre of the plastic sheet that covered the only table in the house. She pulled up a chair and took out her cream coloured, plastic rosary beads, running them through her fingers as she silently prayed. The meal was forgotten as all the conflicting emotions fragmented like an exploding incendiary device in her head.

When Laxman returned to eat, Shani was still staring at the envelope on the table. She had not moved for over two hours and the fervour of her praying had given her a fever. Laxman saw immediately something was far from right with his wife. The intensity of her stare frightened him and made him look at where it was focused. He was still two steps from Shani when he noticed the envelope, unopened on the table.

The devil momentarily released his parasitic grip on Laxman's mind. Relief flooded through his body with such intensity it made him dizzy. But even before the last knot of tension had left him, a crushing doubt returned. An overwhelming fear that challenged all that he knew to be real. The world returned to the dark, cold place he had become so familiar with. He stood beside his wife where their private anxieties fed ravenously on each other and grew into something that was all-consuming. Shani collapsed and fell off the chair into a stunned and shaking Laxman.

He laid her down gently and rushed to the kitchen to pour her a glass of water from a clay jug.

Slowly, she returned to consciousness and he cradled her in his arms in a moment of tender intimacy such as they had not shared for almost fifteen years. When Shani was back on her feet, Laxman picked up the envelope and turned it over in his hands. He carefully put the long, brown nail of his right little finger under the gummed edge of the flap and slit the envelope open. He looked at Shani momentarily before he took the letter out.

Laxman didn't want his wife to see he was suffering and barked at her to go and make a cup of tea. Shani silently left the room, glad of the excuse to leave. She waited, unseen, just behind the door at the back of the house and quietly watched her husband. Laxman unfolded the letter but only looked up to the ceiling and closed his eyes. For the first time in his life he lacked the courage to do something.

Shani quietly walked up to her husband and took the letter from his hands. Tears were rolling down his cheeks. Shani had never seen her husband cry and she had never loved him as much as she did at that moment. She sat down in a plastic chair and read. The letter was simple. There was no return address and no date. Just a few brief words.

'Your son has a big problem.

I can help him, but I will need money.

The more money you can find, the quicker I can make him safe.

I am in Italy and looking after him now, but I will come to Sri Lanka soon.

Have the money ready. It will be at least ten lakh of rupees.'

And it was signed, 'Your son's friend.'

26

S am arrived in Agra at 3 P.M. as the town was stirring from its midday torpor. Agra was a modern city which was once the capital of the Mughal Empire. There was no doubt that the million and a half people who lived there needed a transport system more contemporary than anything the Mughals could offer, but the Cantt Railway Station was so brutally ugly, it was inexcusable.

Over forty percent of the population of Agra is self-employed and this was reflected in the number of small, busy industrial estates. The place was thriving but totally avoidable, so it was with relief that Sam finally reached the Taj Mahal. No polluting vehicles were allowed within a reasonable walking distance of the monument. He saw the queues at the Western Gate and walked round to the quieter Southern Gate, where he was delighted that the sari-clad lady at the ticket window charged him the local entry price rather than the expensive foreign rate. He took his change and walked on to join a group of around fifty, who were released into the grounds of the Taj as a collective herd.

In Sam's experience, not many manmade things had lived up to his expectations. Celebrated works of art and modern wonders of the world usually left him feeling like a lilo with a puncture. That 'Ta-da!' moment, after he had waited so long to see something, was more often an, 'Is that it?' sigh.

The Taj was different. Never had he gazed on anything that captured his imagination in the way the sight before him did. When the rest of his group had moved on, he parked himself on the stone bench made famous by a photograph of a now dead princess. His insides felt like they were melting and turning him into an amoeba. He wondered if he might end up as a puddle around his Bridgestone sandals. If ever man had created perfection, the Taj Mahal was it. A teardrop in the face of eternity, as Gurudev Rabindranath Tagore, described it. Sam didn't have a clue what that meant but it sounded about right.

Only a hundred years ago, the thin-lipped British Viceroy of India had the audacity to melt down the exquisite labour of hundreds of Indian silversmiths to make a rather large wine cooler which sat, gathering dust, in the pantry of his Palladian mansion, a stone's throw from the centre of Derby. That molten act of outrageous arrogance had summed up the British rule of India for Sam. But that palled beside the incomprehensible, eye-popping arrogance of a former Governor General of India, who reportedly wanted to dismantle the Taj Mahal and auction off the marble piece by piece.

Sam was glad that he passed as an Indian, because if he thought he looked English, he would have hung his head in shame.

He left Agra as the setting sun turned the murky waters of the Yamuna into the dappled swathe of a fiery conflagration. The road south took him to Gwalior, where he spent the night in a roadside eatery, euphemistically called a hotel, frequented by lorry drivers who ate and then slept on the wooden benches. It was ten days before the end of July and the summer monsoon rains were still occasionally heavy. The nights were pleasantly cool, but Sam was reluctant to camp out because of the frequency and intensity of the sudden downpours. At night it was difficult to notice the vast black clouds bubbling up from distant horizons, so it became his habit to take an evening meal at a simple lorry-drivers café, then doze for a few hours. If he dozed long enough he would have breakfast before he left. There was always somewhere to get a wash and clean his teeth. He was impressed by the fastidious cleanliness of the truck-drivers, who would strip off and lather up in soapy bubbles that made them white from head to foot. Some would rub their backs against concrete posts to slough off the road grime of the day. Exfoliation Indian-style. Sam tried it one morning and tore the skin on his back in a ragged, four-inch gash. He wondered how many more backs the rusty nail sticking out from the post had punctured. He flattened it with a stone.

A driver saw the wound on Sam's back and approached. It was one of those moments when Sam regretted his inability to read the facial expressions of alien cultures. He didn't know whether the man wanted to buy him a cup of tea or hit him between the eyes. Being a practical man of good nature, Sam smiled, but braced himself just in case. The driver didn't return the smile, but instead, with a soft hand, grasped Sam by the shoulder and turned him around. Sam succumbed. The driver slapped a handful of yellow dust onto the wound and gently rubbed it in. A fine mist of the powder was still in the air as Sam turned to face his tormentor. He recognised its sharp acrid smell as that of turmeric. He had heard of turmeric's antibiotic qualities and understood that the man, far from attacking him, had just treated his wound. But before Sam could mutter his thanks the man had turned and walked away, clapping the remains of the powder from his hands. What a wonderful country India was turning out to be.

There was a new batch of drivers eating, sleeping and smoking beedis when Sam opened his eyes just after 4 A.M. They ignored him as he sat up and stretched. He knew from experience it would be pointless asking for a coffee, so he settled instead for a sweet, black tea, laced with ginger and cardamom. It was the early morning Indian equivalent of a kick-starting Red Bull. 4 A.M. was just too early for breakfast, so he hit the road after splashing his face and scraping the sugar from his teeth with an Indian toothbrush, whose bristles were as unyielding as wire. There was very little traffic but, on a whim, he turned off onto a smaller road which quickly entered total blackness. The surface was good, but the entire visible world consisted only of the small patch of road that reflected a dull yellow from the feeble light of the Enfield.

Sam remembered a time during the miners' strike, back in the '70s, when there had been a power cut. His mother had driven him up onto a hill above Huddersfield. In the valleys below lay much of the industry of West Yorkshire. But that night it was black. A fathomless warm blanket of darkness through which not a spark of brightness could be seen. The lights of his mother's Cortina cast that same feeble yellow glow as the Enfield on the narrow Pennine road. It was with these thoughts dancing nostalgically in his mind that Sam first caught a faint whiff of diesel exhaust. He guessed immediately what it was and eased off the throttle.

Rural tractor drivers all over the world have many qualities, but chief amongst them must be their extraordinary night vision. This is probably necessary because the lights on whatever ancient machine it is they are driving, usually gave up the ghost thirty years before. And there it was, a tractor pulling a trailer, the wooden planks of which were the colour of the night. The only light to be seen was the glowing tip of the driver's beedi.

Successfully surviving on a motorbike is always a gamble. It is a mixture of diligence and dumb luck. Maybe it is the same with life? Sam knew that forty years of mindfully riding motorcycles had increased his diligence and significantly reduced the amount of dumb luck needed. He wondered what was needed in order to move the balance in a similar way with his life.

27

Laxman and Shani had argued constantly since the arrival of the letter a week ago. Ten lakh was a lot of money for anyone. For a poor fisherman who lived from day to day, it was an unimaginable amount. But what is the value of a son?

They agreed they had to get the money, but every time they tried, they were thwarted.

Reluctantly, Laxman had gone to the bank. He had never been inside one before and, when he did, he was made to feel embarrassed at his shabbiness and his fisherman's smell. What counted as manly badges of honour at the beach were dismissed as the marks of a simpleton in the air-conditioned sterility of the main street bank. The manager, in his glass-partitioned corner office, refused to speak to him. And, when a peon discovered Laxman didn't even have a bank account, a private security guard with a brown beret and single-barrelled shotgun escorted him out of the building. People at the counter laughed behind his back as he was pushed out of the door.

Laxman was a proud man. He had always provided for his family. Even in the hungry days, when the monsoon winds blew in from the south-west and piled up a dumping surf, making it impossible to launch his boat, he took work as a daily labourer, carrying bricks or mixing concrete. His hard fisherman's hands and willingness to work made him sought after. But the people in the bank knew nothing of this. He turned in the doorway and, in the manner of a tub-thumping, bellicose politician, stabbed the air with a jabbing index finger and shouted back, "My son is in Italy. Italy!" But his point was lost and the people in the bank fell silent as the door closed behind him.

He fared no better with the moneylender. For people who live off the sea and save their money in village cheetu clubs, or local credit organisations, the moneylender provides an invaluable service. Nobody resents the inflated rates of interest he charges. They admire his ostentatious lifestyle and the fact that he has enough money to lend to them. They appreciate that little paperwork is involved and fail to understand that his crippling rates will drown them in debt if they miss a single payment. Being uneducated in compound economics, and optimistic by nature, the thought of missing a payment never crosses their minds.

But the moneylender Laxman saw already had the deeds to his house as security for the loan he had taken out to pay for Rohan's ticket to Italy. It had been assumed that Rohan would secure a well-paid job at once and find a way to transfer the money back home. That hadn't happened and, after already missing two payments, the meeting with the moneylender was loud and frosty. But the moneylender wasn't really worried. In another six months, at four percent per month, the amount owed would have grown to such a sum that he could justifiably sell Laxman's site to cover his loss. Those who had been lucky enough to find jobs abroad were hungry for land and didn't mind paying over the odds for a plot.

Wealthy relatives were always a good source of unsecured money in emergencies, but the only relative Laxman had with any money was Shani's cousin, who had a shop in Chilaw. And wealth was relative. Ten lakh was more than the cousin could afford without mortgaging his shop and he knew from experience that money lent to relatives was never repaid. If all the relatives he had given money to suddenly decided to pay him back, he would have enough to buy a reconditioned jeep and gift new pews to the church. But it wasn't going to happen. He would have to continue using the bus and secure his place in heaven some other way.

The generosity of people who have little is well-known and in Sri Lanka is probably taken to a different level. But sincere and concerned neighbours couldn't get close to the amount the letter-writer had demanded. At most, the amount usually given was enough to buy the fuel needed to put to sea or medicine for a child. When adults took ill, they would be expected to take a couple of Panadol or wear a poultice of crushed leaves, neither of which really cost anything.

In her frustration, Shani started to blame Laxman for being unable to find the money. Not openly at first, but through hints and veiled accusations which took him all his strength to ignore. Eventually, the blame broke cover and, as she questioned his ability to do what she thought a man should do, she tipped Laxman over the edge. He did something he had never done before. He struck her. He instantly regretted it but found it impossible to apologise. The two of them allowed their stubborn disdain for each other to grow. It was fermented by the tropical sun and the torment of failure into something close to hatred, from which there was little chance of ever returning. They lost their dignity and became broken.

28

I t took Sam two weeks to reach Tamil Nadu, which he knew from his atlas was as close as it was possible to get to Sri Lanka without getting his feet wet. Two weeks which passed pleasantly and easily. The Enfield was a good companion and served him well. He had quickly learned that other vehicles were the least of his worries. Away from the larger towns, the drivers were easy going and predictably irrational. The big problem was with the people beside the roads. Every small town seemed to have a crack suicide squad of militant pedestrians. More than once he saw a face that reminded him of the dead boy in Milan. He slowed down ridiculously as he passed through populated areas.

All his experience at stealth-camping was wasted in Asia. A man sleeping on the roadside attracts little or no attention. In many of the rural areas there was nobody there to see him, so he would pull off the road and fall asleep on the groundsheet. Roadside food was so good and plentiful that he lost all interest in cooking and bought what he needed along the way. Men with glass cabinets, built on handcarts with old bicycle wheels, displayed brightly-coloured foods which they cooked in giant woks of bubbling oil. They could be found everywhere and at all hours of the day and night. India never seemed to sleep and, apparently, constantly required feeding.

Another ubiquitous feature were the roadside shrines. Vehicles would pull up suddenly as another brightly-painted, plaster deity swept into view. The worshipper would quickly alight, say a few hurried prayers then drop some coins into a locked collection box. The ritual having been satisfied, the worshipper would retake his seat and, complete with whatever blessings he had negotiated for, would pull away in a cloud of dust. Sam turned down the opportunity to make offerings at all the religious pit-stops, deciding that an even-handed consistency in his refusal was virtuous. Instead, he put his faith in the diverse deities of friction and the internal combustion engine, a lapse in obedience to either of whom would incur a formidable wrath.

He had managed a couple of early morning runs and was blessed with glorious sunrises, which made the days special. His running shoes had died and been discarded when the gaffer tape holding the soles on had worn though. Instead of another tiresome and futile repair, he ran barefooted. It was surprisingly easy. He started by choosing dirt paths of the type of which India seemed to be made. There were a few larger stones, but mostly he managed to avoid these without spending all his time with his head down working out where his next step would be.

The rhythm of his running changed. With the remains of the artificial cushioning of his Asics decorating a tree somewhere south of Agra, his body had to take responsibility for its own protection. He ran slowly at first, tentatively. Ironically, it felt unnatural. Then he tried bending his knees slightly and taking smaller steps. He remembered a great piece of advice he was once given by a seasoned hill runner; if you are unsure whether to take one step or two, take three. So, he did – and it worked. There was no blistering and his feet quickly grew into their new purpose. Hitting the ground with smaller strides meant his cadence increased. Sam had never been a runner whose natural gait had been giant, heel-striking bounds, but this new way of running soon felt good and quick. It felt like he was using less energy and covered the ground evenly and without stress. Something about it felt wholesome.

He stopped to watch a group of boys using whippy branches for fishing rods. They were fishing for food more than for fun. Their equipment was exactly the same used by boys in western comics. But the children here had a responsibility to bring home their dinner. They kept everything they caught, unhooking them ruthlessly and slipping them into a plastic bag. River monsters they were not.

Tamil Nadu is the southernmost state of India, with just over one and a half times the land area of Scotland. Like most places, its fortunes have waxed and waned. But in contrast to what anyone riding an Enfield through its central arid plains today might think, Marco Polo had once described the Pandyan Dynasty, which ruled the deep south, as the richest empire in existence. Inevitably the British had also played their part when the fabulously named Nawabs of Carnatic bestowed tax revenue collection rights on the British East India Company. 'What on earth were they thinking of?'

The thing that drew Sam to Tamil Nadu, though, was not its culture but the fact it shared a maritime border with Sri Lanka. At their closest, the two countries are just over fifty kilometres apart. They are separated by the Palk Straits, where a chain of low islands known to the world as Adam's Bridge (but to the Indians as Ram Setu, The Bridge of Rama) are visible remains of an ancient land link. The epic Indian poem, *Ramayana*, which in both antiquity and scale makes *Beowulf* seem like a modern-day limerick, tells the tale of how Rama's ape-men built a bridge of stones to Sri Lanka.

Whatever the origin of the islands, large ships cannot pass between them and instead must circumnavigate Sri Lanka, adding days to their journey. It was proposed by the British, as early as 1860, to dredge a canal through the strait. This idea is still being kicked about, but was recently opposed by a religious group, using NASA satellite photographs as evidence to support their belief that the bridge was built by Rama and therefore untouchable. Consequently, the idea of the canal was dropped. This must be the only example in history of a poem scuttling a major engineering project and ranks alongside the Catechism of the Catholic Church, authoritatively defining Purgatory, as examples of how silly we can be as a species.

At various times, there has been a ferry between India's Rameswaram and Talaimannar in Sri Lanka. But it was discontinued in the mid '80s due to the growing power of the Tamil Tigers, and has never been revived since. To get to Rameswaram, from where Sam hoped he might be able to see Sri Lanka, he had to pass through Ramanathapuram and over the spectacular Pamban Bridge which reminded him of something from the cover of an Iain M Banks novel.

He had thought he would arrive at a small impoverished fishing hamlet but was surprised to find a sizeable town, complete with all the usual facilities. There was no mistaking the main function of Rameswaram. The harbour was vast and the number of drab fibreglass boats, lying listlessly at makeshift moorings, almost innumerable. The smell of yesterday's fish sharpened the air, despite the steady breeze.

Like all fishing communities, the inescapable essence of fish had been absorbed into the fabric of the bleached, pastel coloured town. It wasn't unpleasant. The inhabitants probably didn't notice it, but it was everywhere, from the clothing the guard at the railway station wore to the books in the public library. Eau de Poisson.

What was unpleasant, though, was the black canal of human excrement that discharged, untreated, into the sea. Asia can provide examples of pollution that the naïve citizens of more prosperous countries cannot even imagine. Children played on the beach and fishermen tended their boats in a refuse tip flowing deep with sewage. Sam gagged. The children smiled back. He went to explore the harbour, which seemed thankfully free of human waste. His appetite had temporarily deserted him and he walked with his mouth tightly closed. He could still taste the smell of the canal.

Fishermen will always find time to socialise, usually after a day's work, and often in bars or just standing around the boats, talking about their day and bragging about their catches. As ants communicate information through brief physical contact and exchange of chemical pheromones, fisherman do so by social interaction. And the stories (and lies) they tell ensure the whole fishing community have their collective finger on the pulse of the fleet. There are few surprises. So, when a group of thirty or so fishermen were furtively gathering around an unusually brightly-coloured boat, at a small jetty to the south of the harbour, it attracted Sam's attention. The fact that some of them were carrying twenty-litre fuel cans did nothing to dampen his curiosity. As he approached, he could sense the tension rising above them like a Vimana. In attempting not to attract attention, the fishermen became the centre of it. They were fishermen, not spies.

As Sam walked over to them a few spat red betel juice on the ground. This was the Indian version of whistling innocently and looking at the clouds with their hands clasped behind their backs. Although Sam's ethnicity could not immediately be established, it was obvious to all that he was not a Tamil. The dust on his feet and the clothes he wore were those of a poor man. His hair was sun-bleached at the ends, but underneath the dirt they could see his skin was fair. To any dark-skinned Tamils who had bought into the 'snow-white-syndrome,' this would have been cause for envy. But to these fishermen who spent all their days darkening under the morning sun, and to whom 'Fair and Lovely' was just a cruel joke, he was simply alien. To a voraciously gods-fearing society, gurus come in all shapes and sizes and nobody would be the first to disrespect the stranger.

The fishermen of Rameswaram were almost all poor and mostly Hindu. The TASMAC liquor shops, ubiquitous in the rest of the state, were scarce. Instead, they were replaced by temples. It is arguable that religion is necessary for the families of men who make their living on unpredictable seas a in a volatile political environment.

The similarities between alcohol and religion are well recorded, both reducing a devotee's immediate suffering and providing pleasant illusions, so maybe it shouldn't be a surprise.

The women would pray just after midnight when their men went to sea, then again when they woke. When the fishermen returned, another prayer was offered. The trouble was that some of them didn't return. The Sri Lankan Navy was responsible for most of these long-term absentees. For many years, India and Sri Lanka have played an aquatic high-noon with the lives and livelihoods of the fishermen. Tit-for-tat arrests occur on either side of the nautical boundary. At any given time, several hundred fishermen languish in decaying prisons or detention centres, largely forgotten about. The fishermen are cynical about the desire of their politicians to resolve the situation. They are aware that they are disposable bargaining chips in a pointless game of oceanic poker, played by scheming and incompetent politicians.

What Sam was not to know, at that time, was that the brightly coloured boat held his future. Because of the high seas capers, there was always maintained a juvenile numerical parity of those arrested and detained. When exchanges did occur, they tended to happen in the presence of both the Indian Coastguard and the Sri Lankan Navy, somewhere in the shallow waters between the two countries. Well-fed statesmen would make grandiose speeches and lie into megaphones. The fishermen on both sides listened silently, then prepared to welcome their emaciated cousins and brothers back to their home shores.

In the haste to arrest foreign fishermen, mistakes were sometimes made. Genuine and important mistakes, such as the number of men arrested. In one highly anticipated high-seas exchange, brought about by an imminent Commonwealth meeting, one hundred and two men on either side were being prepared for release. This was the entire quota of detainees from both sides. Once completed, the scores would return to zero and the count could begin once again. This time, the problem was on the Indian side. A group of four fishermen had been arrested eight months previously for trespassing over the International Maritime Boundary Line. Since no transport had ever arrived for their transfer to Puzhal prison in Chennai, they remained in custody at the Marine Police Station in Ramanathapuram. Because they were not meant to be there, no funds had been allotted for their maintenance and they relied on food and other necessities from well-meaning but frustrated police personnel.

It was obvious that the books were being cleared, nationally, and the Station House Officer saw an opportunity to offload his four Sri Lankan non-prisoner prisoners. Calls to Chennai had been ignored. The Sri Lankans were an embarrassment and it had become apparent that it was up to him to deal with it. Clearly, they could not be part of the official exchange. These were events full of pompous bureaucracy where the presence of four extra and unaccounted-for men would be an advert for Indian incompetence. The Station House Officer had decided that the best move would be to refuel the Sri Lankans' boat, give them water and food and push them quietly into the sea in the general direction of their homeland.

It was the refuelling of the Sri Lankan boat that Sam had stumbled across. A couple of the men spoke English and, on Sam's questioning, shared a little of what they knew. After all, it was no secret. Each of the four thousand fishermen in Rameswaram had their fingers on the pulse. The Sri Lankans were, as they spoke, being driven fifty kilometres from Ramanathapuram, to this spot, squeezed into the back of a police officer's Tata Indica. The Rameswaram fishermen's job was to get the Sri Lankan boat ready for sea. They had been promised liquid enticements. It wasn't really necessary because the fishermen all disapproved of their government's detention of fishermen from the other side. They feared reprisals and were happy to offer help to their cousins of the sea.

Sam realised there was an opportunity for him here that was about as rare as hen's teeth. The Sri Lankans could arrive at any moment. The Indian fishermen had received the instruction to ready the boat about an hour ago and the drive from Ramanathapuram was usually no longer than an hour. As Sam was thinking it through, a small Tata pulled up beside the road, close to the end of the jetty. The change in demeanour of the fishermen told Sam this was the policeman's car.

A young man had done most of the talking so far. It seemed that, despite his youth and unusually bouffant hairstyle, he had some sort of position within the group and it was to him that Sam made his offer. It boiled down to a Royal Enfield in exchange for hiding him, immediately, in the bow of the boat. Sam explained that the paperwork for the bike was in the saddlebag as he handed him the keys. There was no time to tell the young man about the legacy that came with the bike.

Sam reckoned he was excused that task and under the circumstances, guessed the gents in Delhi would understand.

There was never any question that the fisherman would refuse. A wobble of his head affirmed his consent and immediately the fishermen closed ranks to put themselves between the boat and the approaching policemen. Sam barely had time to notice the four thin, bearded men, nervously watching everything. A police officer walked purposefully on either side of them.

Sam was swept off his feet by a swarm of dark, calloused hands and dropped over the gunwale, where he was pushed down out of sight. He was urged to crawl forward on his hands and knees towards the doors of an anchor locker. It would normally have been impossible for him to squeeze into this space, but the anchor had been stolen eight months ago. He managed to work his way through the door and lay silently inside whilst an oily, threadbare tarpaulin was thrown over the closed door to discourage any inspection. One of the Indians sat on top of the anchor locker and dangled his feet over the doors, affecting an air of casual indifference. The fishermen were revelling in being part of a conspiracy, especially against figures of authority. It was a tale that would be proudly re-told for many years to come.

The policemen were more nervous than the Sri Lankans. They felt exposed and, although their uniforms gave them a status which would normally have been feared by a group of fishermen, everybody knew it was a loss of face for the police and the Rameswaram fishermen leveraged as much mileage from it as they could. Their obvious glee only served to hurry the policemen on.

The Sri Lankans were helped on board and the heavy bag of rice parcels, together with four five-litre bottles of water, were handed to them. The last of them to get on board bent down to respectfully touch the feet of the senior police officer. The policeman could not refuse such a sign of humility and muttered something as he touched the back of the fisherman's head. At this, the other three Sri Lankans climbed back off the boat and lined up to have the blessings of the policeman conferred upon them. It would then have been crass not to do the same to the junior officer, who was by this time already half way down the jetty. He came back and the ritual was repeated. Awkwardly. There was no animosity from the Sri Lankans towards the police. Their respect and gratitude were genuine. These officers had fed them for eight months. Men at the uncomfortable end of Asian society, are well able to distinguish between a cruel man and one who is simply doing the bidding of another.

29

A second letter arrived from Rohan's would-be saviour. Like the first, it was as anonymous as failure and said the writer would be in Sri Lanka sometime during the following week. It also said to make sure the money to help their son was ready.

Shani alternated between fevered prayers and wails of anguish, which she directed at where she thought her God lived. Laxman sat in the darkest part of the house staring wide-eyed at the walls. He would suddenly jump up and pace the room in utter despair. Then he would stumble outside, unaware of where he was. He would shout like a rabid drunk at neighbours and anyone cycling past. The fishermen from the beach came to offer him comfort, but quickly saw it was useless and went to fetch the priest.

The priest arrived in a white van, accompanied by a novice. Both wore white robes gathered at the waist by wide, black sashes. Black-belts in Mysterious Arts. They entered the house without removing their sandals, as their position entitled them to. Both were offered chairs and Shani began to tell the story of their son. She was unable to speak coherently, being overwhelmed by the presence of men of the church and torn apart by her bitter anguish. Laxman stood in the corner of the room rocking gently from side to side like an upside-down pendulum dressed as a man. When he was unable to take the torment any more he stepped forward with such violence that the junior priest almost fell back, out of his chair. He thrust the letters at the priest and said, with an intensity that silenced the mynas in the garden, "We need money. Ten lakh!"

The directness of the man frightened the priest, who was more used to a deferential tone when approached by his parishioners. He started to mumble apologies and said that, although the church was unable to offer financial assistance, he would happily lead the family in prayer, and that he was certain the Lord would provide. Laxman was in no frame of mind to listen to this. He knew the bishop lived in a palace and the church owned coconut estates that it would take more than a day to walk around. He also knew that the bishop's Mercedes cost ten times what he needed to save his son. With as much patience as he could find lurking in the frayed corners of his mind, he explained to the priest that there was no time for prayers and he needed the money now to save his son. Again, the priest refused and offered to pray with Laxman.

Something in Laxman broke irrevocably. It was one twist too many on the unseen ligaments that were mentally garrotting him. He hit the priest and anyone else within striking distance and then went on a blood-curdling rampage of destruction, limited only by the lack of material things to destroy. Everyone retreated to the road as Laxman thrashed around the house, banging his head against the walls until blood splattered on the polished concrete floor. Finally, he stood naked in the doorway, screaming fishermen's curses at the world.

Normally, in any fight, a man might make crude suggestions what he would like to do to his opponent's mother. A Sri Lankan fisherman, however, will go into much more detail. He will typically go on to describe the ambient moisture content of some of her more private anatomical features. It was all too much for the priest who fled to his van with the novice and screamed at his driver to drive.

It was too much for the fishermen, too. Domestic violence was commonplace, but to hit the priest? That was taking things too far. They turned their backs on Laxman and returned to their boats. A neighbour took Shani to her house. She would not return with her daughter until Laxman became reacquainted with his sanity.

30

S am heard the engine reluctantly fire into life and then felt the
steady throb and hum through the fibreglass hull as it settled
into a steady tick-over. The heat in the anchor box was almost
unbearable as the sun baked the panel above his head. He quickly
became slippery with sweat but dared not move. Only when he felt the
motion of the boat as it put to sea, and the steady slap on the hull as the
bow cut through the water, did he begin to breathe easily.

The Sri Lankan fishermen, who were anxiously silent until they
reached open water, suddenly became animated when the reality of
their liberation fully dawned on them. They were chatting excitedly,
then one of them led the others in a song. Two beat out a rhythm on the
engine box with their fingernails and the palms of their hands. Despite
his discomfort, the fishermen's happiness was infectious. Sam grinned
to himself and tried to imagine their faces when he crept out from
his hiding place. But, for now, he had to stay still. He reckoned they
needed to be at least five kilometres out to sea before it would be safe
to emerge. If the boat was capable of cruising at around ten knots,
twenty minutes should do it. He would try to give it half an hour to be
on the safe side. But it was getting hotter and the fibreglass dust was
reacting with his sweat and making him itch maddeningly. With a huge
effort, he managed only fifteen minutes.

Sam was under no illusions that if they wanted to, the four men
could throw him overboard. He cracked the door open a smidgen and
tried his best to peer out. His head was at the port side of the locker,

but it was too tight for him to bend back to see properly. He wondered how on earth he had managed to fit in and had a debilitating flash of claustrophobia. His sweat turned to ice and he felt trapped. The panic was overwhelming. He kicked open the doors and pushed himself out onto the deck, knees first.

The song the fishermen were singing stopped as suddenly as if a needle had been lifted from the vinyl. The happy syncopation of their drumming was abruptly terminated as they fell over each other leaping towards the stern of the boat. Their mouths hung open in shock as they crouched low with their feet wide apart as if ready to attack. Sam lay on the deck, gasping. If his entry had been alarming, his subsequent appearance was so far from threatening, it was laughable.

The bravest of the fishermen slowly put down the boathook he had grabbed and bent down towards something which was hidden from Sam's view by the engine box. Sam froze. He thought he was about to be dispatched by an unseen weapon. "No. No," he yelled as he held his hands up in front of his face. "I am a friend." He closed his eyes tightly as something touched the back of his fingers.

The laughter of the fishermen was a cruel taunt. Only the persistent nudging of something against his hands made him edge back and blink open his eyes. The claustrophobia made him slow to process the sight of four fishermen doubled up with laughter. One of them held out a paper-wrapped rice parcel. Fear had robbed Sam of his sense of humour and it was almost a minute before he began to see the joke.

A second fisherman passed him a water bottle which he gratefully accepted. Nobody spoke as the fishermen, one by one, sat down and opened their own rice parcels. Sam raised the bottle to his lips. He had been in Asia long enough to know that it was indescribably bad form to wrap his lips round the top of it. Instead, he tilted his head back and expertly poured the water into his mouth from a height of an inch or so. In such a manner, a man could happily share his water with a leper.

"Eat," said one of the fishermen.

Sam nodded his gratitude and, after taking another long glug of the tepid water, sat down at the corner of the engine box and opened his packet. He undid the twists from the top of the lunch sheet and spread it out on the paper cover. His rice and curry maintained the shape of the parcel until he stabbed the top of it with his index finger. It collapsed into a display of rice and a variety of vegetarian curries that had been hidden inside. The men ate in silence but, once the meal was finished, the questions began.

Two of the men spoke a little English. Not enough for Sam to give them any details, but enough for him to pass on the bones of his story. He felt complicit in their own subterfuge and saw little reason to hide anything. Their plan was to head to their home port, Chilaw, a busy fishing town on the west coast of Sri Lanka. Thalagamma, the name of the village on the back of Sam's envelope, was a twenty-minute bus ride south, towards Colombo. The men knew the village but not W.M. Laxman Perera. Their boat was sure to attract a lot of attention as soon as it was recognised, so the men said they would drop Sam off, away from the fish market, where the bigger boats normally berthed. There would be fewer people around on the land side of the lagoon and Sam could easily walk to the main road and catch a bus. He was told to look for a number 4.

The men were heading in a south-easterly direction. They wanted to reach Sri Lankan territorial waters as quickly as possible, but they needed to be south of Kalpitiya, where there was a naval base. Once they were at the same latitude as Puttalam, they would hug the coast. This was all sketched out for Sam in the dust on the deck. The names they used were just sounds, but he nodded enthusiastically. Sam gave a universally understood thumbs up. The men grinned and reciprocated. Chilaw would take twelve hours, so they expected to arrive home just before dawn. A perfect time for a fishing boat to arrive without arousing unwanted attention.

The crossing was uneventful. Nobody slept. Lights from the Sri Lankan coast could occasionally be seen. The fishermen were like homing pigeons who instinctively knew their way. He checked the stars, which were huge and bright, and confirmed to himself their direction. The fishermen checked nothing. They could smell the way home. The

Indian coast was not much more than a trip to the corner shop for them. Sam wondered quite how often they had made 'accidental' forays into Indian territorial waters. There was nothing accidental about anything these men did aboard their boat. They were at one with it. At total ease with every nuance and bump and creak.

On the horizon to the west they saw the distant lights from occasional large boats, but nobody bothered them. They steamed without lights, which would only be turned on when they approached the mouth of the Chilaw lagoon, from where a few early morning trawlers were sure to be leaving.

When the night was at its darkest, there was a whack on the starboard side, just above the water line. Sam jumped up and looked in alarm at the others. He was unable to discern their features clearly, but saw that, although they were awake, the smack on the boat barely registered on their faces. There was no sudden movement, no apparent panic. Then there were another two thwacks on the starboard topside. This elicited a response, but not what Sam expected. Two of the fishermen who sat on the deck with their backs to the starboard gunwale leant forward lazily, just enough to bring their heads beneath the level of the gunwale. Just in time.

A brief flash of silver flew out of the darkness and cleared the boat before Sam had a chance to properly register it. Then another, and another. They were no more than the briefest of flashes, ghostly and fast, in the star light. Then there was a smack on the deck, followed by a thrashing and slapping. The noise that flesh makes hitting fibreglass. The sound was coming from the other side of the engine box. Sam stood up and leaned forward to try and see what was making it. As he did so, he was hit in the face by a flying fish.

It didn't hurt, but the shock of it made him scream a high-pitched curse that he hadn't used since he was a schoolboy. The fisherman laughed as Sam sat back down and picked up the stunned fish. He had heard about flying fish but had never expected them to be so beautiful. It was not dissimilar to a herring, but with the wings of a swallow. Its body was stiff and the pectoral fins were fabulous ribbed appendages with a translucent skin stretched taut between the bony lepidotrichia. It quivered in his hands. The fishermen were still giggling as Sam gently released the fish back into the water. He joined in their laughter and the night seemed less dark.

There was still no sign of the sun, but lights on the shore to the east were becoming more apparent. Eventually, the occasional headlight from night-time vehicles could be seen. Sri Lanka could be no more than two or three kilometres away. The fishermen confidently pressed on down the coast, recognising landmarks and features that were hidden to Sam.

When the man at the wheel made the boat turn sharply east, the excitement of the fishermen was obvious. For almost the entire journey, the swell had been coming from the north-west and had been mostly unnoticed. Now, as they turned to port and the waves began to stack up as they approached the shore, the ride became uncomfortable. The boat pitched and rolled its way into the calmer waters of a river mouth which was hidden from view by shallow, sloping beaches to either side of the narrow opening. To the south of them, the lights of a town were clearly visible and, to the east, the first blush of pink kissed the morning sky.

"Deduru Oya," said one of the fishermen. Sam thought it might be the invocation of a blessing, so he repeated it, his pronunciation anesthetised by his thick European tongue. He sounded like a penguin coughing. The helmsman expertly navigated the sandbanks and brought them into a wider stretch of water that was obviously the start of a lagoon. The Deduru Oya.

Boats were making out to sea hugging the westerly bank, which looked to be the home of the fishing fleet. Their boat stayed close to the east bank, beside which lay the centre of the town. Hand signals and exaggerated silent pronunciation, which the fishermen usually reserved for speaking to the deaf, informed Sam which way he should go once he was dropped off.

Ahead, several larger boats were berthed at a concrete mooring which ran parallel to the shore. Behind it Sam could see a road, along which there were numerous streets running off perpendicularly. They led to the lights of the town but were lost to sight behind bends and parked vehicles. The throaty roar of diesel engines being started could be heard above the early morning background throb of the town waking up. The small boat easily manoeuvred into an empty berth and the fisherman at the bow grabbed a steel ring set into the concrete and pulled the boat alongside.

There was no time for thanks or goodbyes. Sam jumped ashore and the bow-man firmly pushed the boat back out into the lagoon. He turned to wave, but the fishermen were already gunning the boat towards the far shore and were in an animated conversation once again. He waved at their backs, smiled thinly and felt very alone.

In a few hours, he was going to meet a family he didn't know, who spoke a language he didn't understand, and try to tell them that he had killed their son. He withered at the thought of drawing diagrams for them and playing a macabre game of charades. He steeled his resolve in the knowledge that, however hard it was for him, it would be unimaginably harder for them. Would they attack him? If they did, would he really mind? If they left him bleeding and battered, would it go any way to assuage the blameless guilt he was feeling?

What had begun as a perceived duty, an honourable course of action, had changed into something that, when completed, he hoped would act as a punctuation mark in his life. He had hoped that the act of handing over the money to the boy's parents would bring something to a close. But the closer he got to doing so, the more he worried that it was only as a gesture, a display of futile vanity. The adventure had moved on from a road trip with a purpose to something more akin to a quest and that quest was for wisdom and, unlike a road trip, had no end. He would pass the money on because it was the right thing to do. It was virtuous and anything that happened to him was therefore of no consequence.

The money had been a weight for too long now although, he had to admit, it had brought him clarity when decisions needed to be made in Milan. If it were not for the money, he would probably be back on Skye and maybe even awaiting the delivery of a new motorbike. He knew that if he hadn't made the journey to Sri Lanka, he would be closer to death. Spiritually, if not physically. Death by boredom.

He went looking for something to eat. Stepping over an unfenced railway line and walking south along the road beside the lagoon, he passed houses and anonymous buildings, mostly hidden behind large concrete walls. Posters for chemistry lessons and small white death notices were carelessly pasted to the walls. Fabulous trees could be seen towering high from behind them. In some, fruit bats, the size of young foxes, were returning to roost. The crows greeted the new day with a cacophony of ugly squawks and reluctantly made room for the winged mammals of the night.

After a few minutes, Sam came to a crossroads. To his right, the railway track crossed the ramp to a long, low bridge which spanned the lagoon to the fish market on the other side. He thought he heard wild whoops and yells from that direction, diluted by the dawn. It had to be the rolling joy at the return of the prodigal sons. Traffic was steadily coming down the road to his left to cross the bridge. Shops and cafes were opening and there was a smell of baking that mingled with the background odours of fish and fermenting garbage. Sam turned left and immediately found a café. The front of it was cheaply fabricated from green, anodised aluminium and glass that may or may not have once been clean. To the right of the door was a man preparing food in a cubicle of glass partitions which came up to the level of Sam's face.

Despite the early hour, the cook was drenched in sweat and it dripped freely onto his work. He was vigorously stretching a dough mixture. He slapped it onto an oiled aluminium table then quickly whipped it off and twirled it expertly in the air twice before slapping it down again. The process was repeated until he had a roughly round, paper-thin sheet of dough, wider than his shoulders. After a final twirl, the dough was slapped onto a cast iron hot plate, where it sizzled briefly. He cracked an egg into the centre of it and threw the shell into a bucket on the floor beside him. The blue plastic bucket was already overflowing with discarded shells.

Onto the egg, he added a small spoonful of pepper and salt and punctured the yolk with the grubby handle of the spoon. There was a small pile of blackened, seasoned onions cooking gently on the other side of the hot plate. He took up a spoonful of these and threw it at the egg. Then he carefully folded the dough repeatedly until it was roughly the dimensions of a small mobile phone. This was added to the end of a row made earlier and left to brown. He flipped the others over and took two from the line to pile on a high glass shelf on his side of the partition. There were dozens of these little dough parcels. Some rectangular, some cylindrical and others triangular. Sam guessed the shapes were dictated by their fillings but was unable to tell what they might contain. He ordered one of each and two of something that smelled like coffee, which was being poured from one stainless steel jug into another through a yard of thin air.

His order was arranged onto a plate, which had been covered by a polythene lunch sheet, then placed on an empty table next to the door. A red plastic bottle in the shape of a long tomato was put down beside the plate. The waiter stared at Sam, but there was nothing intimidating in his gaze. He was just being curious and lived in a society that didn't hide its curiosity. Sam was the first foreigner he had ever served. Sam smiled at the waiter, who remained standing beside the table.

"The coffee?" When he received no response, Sam added, "No sugar."

A solitary coffee was brought to the table in a small glass mug. Sam looked at the waiter expectantly, but the blank look told him there was no more coffee coming. So, he held two fingers up and tried his best to explain that he had ordered two coffees. The waiter returned with two frothy coffees. Sam smiled and said his thanks. A drop of sweat from the end of the chef's nose hit the hot plate with a sizzle.

The triangular parcel of dough looked like a good one to start with. After a large bite, less tentative than it should have been, the only identifiable food inside was a piece of potato. What was immediately identifiable, however, was where the contents should be placed on the Scoville scale. It was up there with law-enforcement-grade pepper spray. In a panic, he picked up his coffee. He immediately felt, from the temperature of the mug, that it was too hot to deaden the chilli pain. In desperation, he squeezed out a sploosh of tomato sauce and dipped the rest of the napalm wedge into it, greedily licking off the sauce as a balm for the burning.

Unfortunately for Sam, tomato sauce is a rare thing in Sri Lanka. Every roadside eating place has a jar of what, to the uninitiated, looks like tomato sauce, but it hardly ever is. Instead, what Sri Lankans enjoy dipping their short-eats into is chilli sauce. Having compounded his problems, he was left with no choice. The coffee had to be used, regardless of any permanent damage that might ensue. Anything was preferable to the chilli torture.

Sam took a large mouthful and swilled it around his mouth. The burning of the coffee with the agony of the chilli was almost unbearable. The only saving grace was the four spoons of sugar that had been added to each coffee. The sugar alone went a small way towards calming the situation. It was at moments such as this when Sam used to enjoy telling his ex that what he was experiencing would make childbirth seem like a walk in the park. Invariably, she would hit him.

Only the smell of the dough burning on the griddle brought the chef round from his quiet enjoyment of Sam's discomfort. His expectations, together with those of the waiter, had been met. Amongst the most common stereotypes Sri Lankans have of foreigners was of their inability to eat normal Sri Lankan food. Sam had not disappointed them.

For once, Sam was unable to smile. The pain died down only after he had gargled with the contents of a carton of long-life milk which he had snatched from a cooler in the corner of the room. Only then did he think about trying some of the other shapes on his plate. The egg one was surprisingly good. It had an interesting rubbery texture with occasional bursts of intense flavour from the added spices and the sweaty chef. He even dipped it tentatively in some of the red sauce and washed it down with the super-sweetened coffee. Maybe essence-of-working-man was a secret ingredient some of the celebrity chefs back home could experiment with. The thought of that brought the smile back to his face.

Then, with a groan, he remembered he had no Sri Lankan currency. At the side of the room was a wooden counter, behind which sat a large man wearing the only clean shirt in the building. He dispensed single cigarettes and biscuits from large plastic jars. His main role, however, was to take the cash, which Sam noticed he threw casually into a drawer beneath his table. He approached the man and took out the remaining Indian notes from his pockets, making his ears disappear as his shoulders came up and his eyebrows arched in an exaggerated caricature of cringing apology.

Mr Clean-shirt looked back at Sam as if he was something brought in on the bottom of a customer's flip-flops. It wasn't personal though. That was his job – to take the cash and hand out contempt in return, with the change. His position in life made it mandatory. But he resented the position Sam had put him in. The food had already been eaten and it appeared that all there was available to pay for it were Indian rupees. Only the memory of Sam's recent pain made the situation tolerable for him.

He leered as he said to Sam, "Hot, neh?" and shouted something to the waiter, who replied with a list of Sam's order. Sam was in no position to argue, but he had noticed that when his plate had been removed, one untouched wedge was replaced on the chef's glass shelf. What Sam didn't know was that this was normal practice and he wouldn't be charged for it. After counting the Indian notes twice, the money man punched some buttons on an oversized calculator and tucked them into his shirt pocket. He reached into his drawer and took out a selection of colourful Sri Lankan currency. Two green, one purple, three orange and a few of silver coins. Sam gratefully took them and lauded the shopkeeper with unacknowledged gratitude.

In a small room behind the café were two raised footprints in a polished cement floor. Between them was a hole. The white of the porcelain in the hole was barely visible through dark brown stains. On the floor beside the hole was a tiny, red bar of soap in a plastic dish together with a bucket. A tap in the wall could be used to fill the bucket with water. Sam had experienced more fragrant and user-friendly toilets in his life. It took him a few moments to work out there was no imaginable sequence of using the available sanitary equipment that would leave him feeling cleaner when he left than he had been when he entered. In the end he valiantly experimented, resulting in an obvious increase to his comfort level, but the jury was still out on the effect it had on his personal hygiene.

At the end of the road was a roundabout. Traffic was being thrown out from the chaotic vortex in all directions. On the opposite side of the roundabout was a bus station. Large, red, single-decked buses of various vintage were shunting and grinding in a dusty vehicular mosh-pit. Sam boldly strode over the yellow pedestrian crossing, where the traffic was halted by a policeman wearing a white crash helmet and dark sunglasses. Some things never changed.

Outside a bus, with the numbers 0-4 on the front, he joined the melee to get on board. In Sri Lanka, the order in which people get to the front of a queue has more to do with their size and the sharpness of their elbows than any position in the line. But what amazed Sam was the absence of any signs of animosity this bullying elicited. It was a happy-go-lucky free-for-all. There were seats enough for everyone because the number 4 began its journey right here in Chilaw.

Sam eventually found a seat towards the back, behind an open door on the near-side. The floor and seats were made of bum-polished aluminium, installed for utility rather than comfort. Function held centre stage whilst form cowered in the wings. Oily cardboard boxes, tied up with coir fibre twine, were pushed under seats and sacks of goods were piled in the aisle. Schoolchildren, dressed in white uniforms, carried their schoolbooks in garish, Disney-endorsed shoulder-bags. The girls had long plaits, which they tied at the ends with red ribbons. They were shy and would not look at Sam.

The children were quite beautiful and if there was innocence left in this world, Sam thought they embodied it. The boys were brimming with adolescent bravado, but were respectful of other passengers and mindful that, if they stepped out of line, any adult would happily clip them around the ears with no fear of parental repercussions.

Office workers, probably bound for Colombo, tried to read the morning paper and affected a careless disdain for lesser mortals. Teachers, in their colourful flowing saris, perched with elegance on the metal seats. The style of their saris was different to the ones he had seen throughout India and displayed their Sri Lankan torsos in all their folds and well-fed magnificence. Here was a race who had been fed from childhood on the mantra that big is beautiful and skinny is a sign of poverty or sickness. If you had love-handles, you were honour-bound to show them.

A conductor made his way down the bus. He kept the different denominations of notes apart by folding them longitudinally down the centre and tucking them between his fingers. The different coloured notes were kept separate. Digitally. His ticket machine reminded Sam of the bus journeys of his childhood. He told the conductor the name of the village he wanted to get off at and handed the man an orange note. In return he got a ticket and more colourful change. He asked the conductor where Thalagamma was but was ignored. A common reaction from people who are embarrassed by their lack of English is to ignore the person asking the question. It can look like arrogance but isn't.

"It is twelve kilometres away," said an office worker, sitting on the opposite side of the aisle to Sam. "I will show you."

The twelve kilometres passed quickly, with much accelerating and braking. If the person getting on or off the bus looked fit enough, the driver wouldn't stop, but would only slow down, necessitating those getting off to undertake a leap and a run, and those getting on, a run and a leap. The office worker kept up a steady stream of questions without waiting for answers. The questions were more personal than Sam would have expected and couched in language that was from a bygone black and white age. The man was repeating questions he remembered from the colonial English text books of his school days.

"Where are you going, good sir? Are you married? Kindly allow me to introduce myself. What is your good name? It is a pleasure to make your acquaintance. This is Thalagamma."

"This is Thalagamma," he repeated, gently shaking Sam by the shoulder.

The bus came to a juddering stop and waited for Sam to climb down the three metal steps to the gritty dust beside the road. Sam took the bus driver's insult in good humour. The bus halt was on the land side of the road and Sam instinctively knew that the man he had to meet, being a fisherman, would be on the sea side. Opposite him was a small road leading to where the beach must be. There was a market selling fish and vegetables. Some of the stallholders were setting out their wares. The fish market looked fascinating and he could see the bright red flesh of a huge tuna that had been sliced in two. The blood mixed with melting ice and ran off the metal table onto the floor. Glistening piles of smaller fish were piled high on the vendors' tables and others were being prepared by men and women with long, curved knives on tree-trunk chopping blocks. Where a particularly tough bone needed cutting, they would smack the spine of the knife with their palms. If that wasn't enough, they would hit it with a wooden block to separate the vertebrae.

Parked by the junction were five three-wheelers. It was a quiet time of day, when people had already been brought to the junction but hadn't yet started returning. Four of the drivers, all men, were sitting around an upturned beer crate on which a large board had been placed. They were flicking wooden draughts from the base line of a complicated pattern of lines and circles. Surrounding the board was a raised wooden perimeter from which the draughts ricocheted. In each corner was a hole, just larger than the draughts on the board, for them to fall through. It was like billiards for four players, with fingers for cues and plywood for the slate bed and green baize. The only man not playing was looking on intently and participated by occasionally shaking a fine white dust on the board. Sam was hesitant to interrupt, but one of the players noticed him approaching and smiled readily.

"Can I help?"

"Can you tell me where Wella Mawatha is? I am looking for Laxman Perera. W.M. Laxman Perera."

Two of the other players looked up. "Are you from Italy?" one of them asked.

"No. Scotland."

"Ha," the player said, before resuming his game.

The news of Laxman's flirtations with the devil were well-known. Rohan had been a friendly boy and was well-liked. In Thalagamma, everybody knew everyone. Also well-known was the fact that someone from Italy would be coming soon, asking for money to help Rohan. The incident with the priest had made this public knowledge. Two village men with a fondness for liquor had already approached Laxman and claimed they had knowledge of Rohan's predicament and demanded the ten lakh. They had been chased away, beaten and told to sober up.

Sam was offered a ride by one of the drivers, but said he preferred to walk. Laxman's house was nearby and he wanted to gather his thoughts and approach at his own chosen speed.

31

Despite her husband's recent insanity, Shani was unable to spend long away from him. Since their wedding, the only time they had been separated was when Rassika was born and Shani had been taken to a hospital in Colombo when complications with the birth occurred. Recently, Laxman had turned into a yakka, but he was still her husband, and in her own anxious way, she cared for him and badly wanted to tend to the wounds on his head. She wanted to comfort him, if only he would let her.

Last night she had returned home from the neighbour's. Rassika was staying away until her mother called to say it was safe for her to return. Shani had found Laxman sitting motionless on the floor holding his head in his hands. He was filthy and had not eaten, nor barely slept, for two days. His skin was dry and powdery and there was a crispy, brown scum around his bloodshot eyes. His sarong was tied around his waist in an ugly knot of the kind used by a man who no longer cares. Shani went to the well behind the house and brought him a large glass of water. Once he had drunk it, she persuaded him to sit on the step beside the kitchen, washed him from head to foot then helped to change his sarong. He was sipping water all the time she was attending him and slowly his body began to grow back into his skin until, at last, he sat up as straight as only a proud man could.

Shani knew water was more important than food. The fishermen could all survive at sea without food for a few days if an engine broke down. But without water, these same men would be desiccated by the unforgiving sun in two or three days. She remembered when a missing boat from the next village had been found in calm waters not more than an hour from the shore, everyone on board was as black and shrivelled as a goraka.

When Laxman was well enough, Shani called for her daughter and made them all a meal of dahl. She sent Rassika to the kade for 2 lbs of warm, crusty bread. Laxman ate little, but she knew he was regaining his strength. She prayed that what was left between his ears would be as easy to rejuvenate.

At 4 A.M. the following morning, with Laxman sleeping on the floor, she rose and began to sweep the leaves and fallen fruit from the sand around the house. Then she cooked a meal of rice and dried-fish curry. Laxman loved dried fish and she knew he would eat more of that than anything else. To a westerner, dried fish looks and smells like something that has gone bad in the sun. Essentially, that is what it is. The trick in making it well is to allow just the tiniest hint of rottenness to happen before the curing of the salt and sun has a chance to preserve it. The best dried fish is permanently tainted.

Rassika sat with her father as he ate his breakfast and then happily went off to school with her friends.

Village dogs are never treated as pets. They have a job to do and that job is to warn their owners of the presence of strangers. Mostly, strangers might be trying to steal a chicken or climb a tree to take a few coconuts. The dogs knew what should happen at night and what shouldn't. They knew not to bark as Boniface, in the early hours, drunkenly left the house of the woman down the road whose husband was away working in the Middle East. But when a boy from the next village quietly leant his bicycle against the fence around the back of the garden, they knew that it was expected of them to howl and snarl for all they were worth.

One dog would set off the next and the boy would have to make his escape as fast as his legs could pedal. He had to endure a rolling wave of thunderous growls all the way home. Once the dogs had started, only blood or boredom could make them go back to their watching brief of night-time comings and goings.

Occasionally, the dogs would set up a kind of aural Mexican wave during the daytime. They reserved this behaviour for special occasions, when someone significantly at odds with what they expected came boldly into their midst.

Sam arrived in front of Laxman's house to such canine pandemonium. None of the scraggy beasts were bold enough to take a good bite at Sam's legs, but he was not to know that. They bared their teeth, tucked their tails between their legs and tried to look intimidating. They postured and danced in the gateways of their owners' houses until Sam had passed well beyond their turf.

Laxman went to see what was upsetting his dog. He took a stout stick from beside the door, waved it in the air and yelled alarmingly at the beast. The dog whimpered and slunk off, hugging the ground behind Laxman. Sam wanted to thank the villager for dealing with the dogs but, as he approached, a look of panic gripped the man and he rushed into the house with an expression of alarm. This puzzled Sam but, intent on giving his thanks anyway, he followed the man to his house. He was met by a small woman who appeared in the doorway.

"Itallee?" she asked Sam.

"Itallee?" he repeated. "Ah, Italy. No... Well, yes, I suppose, really... But I am from Scotland."

This made no impression on the woman who simply repeated, "Itallee?"

"No, no. I was there, but I am from Scotland."

"Itallee?" She asked again and tears welled up in her eyes.

"Laxman Perera? W.M. Laxman Perera?" Sam replied.

At hearing the name of her husband, Shani screamed and ran back into the house. Sam was afraid the slippery slope to insanity was already underfoot. Then the man appeared back in the doorway and stood defiantly with his chest thrown out and his hands in tight fists by his side.

"W.M. Laxman Perera," he said, with the volume and projection that any West End theatre veteran would have been proud of. Then he stabbed his chest with the index finger of his right hand. Sam had found his man.

32

That all was not well at the Perera household was painfully obvious. Sam stared open-mouthed and wondered what madness he had arrived at. For his part, Laxman was relieved that the wait was over, but terrified the excuses he wanted to make to the stranger would not sufficiently soften his heart. Help was nearly always easier to find when you and cash looked for it together. Laxman knew that this time, when he needed to find help more than ever before, there was no money.

Shani was frightened that, once her husband's poorly-developed attempt at intelligent persuasion was exhausted, he was likely to resort to his more usual technique. He had two standard arguments, and both had five digits that could screw up into a fist. She had to act quickly. After briefly disappearing into the house, she returned with a plastic chair which she put outside the front door. She said something to Sam which he understood as an instruction to sit. Laxman sat on the step and stared silently at Sam who was desperately wondering where to start his story. Shani stood, hovering nervously at her husband's side. No amount of praying had prepared her for this. The stranger looked kind, which was gratifying, but, because of that, she wondered if he was strong enough to help her son.

It confused both Laxman and Shani that the stranger was white. He dressed like an Asian man, but if they took his clothing away, they were sure the bits underneath would all be white. Having a white man ask for money was unexpected because white men usually *gave* money. Maybe he was Italian?

Occasionally, a white man would come to the village with a bag of schoolbooks and pens for the children. They would smile a lot, then disappear and were never seen again. Once, a white man came in a big car with two Sri Lankans from Colombo. He gave the fishermen some electronic navigation equipment, had his photograph taken with them, then he too, disappeared. The fishermen swapped the equipment for bottles of Arrack as soon as the car was out of sight. White people were odd, but none had ever asked for money before.

After a moment of silence, whilst Sam tried to make himself comfortable in the chair, they all started talking at once. It was immediately apparent to Sam that they would need someone to translate.

Sam put his hand up for silence, and said, "I speak English. English. Do you speak English?"

An incomprehensible babble started again. It was silenced only by Sam raising his hand once more.

"Sri Lankan," then pointing to his mouth, "no." He sighed. "English, yes." He nodded, desperate for a sign of recognition.

Shani understood. Pointing to her own mouth, she said, "Ingreesi, no. Sinhala, yes."

"OK. We need to find someone who can translate for us." Then he gave it his best shot at looking puzzled and put his hand on his forehead and pretended to scan the horizon. Laxman and Shani both followed his gaze expectantly. After repeating his incantation of 'Sri Lankan no, English yes,' a few more times, Shani appeared to understand what he was asking for.

She had an animated conversation with her husband and then ran out of the garden and disappeared down the road. Laxman and Sam stared at each other silently and Sam worked hard to find a smile. After a few minutes, Shani returned holding a 5 or 6-year-old girl by the hand. The girl's anxious mother was trotting along beside the two of them, dancing around and fretting about the dangerous situation she imagined her daughter was being put into.

"Ah," said Laxman, "Sinhala, yes, Ingreesi, yes." He jabbed a stubby index finger towards the girl.

"Oh, dear God," was all Sam could manage. The thought of getting this child, in a pink party dress and with colourful ribbons in her hair, to tell a couple that he had recently killed their son was just too surreal to contemplate.

"No, no, no. Not the girl. Sorry, I need someone older. Much older."

The girl looked as sad as her mother looked happy and was immediately whisked away by her very relieved parent. Laxman looked crestfallen. Shani looked frightened. Sam looked to the sky for inspiration. Then he remembered something on the boat from India. When telling a story about his family, one of the fishermen had emphasised the age of an older man by twisting the ends of an imaginary moustache. Sam tried it and, to his immense relief, both Laxman and Shani immediately understood. Again, Shani left the two men together and this time was gone for fifteen minutes.

The atmosphere between them grew heavier as the minutes passed and neither spoke. Laxman stared hard at Sam. His face showed no emotion. This was harder to deal with for Sam than if Laxman had shown open hostility. He was unable to read what was going on in the man's mind. His attempts at *bonhomie* with a half-hearted smile were futile. It was as if Laxman was staring deep into an empty box.

Sam was wondering how much more he could take when Shani returned in a beige Baby Austin. It was years since Sam had seen an A30 and he was surprised by how narrow the tyres were. It was probably of a similar vintage to him. The semaphore indicator on the driver's side swung out and the car pulled up outside Laxman's gate. Shani was unable to open the door from the inside. She had never been in a car before. A short, heavy-set man with a wide, smiling face and a shock of white hair got out of the driver's side and walked around to open the door for her. Sam was amused to see he had a spectacular white moustache that looked like it might be waxed at the ends. It gave his face an unmistakable set of amiable jollity.

Of equal magnificence was his stomach. But, unlike western paunches, this one was rice-fed and looked as tight as a drum. As he walked, he swung his arms out to the sides with the confident swagger of a much younger man. He wore a loose pair of cargo shorts and a white polo shirt and looked like he could make himself at home wherever people didn't take themselves too seriously. Sam decided he liked him.

As Sam stood up, the new man approached and introduced himself with a surprisingly soft, feminine handshake. Sam guessed he was more used to slaps on the back and the chinking of glasses than the formality of a handshake. His name was Ivan. A chair was brought for the distinguished new visitor and he, Sam and Laxman sat in a triangle whilst Shani stood in the doorway.

Nobody knew where to start. Small talk would have been ridiculous, but Ivan made a valiant attempt to fill the silence. Sam's intolerance of idle chit-chat kicked in and he held up his hand. He thanked Ivan for coming to help and, without further hesitation, told Ivan his story. Ivan tried to smile, but his eyes betrayed him as they flicked quickly between Shani and Laxman and then back to Sam. When his story was finished, Sam sat back in his chair, relieved at having shared it in full for the first time. He understood the burden he had just put on Ivan's shoulders and the terrible grief that was about descend upon the confused parents.

Ivan sat forward, put his hands on his bare knees and looked very directly at Sam. For a moment, his smile faded.

"So, you are not here to collect the money?"

"Money? No. I mean, yes. I want to give it to the boy's parents. But it isn't just that. I had to face them, Ivan, to tell them what happened. How it was an accident and that I am truly sorry for the part I played in it."

"So you do not want to take the money from them?"

"No, I want to give the money to them. I don't want it."

"Oh, I see," said Ivan, clearly not doing. "And you are not going to help their son?"

"Ivan, did you not listen to me? Their son cannot be helped. He is dead." When he had said the word 'dead' he had lowered his voice almost to a whisper. He instantly regretted doing so. It felt as if he was passing the burden that he had carried for so long to a stranger.

"... dead." The word hung like a judgment in the air.

Shani moved behind her husband and held onto his shoulders. Who was giving strength to whom was impossible to tell.

"Yes, I see." Ivan sank back in his chair, deep in thought. The ends of his moustache began to twitch. His hands went into automatic, put a cigarette between his lips and lit it. He inhaled the smoke in a distracted manner and stabbed two fingers in Sam's direction.

"You didn't write the letter." It was not a question.

Ivan slowly nodded to himself as the smoke from his cigarette made lazy folds in the still air between them. Then he explained to Sam that on the short journey here, Shani had told him about the two letters and that they were expecting a visit from a man who needed money to help their son in Italy. It was Sam's turn to be shocked.

"No, Ivan. That is just not true. Their son is..." he looked at Laxman than back at Ivan, "... dead. I killed him. Anyone who is wanting money to help is lying. They cannot help."

Sam stood up and paced back and forth, deep in thought. Shani became alarmed. She thought Ivan had told Sam that there was no money. She approached him in such a resolute manner that he backed up to a wall and braced himself for what was coming next. What did come next was unexpected. Shani prostrated herself on the sand in front of him and began to touch his feet with both hands. She repeated this several times then wailed at the sky with her hands stretched high above her head.

Ivan came to his rescue and lifted Shani to her feet, calming her. It was time to end the confusion and Ivan sat Shani down in Sam's empty chair, which he had placed beside Laxman, and began to tell them Sam's story. Parts of it, anyway.

Never had Sam seen such distress. The hairs on the back of his neck stood, electrified. At this moment in time, here was the centre of the universe. Nothing else counted. Life before or after was meaningless. The world was changing in front of him. Shani was drowning in her grief and the waves that overwhelmed her were relentless. There was no debris or flotsam to grab onto, no lifeline. She was slipping beneath the surface and struggled to breathe. The sand in the garden was an unwelcome support that stopped her from disappearing forever and she writhed and twisted in a cloud of fine dust as if searching, wretchedly, for a door to another world.

She screamed. Her lips moved but there was no sound. Sam had to look away as she reached out for her son and fell back to the floor when she found he wasn't there. The visceral cord that joined them had been severed.

Laxman's grief was vented in a rage that was silent and terrifying. He closed his eyes as the muscles in his face contorted it into something that was both dreadful and magnetic. The world disintegrated behind his furiously closed eyes. Only his solipsistic madness stopped him from destroying it. Nothing else existed. Short tufts of hair stuck out between his fingers as his palms rendered the darkness and he tried in vain to crush his skull.

Whatever ideas Sam had of virtue were being shredded in the face of such rawness. This was no longer an academic exercise. Not a theoretical indulgence for his delicate ego to dally with. This was real life where consequences could no longer be hidden or contemplated in comfort. Until now, grief had only been a word, part of a glib description he had stuck a label on some future part of his adventure. Now it was real and, if wisdom truly was the anticipation of unpitying consequences, he had been memorably stupid.

The contrast between this livid scene and the melodramatic first-world problems of his own failed marriage could not have been greater. He knew then that part of him was the woman who had been his wife and that her delicate shimmering bubble lived within his own, reduced but, ever present.

The drama had brought a crowd of curious neighbours to the gate. Ivan, who commanded respect from all, backed them away and silenced them with a wave of his hand. His big house and Baby Austin gave him the power to do that. To them he was Ivan Mahatheya – Ivan Sir.

When the first wave of despair had slowly subsided, Laxman looked confused. He started speaking to Ivan hurriedly. The palms of his upturned hands questioned the air, demanding an answer. Ivan carefully explained to him that the author of the letter had to be a cunning crook who was trying to take advantage of a situation he had somehow stumbled across. Laxman and Shani impatiently demanded more answers. The volume of the conversation was rising. The audience was getting excited and struggled to get as close as possible to the drama.

Sam was deep in thought. Who else in Milan knew both the address and the circumstances of the boy's death? The only ones who saw the address were him and the kids in the café who had translated it for him. He prided himself on his ability to judge others and, to him, those kids were delightful. Young, bright and happy. He refused to believe it could be any of them. But there was no-one else.

Then he remembered. Su-something, she had called him. The full name didn't immediately come to him but the image of white letters on an orange background did. The man (was it a man?) who had translated the address from the photograph of the envelope the girl had sent to him. It had to be him. The photograph had shown the bloodstains on the envelope and the newspapers, the following day, were sure to be full of news of the accident. Su… Su… Soo-rain, yes, Soo-rain, had put two and two together and come up with a jackpot.

Sam wondered how anyone could be so heartless? *That* was broken. He interrupted Ivan and Laxman's conversation and told Ivan what he thought had happened. Ivan nodded slowly and lit another cigarette. Ivan's translation brought a second high-pitched wail of anguish and despair as Shani thrashed the air with flailing arms.

The letter-writer had given them the only hope of seeing their son alive. All they needed was money. He had said so. The new stranger told a different story and, much as they respected Ivan Mahatheya, why should they believe the white man? Apart from their curious habit of being punctual, what else did white men ever bring to the table? They ate foreign foods, they didn't wash, they slept with whoever they wanted to and spent their time sitting on the beach in the afternoon sun. They were hippies.

At this point the white stranger gave them a very convincing reason to believe him. He handed the envelope containing the five thousand euros to Laxman. Ivan had decided that Laxman and Shani should be spared some of the details. He had told them that there had been a terrible accident and the money was compensation from a well-wisher. He cautioned Sam against pushing the truth.

Without the open acknowledgement of his involvement, handing the money to the boys' parents became an empty gesture. He tried to decide what was the right thing to do. Was this about him and making himself feel better, or about letting the boy's parents know the truth of their son's death? And if the truth would hurt so much, was it really virtuous?

He wanted to make sure none of his confusion had its origins in self-pity. At last he decided that virtue couldn't be virtuous if it came at such a cost and agreed with Ivan to spare some of the details. Sam knew that other than being the messenger, he was irrelevant.

On the journey here, Sam had spent many hours thinking about the events in Milan. What had happened had left a wall against which any emotional growth was blocked until the wall was dismantled. The first piece was removed when he finally came to the conclusion that guilt was just a feeling. It was an emotion experienced without a value judgment having been made and, as such, he should be indifferent to it. Guilt could only be appropriate if he had made a bad choice, for example, crashing into the boy after having drunk half a bottle of wine. Under those circumstances, his guilt would illuminate the difference between past actions and how he would wish to behave now. When he realised there was nothing he could have done differently, the façade of his guilt collapsed. But he was human and imperfect and so, in the face of undeniable logic, lingering doubts remained. The rest of the wall began to crumble when he accepted that the only way to grow was to discover the true meaning of virtue and to live his life by it.

The money had been strapped to his body for over seventy days and nights and had left an indelible mark. A stigmata. Sam felt light-headed and sat heavily on the floor.

The onerous responsibilities and deeply-held tradition of Sri Lankan hospitality shook Shani temporarily out of her grief and she quickly offered her chair to Sam and rushed to fetch a glass. Somebody at the gate was dispatched with urgent instructions and Laxman helped Sam into the chair. Almost at once, a young man came running back and handed over a slim glass bottle of a fizzy, brown drink. It was already opened. It looked warm and dusty and so unlike the sparkly, iced version that the shiny-happy people, who wanted to teach the world to sing, drank.

Before Shani could pour the gravy-coloured syrup into the glass, Sam mustered the strength to say, "No. Water, please." Shani quickly reappeared with a large glass of filtered well water.

Silence descended on the gathering and all swallowed in support as Sam drained the glass. At some point, Laxman had put the money away. He didn't know the currency or how much it was, but he did know that if a white man had come all this way to give it to him it was a significant amount. He also knew that the less he flashed it around in front of his neighbours, the better it would be. In a village where everyone had their problems, people without cash invariably saw money as the answer. Laxman was astute enough to realise this and humble enough to understand he would not be able to refuse such requests if they came.

Once it was apparent the drama was over, the villagers began to drift away, leaving the four of them on their own in a rarefied silence where dignity scrambled for a toe-hold.

33

Sam's immediate decision what to do next was deferred as Shani began preparations for a meal of rice and curry. None of them had eaten properly for a good while and now seemed like the right time to fix that. It took her attention away from thoughts of Rohan. She needed the diversion as much as Laxman needed the quiet time to begin to collect his thoughts.

She was still not convinced by Sam's story and clung onto hopes of her son's safe return. Until she saw his body, she would never believe he was dead. Ivan was invited for the meal, but politely declined. He gave Sam his telephone number and told him to call any time.

Laxman sat quietly and stared at the ground. His breathing was calm, but he occasionally shuddered and faltered while exhaling, like a sleeping dog does when it dreams. But Laxman was not dreaming. Darkness had taken his mind and he thought about poison. Unlike Sam's, the feelings of guilt he was persecuting himself with were not so easy to dismiss. He had made decisions that he bitterly regretted. Would Rohan ever have gone to Italy if he had not supported and encouraged him? The reason his son was dead was because of his selfish parental pride. He felt guilt for what he had done and shame for what he was. It was the shame more than the guilt that craved the poison.

Sam saw nothing of the food preparations but heard the scraping and grinding which sounded ancient enough to please any Luddite. Then the smells started. First came the tantalising, ephemeral whiffs of the raw spices being ground. These built into a substantial but complex cloud of scents as they were roasted, then fried in coconut oil. What Phil Spector did for sound, Shani managed with food – a wall of smells that drew from the roots, the bark, the seeds and the fruits of the land around it.

Delicate bee-eaters perched high in the bare branches of a dead tree across the road. Occasionally, one would dash out in an acrobatic, sweeping flight to chase a passing insect. After one such foray a wounded butterfly spiralled helplessly to the floor outside the doorway. It beat its wings, but only succeeded in turning in clumsy circles in the sand. Sam picked it up to place it in a bush. He was startled to see that the bee-eater had bisected it. All that remained were the head and wings attached to the short thorax. The fleshy abdomen had been removed, in flight, by the bee-eater with all the precision of an aerial surgeon. Nature was exciting. With these thoughts playing in his mind, Sam surprised himself by beginning to relax. Laxman saw nothing but the dirt in front of him and wanted the world to go away.

Eventually the clay cooking pots were laid out in a semi-circle around a steaming mountain of white rice. Some of the curries were still bubbling from the retained heat of the wood fire. Each round-bottomed pot was kept stable by a circle of woven straw, about the size of a large doughnut. Apart from the rice, Sam could identify little of what was on the table. But the colours, the smells and then eventually the tastes, blew his mind. He had never had a meal like this. Bombs of taste sensations, most of which were new to him, cascaded and sparked around his tongue. Then background flavours, so subtle they were almost not there, flirted with his senses. An overwhelming wave of fire accentuated rather than diminished his ability to differentiate between the instruments in the expertly orchestrated symphony playing in his mouth.

In the UK, when Sam had ordered a hot curry, he had often been challenged by the chilli, but ultimately left underwhelmed by the experience. All fire and nothing else. With Shani's meal, the fire was considerable, but it was backed up by an artillery of flavours that filled the void that chilli alone would have left. There were crunchy little fish, deep-fried whole, which broke like poppadums. There was a leaf mallum, so vibrantly green that it was a new colour for Sam. There was an orange fiery sambal flecked with pieces of dried tuna and crushed raw onions that was wound up tight with lime and garlic.

The curry of a fish, similar to herring, was sublime. The fish had been fried in spices after cooking in a curry sauce bursting with the flavours of cardamom, cinnamon and coriander. The remaining dish was a light-yellow, sticky curry peppered with small black seeds, which acted as an arbiter between the other more flamboyant flavours. Sam quickly learned to eat a morsel of this between the more pungent mouthfuls, much the same as pickled ginger in sushi dishes. This was breadfruit, originally from the South Pacific, and its spread throughout the tropics was largely due to the endeavours of one William Bligh, captain of HMS Bounty.

Since no cutlery was brought out, Sam ate with his fingers. The food never went above the second joint of the fingers of Laxman's right hand. He picked at his food without enthusiasm and chewed the little he put in his mouth with a slack, immobile jaw, but nonetheless, he ate with precision. Sam ate like an oaf and the curry ran down his fingers almost to his elbow. Shani ate in the kitchen, together with Rassika, who had by now returned from school. The silence from the kitchen informed Sam that Rassika had been told the news about her brother. Sam cleared his plate and a glass of water was brought for him.

After the meal, Laxman lay out on a plastic woven mat which he unrolled on the cement floor. He doubted he could sleep but if he pretended to, at least the world might leave him alone. A second mat was unrolled for Sam. He thought it rude to do anything but please his hosts and lay out next to Laxman. There were no pillows and Laxman lay on his side supporting his head on his forearm. Sam didn't know what else to do.

Crossing continents and confessing to killings can be tiring business and when he awoke it was late afternoon. Laxman was gone and Rassika was sitting at the table in the corner of the room doing her schoolwork.

"Amma," called Rassika, as she saw Sam stretching and sitting up.

Shani appeared from the kitchen and started speaking to Sam. The words came out like projectiles from a Navy Railgun, but there was no anger in her voice. This was how she talked. The monologue never faltered, but she busied Sam out of the front door and pointed him down the road in the direction of the beach.

"Laxman?"

"Laxman," she replied, with a wobble of her head.

"Father is beach going," said Rassika, and gave Sam a smile that could bring sunshine to the night.

Shani beamed with pride at her daughter. "Ingreesi, yes."

Sam blinked in the afternoon light. Two steps on the hot sand were enough to make him return for his sandals. Although his feet were tough, they were no match for the baking ground beneath them.

He followed the path in the direction Shani had pointed, down a gentle gradient for a few minutes, until he could hear small waves breaking on the shore. The coconut trees which had surrounded him suddenly opened up and the path came out onto a long, sandy beach which disappeared to the north. The green of the coconut trees, the yellow of the sand and the turquoise blue of the ocean converged in a misty, far-away point.

To his left was a simple church with concrete block walls painted white and light blue. The roof was covered by brick-red clay tiles and a large wooden cross had been fixed in the sand immediately above the high-water mark. At the back of the church, facing the open front and the sea, was a glass case containing a statue of the Madonna. Beside the church were five brightly-coloured fibreglass boats, pulled up above the high-water line. Further up the beach was a motley collection of oily tarpaulins, stretched tightly over wooden poles which were driven into the sand. These offered shade to the fishermen, sitting around on wooden boxes, fastidiously baiting hundreds of hooks, preparing for going to sea later.

Laxman sat alone, attempting to do the work of two. In the time he had been out of action, his crewman had left to find work on another boat. It was expected. Men had responsibility to put food on the table for their families and if the skipper was unable to work the crew moved on. In this way the men formed a close, but internally mobile group that collectively fished the same boats from the same beach. The only time the group itself changed was when one of them died or went to the east coast to try his luck with the larger multi-day boats. Laxman's crew had gone east.

It seemed natural for Sam to sit down beside Laxman and share his work. He was clumsy at first and Laxman's irritation bubbled close to the surface on a couple of occasions as Sam made a mess of hooking the small sardine-like fish that were used for bait. When Laxman worked, the bait on his hook was a thing of beauty. None of the hook was visible, being completely buried in the soft flesh of the bait fish. A short length of soft cotton twine bound the fish's body together and the monofilament line looked like it came out of the upper tip of the forked caudal fin. The bait was laid out in careful order on a lipped shelf that ran around the outside edge of the open wooden box into which all the line was placed.

Laxman had already prepared the boat. It had been cleaned and filled with fuel – thirty litres of kerosene and two litres of petrol to start the Suzuki 15HP outboard. There were no auxiliary motors on any of the boats, so Sam guessed the engines would be meticulously maintained.

Most of the other men had finished baiting their hooks and had wandered off, or stood around smoking beedis or chewing betel, before Laxman and Sam came to the end of their line. When the last hook was baited, Laxman threw a cloth over the box and tied it firmly in place. There was nothing more to do until he put to sea.

The heat was mostly out of the day as the two men, skipper and his new de facto crew, walked back to the house. Shani was expecting them and had a meal prepared of dahl, a spicy hot onion sambal and fresh bread. It was simple village food and had sustained generations of men like Laxman for the demanding work they did. They ate in silence, then lay down on their mats for a few hours until it was time to put to sea.

All the fishermen arrived at the beach within minutes of each other. Kerosene lights were burning and tainted the air with their distinctive pungent smokiness. The men worked together carrying the loaded bait boxes to the boats. Each boat had at least two five-litre bottles of drinking water. When all the boxes and other essentials were loaded, the first boat was turned around to face the sea. All the men helped. The skipper and his crew stepped into their boat and the men beside them waited for the perfect wave before pulling and heaving the boat down the short, steep beach and into the water. They didn't mind getting wet. Two of them waded out, pushing the transom of the boat into the receding wave until there was enough depth for the skipper to drop the outboard and pull the starter. Once at sea they would head directly away from the shore until the waves became a gentle swell. Then the skipper would turn the boat around to face the flashing red light on top of the church's wooden cross. What prayers were needed were said and the boat would spin around and head out into the darkness, being lost to sight almost immediately.

Laxman's boat was the next to last to leave. There was a shore-based crew of helpers who performed the manual task of launching the last boat. They were rewarded each day by all the fishermen with a few fish to keep their families from starving. These same men would be there at dawn to help drag the boats up the beach and, if there was a big enough catch, to help sort it.

Once at sea, they headed due west for more than an hour before Laxman cut back the engine and switched on a short, plastic torch which begrudgingly emitted a faded yellow light. It gave off just enough of its precious illumination for them to perform their tasks. Laxman set the throttle to tick over and beckoned Sam to take his place. He pointed in the direction he wanted to go and placed Sam's hand on the tiller. Other than the stars, there was nothing to guide them. Laxman took the cover off the baited long-line and fastened the end of it to a buoy made up of three plastic five-litre oil cans lashed together. Between them was a piece of bamboo with a flag tied to the top of it. He threw this off the port side and the long-line dutifully followed at the pace dictated to it by the outboard. They were heading due north, running parallel to the unseen coast. Even with the poor lighting Sam could see that the current was running strongly away from the land. By shooting the line to port, Laxman had ensured the trailing line would be pulled away from the boat by the current rather than onto the propeller. Sam was receptive and was learning quickly.

It took almost an hour to shoot the long-line. The baited hooks landed with regular splashes over the side but were immediately lost in the darkness of the ocean. Laxman buoyed the end of the line and resumed his place on the tiller. He turned the boat hard to starboard and ran at full speed for a couple of minutes. Then he cut the engine and, as the boat settled off the plane and back into the water, he dropped an anchor over the gunwale. The anchor was home-made from a granite boulder lashed around with old ropes. The end of the anchor rope was made fast to a large wooden cleat bolted to the short foredeck. From a plastic can which had been cut in half and was stowed at the bow, Laxman took out two polystyrene blocks. Around the blocks were wound fishing lines strong enough to tow the boat. A lead weight and a large hook completed the simple hand jigs. They baited their hooks with thin strips of cuttlefish and began jigging off the bottom.

Sam guessed they were over a reef of some sort, because the depth was only around 20 metres. How Laxman knew they were over the reef was a mystery that Sam would never fathom. The reef was almost twenty kilometres out at sea and no more than fifty metres wide – an incredible feat of seamanship. Seeing skills like this, Sam had no aspirations to be skipper. He was content to be the best crew he could be. A Sri Lankan deckie-learner.

Laxman started pulling in fish almost immediately. When the weight touched the bottom, he would tug the line up and down by an arm's length. When a fish took the bait, it was hauled to the surface, removed from the hook and thrown on the deck before the line was baited again and dropped back over the side. There was no subtlety to fishing like this. Laxman was not doing it for sport. He was fishing to feed his family. No fish he was likely to hook on the reef stood any chance of breaking his line, so there was no point in playing with it. It was efficient and done entirely without joy.

Laxman had four fish flapping on the deck before Sam felt a bite. He copied what Laxman did. The line was suspended from the hand at the top of a circle described by both outstretched arms. The hand at the bottom of circle grabbed the line and quickly went in an upward arc until it was now at the top. The opposite hand was now at the bottom and would grab the line. In this way the fish was hauled to the surface and the line remained tidily out of harm's way, coiled between the hooked thumbs of the two hands.

The first fish Sam brought aboard looked like a kind of mullet. The second, third and fourth were the same. There was apparently little variation to the reef fish. Then Laxman hooked something a little bigger. He hauled it in at the same speed as before, but there was clearly more effort involved. Sam strained to see what would emerge on the end of the line. It was a small stingray. Laxman grabbed a crudely-fashioned gaff and hooked the fish through one of the wings to haul it aboard. He cut off the barbed tail and threw it overboard. Then he cut the line close to the fish's mouth and quickly tied on another spade-end hook. The fish was landed and the line re-hooked, baited and fishing again in a time that took Sam's breath away. Laxman was a finely-tuned fishing machine. When he spat gobs of red betel juice into the sea, Sam felt sure it was probably done only to attract the fish.

There were around forty fish aboard, most still flapping around, when Laxman carefully coiled his line back around the polystyrene block. Sam did the same as the anchor was hauled aboard. It was only when the engine was started again that Sam appreciated the silence of the last couple of hours. Now it was gone, removed in an instant by the tinny rattling of the outboard. For ten minutes, Laxman gunned the boat at its full speed. He never varied the course. Clouds had started to obscure the sky and what stars were visible offered no clues to Sam which direction they were heading in. But then, without a moment's hesitation, Laxman cut the engine and reached casually over the side of the boat and lifted the buoy that marked the start of the long-line. How did he do that?

Now the hard work started. The line was to be hauled in by Sam. Laxman would deal with any fish and lay the line in the empty box. What was left of any bait fish would be stripped from the hooks, which would then be laid in order over the lip of the box. There was no time to unhook the fish. The lines would be cut. Most of the fish had swallowed the bait and were hooked deep inside. The variety of fish on the long line was much greater than those caught on the reef. There were two small sharks, another ray, some small tuna and a variety of other species Sam didn't recognise. The prized catch was a seer fish, the size of a decent salmon. That alone would have made the trip profitable.

Sam's arms were aching, and the blisters made by pulling the fishing line, on the web between his thumb and index finger, had gone soft in the seawater and burst. As the sun finally began to rise over the shoreline, Sam looked at his hands and saw two patches of bright pink flesh surrounded by the yellow, curling edges of burst blisters. They stung, but the sight of the night's work, now dead on the deck, brought a smile to his weary face.

Laxman's expression gave nothing away, but if he wasn't so sad, he would have been thrilled. This was an exceptional catch and was no doubt due to the white stranger who had brought luck on board. Sam didn't feel lucky. He just felt exhausted. He had given his body the kind of workout that it had not had for many years. There was no part of him that was not aching. He knew he would be tender later today but that, given time, he would be hardened in a way he never had been before. The thought pleased him and made the pain bearable.

The swell had grown through the night so that surf was dumping on the beach by the time they neared the flashing red light of the church. Three of the boats had already landed and there was a hive of activity as the catches were laid out for the buyers to inspect. A lorry had arrived to take the bulk of the catch to the markets in Colombo. Men on bicycles, with large boxes bolted to steel frames at the back, were buying up the smaller fish. They had called at the ice factory and lined their insulated top boxes with ice on the way to the beach. These men would spread out and deliver fish to the houses inland, weighing them on hand-held scales and cutting the fish at the side of the road. For bags, they used banana leaves, which were folded and tucked under strings around their fish boxes.

Sam was concerned about beaching through the surf, but Laxman was unfazed. He circled slowly just outside the surf zone and kept his gaze out to sea, looking for the perfect wave on which to catch a ride. He was not to be hurried. He knew what he was looking for and would not be tempted by anything less. Eventually, when it came, he fired the engine as hard as he could, propelling the boat headlong towards the shore. When Sam realised they were going to crash into the beach, he braced himself for the impact. Laxman had timed his approach perfectly and they hit the beach the moment the chosen wave was at its highest. Instead of the spine-tingling smack Sam had been expecting, the boat beached with grace and a slight upwards turn as it rose out of the water and up to the lip of the beach. As the last gasp of momentum was scrubbed from it, the boat tipped over the lip and came to a stop where it would be safe until tomorrow. As Sam turned and looked with relief at Laxman, he saw that in the middle of landing, somehow, the fisherman had lifted the outboard. Laxman was *the* man.

Their catch was admired by all but commented on by none. It would have been bad form to do so. The fish were displayed on a tarpaulin beside the boat and sold in less than ten minutes. Together they cleaned the boat and stowed the gear away. The long-line box was carried to their shelter and they walked side by side, back to the house. On the way, Laxman counted out five green notes which he handed to Sam who knew better than to refuse them.

It was a good night. Sam put it down to beginner's luck.

34

After a second night's fishing with Laxman, a routine was developing. Sam would go for an evening meal with the family and then work the night on the boat. He had been offered the use of an abandoned shack on the beach which, because of its simplicity, was easily repaired, using no more than woven coconut leaves and coir fibre twine. The fishermen all helped.

A plastic chair and a wooden folding bed were provided. He bought two cotton sheets from a store in the village. In the afternoon, as he lay resting, the wind from the ocean blew in through the open door tickling him with its cooling, salty breath. He drew his drinking water from a nearby well. It had a slight salty taste but was used by all the fishermen. His toilet was the shoreline. Just before daylight, it was normal to see fishermen walking to the water's edge, lifting their sarongs and squatting on the sand. They washed themselves with sea water. Their connection to the sea was so powerful, Sam wondered if these men had blood or salt water running through their veins.

There was a small kade which sold bread and simple provisions. At breakfast time one of the village women supplied home-made string hoppers in small plastic bags which the shop sold with coconut sambal and a dahl. The dahl was also served in small, red plastic bags, tied tightly in a knot to stop the gravy from spilling. With his experience of hobo stoves, it took Sam no time at all to get used to the local clay version. They were things of beauty and fascinatingly efficient. The handmade clay pots, which he experimented cooking his meals in, were made to fit perfectly in the opening of the stove, which had cost him the equivalent of a pound. It was the simplest life he could ever have imagined. The only thing he had of value was his freedom. He had as much responsibility as a new-born baby and there was nothing, other than his own moral code, that he had to obey. He would find happiness from making good choices and accepting their consequences. What was beyond his control was irrelevant. If he didn't work, he didn't eat, but the only mouth he had to fill was his own. This was probably what he had been searching for all his adult life. He tried hard to but was unable to think of a single material thing he wanted.

Sam looked to a future where he would learn from life and think about things freely without the debilitating hindrance of a modern western lifestyle. He would spend days, weeks if necessary, contemplating whether weapons of mass destruction or advertising were the greatest global evils. He would meditate and try to find those deep corners of himself that affluence and supermarkets had clogged with fluff. He would quite probably learn Sinhala and would never fill in an official form again. His focused attention to the details of life provided a constant and mindful punctuation which slowed down his perception of the passing of time and made it rubbery.

On the fifth day, as he walked to Laxman's house for his evening meal, he could see that something was wrong. Laxman and Shani were arguing loudly beside their gate. It looked like Laxman was trying to leave and Shani was tugging him back, screaming at him in her machine-gun voice. They both calmed down as Sam approached, but it was only a brief respite. Rassika was pleading with them both, suffering the excruciating embarrassment of an adolescent girl mortified by her parents' behaviour. Rassika ran to Sam and grabbed him by the arm, pulling him as quickly as she could towards the warring couple. She sensed Sam was her only hope of bringing peace to the garden.

"Italy man come," said Rassika. "He come and go."

"Soo-rain?"

"Italy man. Amma give him money. Now he go."

"Oh, God, no."

Soo-rain was fortunate enough to have arrived when Laxman was out. Shani had given him the five thousand euros and he had left, quickly, promising that her son would be home as soon as possible. Now Laxman wanted to find the man and kill him. Over the last five days Laxman had decided that Sam was an honest man and had reluctantly accepted his story was true. Rohan was dead. He had tried to make Shani understand, but she was a mother, and refused to give up hope. The man from Italy had given her a chance to see her son again. The money from Sam was proof that her prayers had worked.

A three-wheeler came speeding towards the house from the direction of the main road. Shani released her grip on Laxman as the three-wheeler spun around, the tinny, two-stroke engine revving hard. Sam thought he recognised two of the fishermen in the back, but their grim expressions made him doubt it. Laxman leapt onto the rear seat in a space that was hastily made for him. He didn't look back to see Shani screaming silently. All her voice was used up. The look of terror on Rassika's face, made Sam feel sick.

He stumbled back to his hut and lay down. His mind in turmoil. The horror of what Laxman might do and the unbearable anguish Shani was suffering made it impossible to stay still for long. He set off running up the beach at an aggressive pace, heading for that point on the horizon where the world disappeared. He ran barefoot above the high-water mark where the coarse sand was dry and firm. And he ran on. Children waved at him and dogs ran towards him barking. He never saw them. He was confused and almost began to feel sorry for himself. Sorry for the new life he had found which was being torn away before it had really started. But he quickly dismissed that for the lie it was. So, he ran harder and tried to lose any desire for what fate had teased him with. The running felt good. It cleared his mind, as it always had done. The steady motion of his limbs gave a solidity to his thoughts that made them more manageable.

The horizon kept slipping away from him, but it was nightfall that finally made it disappear. It gave him the excuse he needed to turn around. He took a long drink of brackish water from a well beside a fisherman's house and slowly started running back to the place he had just begun to call home. It was late when he saw the blinking red light on the top of the cross. Four boats were on the beach. Laxman's was gone. The breeze was light, but nobody else had put to sea. The hooks of the long-lines remained bare.

He walked up the path towards Laxman's house, but it was in darkness. A silence had descended on it that it would have been impossible for him to break. Sam walked back to his shack, filled with dread. He closed his eyes, but sleep was not easy. He must have dozed though because, at dawn, when he walked to the water for his ablutions, he saw Laxman's boat was back in its place. The incoming waves had washed away any trace of it beaching. Sam began to wonder if he had counted the boats wrongly the night before. It was a natural enough thought that he had made a mistake. He wanted to believe it, but he knew he had not been wrong. Laxman's boat had not been on the beach and now it was. Sam made his way up to the fisherman's home.

Shani was plaiting her daughter's hair and tying red ribbons in the ends, adding the finishing touches to her school uniform. Rassika's schoolbag was heavy with textbooks. After bending down to touch her mother's feet, Rassika ran out of the gate to join two other identically dressed girls waiting impatiently. She waved back at Sam as the three girls skipped up the road.

Shani had begun her rattling talk before Sam even got to the house. The volume was turned down though, maybe in deference to the hour of the day. The words made less sense than a cough, but her hands told him Laxman was not in the house. She looked nervously about her as she spoke and something about her manner told Sam he was unlikely to be eating there again. For whatever reason, he had overstayed his welcome. Shani was standing in the doorway, but her feet were already pointing back inside the house. She was talking to him over her left shoulder. Her words may or may not have been nuanced, but her body actions told him clearly he was no longer welcome.

Unable to do anything else, Sam went to buy some breakfast from the small shop by the beach. He would cook a pot of dahl and eat it with a loaf of bread. Then he would kill the long, hot hours either side of midday until the fishermen returned to bait their hooks.

At the kade, instead of the usual one or two customers lazily passing the time of day with Kalum, the shopkeeper, there was a small commotion. All of Kalum's family were helping him to get an order ready. The disposable income of Kalum's customers meant they bought just enough for the next meal. Even tea powder was sold in small newspaper cones that barely contained more tea than a teabag. It would be common for them to visit the shop four or five times a day. So, as well as providing their necessities, it was a social venue. Nobody was ever in a hurry to leave. The gene that turned normal flies into blue-arsed ones seemed to be totally absent from Sri Lankans.

There was a man at the shop whom Sam had never seen before. He wore a dirty, white vest and a cheap, batik sarong. He was buying the contents of Kalum's shop. In fact, he was buying so much Sam realised Kalum must have taken in extra stock just for this sale. A blue Piaggio three-wheeler, much boxier and beamier than the normal Bajaj models, was being loaded with sacks of rice, sugar, flour and dahl. There were gunny bags of small onions and garlic. Plastic bags full of tea powder and biscuits and betel leaves were stacked outside the shop.

It had always amused Sam how disproportionate, to his western eyes, the choice of biscuits and soap were in Kalum's kade. Like sausages in a Polish convenience store, biscuits and soap accounted for thirty-five percent of the floor space. But today the dusty tin shelves were bare. Sam had previously seen bars of soap being cut in half for customers who were unable to buy the full cake. There was a waxy wire hanging from one of the shelves just for this purpose. But today the man in the vest had bought more than a hundred bars. Sam wondered how big and how dirty his family must be.

The three-wheeler departed, filled with sacks, boxes and bags of provisions. There was no room in the back for the man in the vest. He perched tentatively on the corner of the driver's seat as the driver carefully manoeuvred the ruts and pot-holes in the path. And still Kalum was reading from a list and shouting orders to his wife and young children, who were stacking smaller items in old cardboard boxes and tying them up with string. This was some shopping list. In less than ten minutes, the three-wheeler returned for the rest of the supplies.

The man in the vest spent a few minutes going through the list with Kalum whilst the driver loaded the rest of the goods. The price was totalled three times and when agreement on the sum was finally achieved the man removed a black plastic bag from the lockable glove box in the front of the three-wheeler. The bag had the word 'TULIP' on it in capital gold letters. He took out four large bundles of tightly stacked notes, bound with rubber bands, and handed them to Kalum. Then he reached under the leather belt fastened tightly round his sarong and pulled out a large, old brown envelope from which he took several more notes. Kalum's wife counted the bundled notes whilst Kalum and the man in the vest waited patiently. Nothing else was said until Kalum's wife simply gave a very slight, silent head wobble. The three-wheeler departed, having bought the equivalent of the total sales for Christmas, Easter and the Church Feast all rolled into one. Whatever was happening was something big.

Sam joined the queue with two other women. He raised his eyebrows to one of them in recognition of the huge sale, but she blanked him, walked past, and bought the last loaf of bread. All that was left to eat were a few dry string hoppers and a sugar-coated crocodile bun. Sam declined them and walked back to his shack.

35

When Sam saw the other fishermen baiting their long-lines, he took some small fish and began baiting Laxman's hooks. It was hotter than usual because the tarpaulin from the top of their baiting shelter was missing.

A step-through Honda 90, known locally as the Horse model, arrived. It was one of the newer, 'light- on' versions, but still had more than a dozen years of hard work under its belt. In most countries, it would have been condemned, but in a Sri Lankan fishing village, it was barely run-in. If a for-sale advert for it were to be placed in the local paper, it would probably be described as being 'in topping condition'. Laxman was riding pillion. When he saw Sam baiting the hooks, he gestured for him to come. As Sam stood up, the young man who had been riding the Honda, took his place and continued baiting where Sam had left off.

All the fishermen were surreptitiously watching them as Laxman handed Sam a folded piece of paper. On one side of the paper was some of Rassika's maths homework. It had been marked. There were large red ticks beside the simple sums. Sam guessed correctly that whatever information Laxman wanted to give him, it was not that his daughter had done well in her maths test. So he turned the paper over and read a simple message written in English capital letters. It said, 'Mr Sam, the boat leaves at one in the morning. Please be ready. Your ticket is OK.'

"What?" said Sam. "What boat? And where is it going to?"

"Italy," said one of the fishermen, without looking up from his work.

"Italy? Why do I want to go to Italy? I have just come from there!"

"Itallee," repeated Laxman. He had the straight-lipped smile of a betel chewer with a mouth full of the toxic juice. His stare was unflinching, but benevolent.

Sam could see he was being given no choice. First, he had been made to understand that he was no longer welcome at Laxman's house and now his job as crewman on Laxman's boat had been taken by another. He was being cut off, his fate had been decided and he didn't know why. He had done nothing wrong that he was aware of and had joined in this lifestyle with a genuine enthusiasm which he had hoped Laxman and the other fishermen would have picked up on. He felt angry and disappointed and his usual affable charm deserted him. Instead, a petulant animosity came bubbling up from some place he had forgotten about. It was impossible to hide his feelings. He turned on his heels, throwing the note to the ground and walked belligerently down the shore away from the fishermen, muttering to himself.

As he put distance between himself and the others, he calmed down. The overwhelming feeling that remained when the anger had left was one of frustration. Try as he might, he was unable to understand what he had done that was so terribly wrong. If he had upset anyone it must have been seriously, because there was no question about it – he was being excommunicated.

Unable to identify his mistake, he was unable to rectify it. His newfound quest for virtue dictated that intolerance of uncertainty should be avoided. He forced himself to believe that superficial things outside his control were neither good nor bad and reluctantly accepted Laxman's news as his fate.

For his part, Laxman was not expecting any gratitude. When a gift was given and received with a clean heart and a gentle respectful touch of the forearm, nothing more was needed. Unnecessary displays were just insincere thanks for a gift reluctantly given. But Sam's behaviour had surprised him. Usually foreigners said, "Thank you," as easily as they breathed. It meant nothing. But Mr Sam hadn't done that. He even looked angry. Since manhood, Laxman had given away many things. Some of value and some which cost him heavily in sweat and time. But he had never gifted anything so valuable or as hard-earned as that he had just handed to Mr Sam. Why couldn't the white man see that?

There was some activity at sea shortly after it got dark. Lights briefly appeared on a large boat anchored just off shore. Then the lights were killed and the darkness reclaimed the horizon. It took Sam less than thirty seconds to pack, which, even for him, was a record. Just after midnight, various three-wheelers and motorbikes deposited a growing number of people on the beach close to the boats. Some went to the church to pray, others stood around nervously in the shadows. Two of the boats were turned around at the head of the beach, but the bait boxes were left ashore. Small groups of people were ushered quietly into them from the darkness.

Sam counted fifteen people in one boat, together with two crew. The fishermen on the shore hauled at the heavy boat and slid it down the beach and into the water. The boat looked dangerously overloaded, but it behaved impeccably in the expert hands of the Thalagamma fishermen. By the time the first boat had returned from depositing its human cargo on the anchored boat, a second had put to sea with a similar number of nervous passengers. When the first boat was ready to make its third trip and Sam, looking behind him, suddenly realised that this would be the last, there were only six passengers remaining on the beach. Sam and the crew would make nine. He realised he knew nothing about what was happening to him.

He silently mouthed the words written on the purple piece of paper, in his back pocket, 'Continue the Adventure,' and stepped into the boat. He realised Laxman was not there and wished he could say farewell to his one-time skipper and friend. One of the fishermen mistaking the look in Sam's eyes for panic held him in the boat in a grip that could not be compromised.

"Where is Laxman?"

"Laxman gone," said the fisherman with the grip of steel. "No here." Sam wilted, and the fisherman released his hold, knowing it was no longer needed.

There were no farewells or hearty slaps on backs as the fishermen left Sam on the big boat. The diesel engine was started, the anchor weighed and Sam could see, under the warm yellow light of the kerosene lamps ashore, the fishermen loading their long-lines onto the beached boats. He thought he saw Laxman and waved hopefully. The figure looked directly at Sam but did not wave back. Then everyone aboard was ushered down a steel ladder into the holds below deck as the boat headed out to sea. Sri Lanka disappeared.

The man at the wheel was still wearing a dirty white vest and a cheap batik sarong made fast at the waist with a tight leather belt.

36

The following day, they were all kept below decks. It was hot, but not unbearably so. The hatches were open, which helped to ventilate the waste gasses from more than sixty human beings. It was a modified fishing boat, so there were no portholes. Sam had to satisfy himself with the occasional glance out of one of the hatches to glimpse what he could through the large, rectangular scuppers. All he saw was water reaching to the horizon and occasional white spray from the bow as the boat made steady progress through a gentle swell.

The engine fired steadily and slowly and without apparent trauma. It set up a reassuring vibration which throbbed through the boat. His fellow passengers were a mixed group. Sam counted five older ladies, who everyone called Aunty. There were sixteen younger women, around their early twenties, and between thirty and forty young men, three of whom apparently knew their way around the boat. Sam assumed they were crew. There were also five young children. It was hard to get an accurate count because the children kept running around and standing on prostrate adults, reclining wherever they could. Some of the young men also found it difficult to keep still for long.

Shortly after dawn, the aunties, who automatically assumed galley duties, brewed tea using large plastic jugs, tea powder and indecent amounts of sugar. They poured the brew through a stained, stainless steel strainer into a variety of old, colourful cups. Sam put his aversion to sugar aside and happily accepted a cup from a dynamic little woman with white hair and a pronounced stoop. Quite what she was going to do in Italy was beyond him. She mothered everyone and, within an hour, everybody was calling her Achchi, a ubiquitous name used fondly for a grandmother. Four Aunties and one Achchi.

After the skipper, Achchi came next in the on-board hierarchy. She had the energy to handle the entire domestic operation single-handedly. The children were given biscuits with their tea, as was one of the young women, who, it turned out, was pregnant.

The alterations made to the boat were practical, but the internal butchery meant that it was probably never destined to make the return journey. The bulkhead between the forward bait hold and the fish hold had been knocked through to make one large room. The vestigial remains of the bulkhead had been left intact to offer a small degree of gender separation. A crude timber decking had been assembled on the unforgiving fibreglass floor of the holds and it was on this that sleeping mats were unrolled. A slurry tank had been removed to make room for more storage for provisions and extra water. The normal two thousand litre wing tanks would have been inadequate for such a thirsty cargo. The balance of the dry provisions was stored in the fore peak, accessed by a hatch on the deck.

In the aft wheelhouse were six bunks. Four were earmarked for the skipper and his crew. Sam was offered one of the remaining bunks but declined. Achchi was given one, being next to the galley, which was her natural domain, and the pregnant girl was then given the remaining one, next to Achchi. There was a flushing toilet at the back of the wheelhouse, running entirely off seawater and discharging directly into the sea. It was rarely unoccupied, day or night.

As the sun began to set, the skipper informed everyone that they were far enough away from Sri Lanka and, if they wanted to, they could come up on deck. There was a crush for the ladder. Sam stood back, allowing the others to go first, despite his desperation to fill his lungs with fresh air and catch a glimpse of the open ocean before the light died. The men went first. To Sam's surprise, the women stayed below deck, getting their pleasures from luxuriating, at last, in a male-free environment.

The beauty of the setting sun clearly held no fascination for them. The children lay asleep with the women, exhausted by their play.

The deck was of a tight-fitting hardwood, caulked with a black synthetic filler and looked well-worn but attractive, despite its obvious utility. A pattern soon emerged where the deck was the place the men sat, with their backs against the fibreglass gunwales. Other than in the heat of the day, it was the most comfortable place on the boat. But none of them displayed any sense of entitlement and if someone else wanted their spot they would happily move. When it got too hot, everybody would descend into the hold and doze lethargically. At night, the men slept on deck in the open while the women took over the hold, where femininity reigned.

Lunch was always rice and curry. Simple, but adequate. Everyone ate with their fingers. Sri Lanka seemed to be blessed with the least-fussy eaters in the world. The only rule seemed to be that if it was on your plate, you ate it. The children devoured similar-sized portions to the adults. Lunch was the only meal of the day. As the sun was setting, tea was brought round again. But this time with biscuits for all. The biscuits were plain and sweet. Sam found them perfect for dunking in his tea, much to the amusement of the other passengers who had never seen this white man's eccentricity before. A few of them tried but miscalculated the critical moment. There was much hilarity and only Sam got it right.

After meals, the cramped boat was diligently cleaned by the younger women. The daydreams of the young men were filled with hormonal longings and fuelled by the certainty of the enforced proximity of so many eligible girls for the rest of the voyage. Achchi was alert to this and clubbed one game young man on the head with the wooden handle of a broom. His crime was to gently touch one of the girls on the arm as she was collecting his plate. His amorous ambitions and his libido shrank as the lump on his forehead grew. The others laughed as the girl bashfully withdrew. The plates and mugs were washed on deck by one of the crew with buckets of seawater. The washed crockery was left in the sun to dry. Salty crystals coated the dried plates.

On the second day, returning from the toilet, Sam said, "How are you doing?" to the skipper as he squeezed past the captain's chair to get out to the deck. It was more out of politeness than any desire for another protracted mime. All the two men had done so far was nod briefly at each other.

"I am fine, thanks. How are you?"

"Yeah, good. Good. Comfortable, thanks." Not expecting an answer, Sam asked the skipper how the trip was going.

"I am Lucian." The skipper held out his hand and gave Sam a firm, pumping handshake.

"Oh, yes, Sam."

"We're making good progress, Sam. The weather is fine and, most importantly, this lot seem to be easy – going." He jerked his thumb in the direction of the men on deck.

"This lot? Do you mean you have done this trip before?"

"A few times. Each time, I tell myself it will be the last. But I just enjoy it too much. And, of course, it pays well."

For the next three hours, the two men talked. Lucian was an open man with little that he wanted to hide and Sam had all his questions answered. At times, Lucian's attitude to life seemed to echo his own and he made Sam laugh when he explained he got more satisfaction living his life between his ears than between his legs. Lucian maintained that attitude was everything.

"Don't take life seriously," he told Sam. "It isn't."

He had been a merchant seaman for almost twenty years but had come back to live in Sri Lanka eight years ago. He lived in Negombo, home to one of the largest fishing fleets in the country. When the urge to go back to sea became too much, and the ways of dirt-dwellers began to confuse him, he had bought a boat and started fishing. He loved the life, but it made very little money. Because he lived alone, his extended family thought they had a divine right to share in his wealth. They pestered him with desperate requests for start-up funds for businesses that never saw the light of day. Luckily for them, Lucian believed money in the bank was a sinful waste, so he would usually give them what they wanted, then put to sea and stay out there until the hold on his boat was full of tuna and shark fins.

Sam ran his hand appreciatively over the patinaed woodwork of the helm console. His fingers vibrated steadily with the throb of the engine.

"She's 180HP," said Lucian. "I fitted her myself for the trip."

"Forty feet?"

"Forty-five. A forty-five-footer usually works outside the two-hundred-mile Exclusive Economic Zone."

"How far outside?"

"It depends on the season but usually up to the Bay of Bengal or occasionally the north-west Arabian Sea. Some of the boats go as far as the Red Sea."

"It looks like some go a bit further than that."

Lucian laughed, "I guess they do Sam."

The skipper's nomadic fishing exploits reassured Sam there was a capable pair of hands at the helm and there would not be much happening at sea he hadn't seen before. A normal trip would be up to a month, unless the fishing was particularly good. Any longer than a month, Lucian explained, and the catch would begin to spoil. They had no freezer facility on board and needed to rely only on stored ice. They worked long-lines and large-meshed gill nets. It was the bigger fish species they were after, but the most valuable was the yellowfin tuna or very rarely, a bluefin.

It was unusual for the skipper to own the boat. Normally, the owners sat around in the rest houses, eating rice and curry and drinking arrack, waiting for their boats to return. The average boat only made 12 or 13 trips a year, so there was a lot of sitting around to be done. The boat owners tended to be the fattest of all the men in Negombo. After their enormous lunches, they would rent rooms by the hour and be entertained by ladies who knew how to make fat men happy.

Lucian explained the smaller boats that fished in the EEZ surprisingly made more money than a larger boat like his. This was because they made more trips and the quality of their catch was generally better, due to less time being spent at sea. Their fish fetched a higher price. But the smaller boats were useless for Lucian's other job, which was carrying people to Italy. A thirty-two-foot Sri Lankan boat heading across the Arabian Sea would attract attention. But for a forty-five-footer, it was nothing special. And a forty-five-footer could carry many more fare-paying passengers.

As a fisherman, Lucian might expect to make a couple of million rupees a year. That was OK. About as much as a university professor. But delivering people – he objected to the term 'human-trafficker' – made a lot more money. There were fifty-nine fare-paying passengers on this trip. Each had paid six lakh. Sam worked out that the gross income for this trip was over thirty-five million. Lucian saw Sam doing the mental arithmetic and nodded happily.

"Yes. Yes, a lot of money. The same as twenty years fishing."

"Fifty-nine?" asked Sam, having thought there were more on board.

"Yes, the crew go free. Then there is my mother and me. That leaves fifty-nine."

Two thoughts struck Sam with equal force at the same time. One was that the old lady was Lucian's mother and must be along for the hell of it and, two, that his own name had not been included in the list of those getting a free ride. Most people are not mentally equipped to process two competing thoughts simultaneously and Sam was no exception. His next sentence was a garbled attempt at two half-formed questions, which would have needed something like an Enigma machine to decodify. The equipment in the wheelhouse consisted of a radar, an SSB radio, a GPS and a CD player. There was no Enigma machine, so Lucian wisely stayed quiet, waiting for Sam to make another attempt at getting the right words out. Sam decided to start with Lucian's mother. The other query might lead to yet more questions that he wasn't sure he wanted to find the answers to.

Achchi was indeed Lucian's mother and came along on all his Italian trips. She kept everyone in order whilst he concentrated on getting them there. Once they landed in Italy, there was a boatyard he knew where they would pay him cash for the salvageable parts of his boat. The engine, the navigation equipment and one or two smaller items, which they would remove before scuppering the hull somewhere in the Adriatic Sea. Lucian knew enough about the sea and merchant vessels to negotiate a passage home for him and his mother. They generally worked their way back and often managed to return home in less time than it took them to get there. Here was a man who shared Sam's distain of man-made borders and the bureaucratic niceties of civilised travel. But Lucian had taken the freedom this gave him to a different level.

Sam knew that if Lucian and his mother were dropped anywhere in Karachi, they would be at sea within the day. No illegal passports or long rides on buses for them. All he needed was his dirty vest and sarong and he was as good as home. He spoke the language seamen everywhere understood. Sam envied him that but, whilst having a genuine desire to learn more about his years of travel, what was at the back of his mind, and coming ever closer to the front, was question number two.

"I never paid."

"I know. It was all taken care of."

"How?"

"One of the fishermen I use for loading passengers. Negombo is too obvious. Too many people wanting a pay-off."

"One of the fisherman took care of it how?" Sam was frightened to hear the answer but braced himself when he saw it was coming.

"One of the fishermen paid for you."

Sam remained silent.

"The funny thing was, he paid in euros. Five thousand. I have never had that before. It'll be handy for topping up with fuel in Cairo."

Sam went out to the deck and joined the pregnant girl in throwing up over the side.

37

S am spent long hours sitting in the wheelhouse, drinking muddy
Sri Lankan coffee and learning about the ways of Lucian's world.
The skipper taught him about cruising long distances and how to
economise on fuel. Like life, everything was a compromise, and Lucian
had a perishable cargo which factored high in his decision making.
The hull speed of any boat was calculated by a simple formula, and
this would theoretically be the most efficient cruising speed. But
Lucian had experience enough to know that if he knocked a knot
off the theoretical speed this vessel would give him a better return.
In addition, the engine he had installed was a little underpowered, so
he brought the revs down a smidgen further and settled at a cruising
speed of six knots. They were not in a race. At six knots they would
take approximately two weeks to reach the Red Sea, twenty-three days
to reach the Suez Canal and a further week to cross the Mediterranean
and land in Italy. Lucian didn't have to be worried about his cargo. His
mother would take care of that.

It took them fifteen days to reach the Red Sea. Sam could not pretend
that it was anything other than pleasant cruising. The food was sparse,
but tasty, and adequate for bodily maintenance. The water was tainted
with something unidentifiable, but nobody became ill drinking it.

Although Sam could think comfortably in either kilometres or
miles, knots were slightly troublesome. He found that whenever Lucian
talked about them he would have to convert them into something
he could imagine running. It was distracting, like struggling with an

unfamiliar language. So he decided to divide the sea into the units devised by the French Academy of Sciences and knew they could cover over two hundred and fifty of them in a day. That was until they came to the Red Sea.

The Gulf of Aden is separated from the Red Sea by a strait, approximately thirty kilometres across, called the Bab al Mandab. Dividing the strait into two unequal parts is Perim Island – which Sam was not surprised to learn from Lucian, was once claimed by the British, an action which he was certain was not undertaken as a gesture of colonial altruism. There is a story that, no matter what time of year or which direction you pass through the strait, the wind and current will be against you. This time, the story was true. A steady northerly freshened as they kept Perim Island to port and navigated the narrower of the two channels. In past times, sailors would hug the east coast to avoid the worst of the northerlies, but Lucian decided to stay out of sight of land. Like many mariners, he professed to being apolitical, but pragmatically saw no reason to test the tolerance of potentially hostile cultures.

On the third day, the wind turned orange and forced everyone below deck. It was relentless, and visibility was reduced to almost nothing. The strength of the wind was terrifying for those below deck. Lucian had seen it before. The only thing that could trouble them was sand getting into the engines, but he knew the air-filters were tight and well protected. They made little headway into a northerly wind that gusted at over thirty knots. After a day, all the sand had fallen out of the sky and the horizons reappeared, but the wind dragon showed no signs of slackening its fiery breath. The crew pushed piles of gritty dust into the sea through the scuppers. Sam spent time in the wheelhouse but, other than one or two men lingering on deck after relieving themselves over the side, everyone else stayed below.

It took ten days to steam up the Red Sea, which Sam found staggering. In his atlas, he had never really paid much attention to it. If he had thought about it all, he had imagined it being similar in size to the English Channel turned on its side. But the Red Sea is two thousand four hundred kilometres long and, battering into a headwind day and night, it was by far the longest and most uncomfortable part of the passage. The cargo began to show signs of perishing. On the day before they were due to reach Suez, Lucian urged everyone out on deck and encouraged them to stretch and relax. He knew that for the trip up the canal nobody would be allowed out of the hold.

The Suez Canal took ten years to build and was completed in 1869. It was the French who eventually brought the idea into reality. So it was no surprise that the first official vessel intended through the canal was the Imperial Yacht L'Aigle, carrying the French Empress Eugenie. But the British gate-crashed the party.

On the night before the canal was due to open, HMS Newport, captained by Captain Nares, piloted his vessel, in total darkness, through the waiting ships and stole to the front of the line, in front of L'Aigle. The French had a monumental hissy-fit, but it was impossible to pass the Royal Navy vessel. Captain Nares received an official reprimand, made more bearable by the praise that was quietly heaped upon him by the gloating Admiralty. Despite being staunchly against the Suez Canal from start to finish, it only took another fourteen years for the British to gain control of it.

Lucian gave Sam these facts in a detached manner. The ongoing political skirmishes and baksheesh economy that drove the region were anathema. Of far more concern to him was that at this time of year, south of the Bitter Lakes, the current would change with the tides and the current in the canal north of the lakes would run southerly. Lucian estimated that, once they had topped up with supplies in the Gulf of Suez, allowing for an inevitable bit of dodging and zig-zagging, they would pass through the canal in under twenty hours.

Sam was in the wheelhouse when Lucian made a call on the radio. It was like a supermarket home delivery service, except first on the list was fifteen hundred litres of fuel. What followed was a shopping list for fresh water, sanitary towels and enough food and essentials to keep the cargo from deteriorating too much. Lucian paused the call and spoke briefly to his mother in Sinhala, after which a few more items were added to the list. Two essential pieces of information came over the radio, which Lucian wrote down. One was the price and the other the coordinates for the exchange.

Only Lucian and the crew were allowed on deck when the transaction occurred. It was night-time and most of the passengers were asleep. But, in the relative quiet in the lee of the supply boat, Sam could hear the calm, assured tones of a relaxed conversation. It was one that both parties had indulged in many times before. After the farewells, Sam could hear the crew stowing the dry goods in the fore peak.

They entered the canal just after midnight on the sixth of September. The northerly convoy of vessels would not start until 4 A.M. If Lucian was correct, the convoy would begin to overtake them just before they reached the Friendship Bridge. The start time was fortuitous. They would make the Bitter Lakes by dawn and would be past Lake Timsah by the time the various authority boats began scouring the marinas in search of easy targets for their daily quota of baksheesh.

To a man of the open waters, like Lucian, the canal was just a long drainage ditch. Passage through it would have been as dull as the water that came from it, had it not been for the constant cat-and-mouse games he played with the minions of the Suez Canal Authority. Once, when he had been stopped in the first kilometre of the canal, he had affected an angry intolerance at their unwanted interference and loudly and unrelentingly demanded cigarettes from them. When, bewildered, they at last grudgingly handed over two packets of Marlboros, he had abused them even more with a few choice Sri Lankan curses before casting off. Mostly, however, he just tried to blend in. If there was a busy stretch ahead, he would motor casually from one side of the canal to the other, pretending that he had a place to go to. When the convoy caught him up, he would dodge between them, putting 250,000 tonnes of boat between him and any officials. There were always easier targets to be found. It passed the time for him.

Lucian was strict about nobody being on deck. A toilet bucket was kept below decks and hidden by a makeshift arrangement of sleeping mats suspended on ropes. Privacy was minimal, but nobody wanted to watch anyway. When the bucket was filled, someone would call to the crew and one of them would haul it up on a coir fibre rope. They all heard the splash as the contents were thrown over the side. It wasn't pleasant, but nobody complained.

There was little lighting, but Sam took the opportunity to study his fellow passengers in the intimate fugginess below deck. Was there another race on earth as uncomplaining and willing to suffer hardships as the Sri Lankans? He had not heard a single cross word on the entire voyage. Everyone was polite and respectful. Other than thwarting the odd experimental hormonal foray into the opposition's territory, Achchi's skill as a peacemaker had not been needed. Everyone bore their discomforts and inconveniences with good grace and a fortitude that humbled Sam. There had been no tantrums or unwanted displays of high-maintenance behaviour. People just got on with it. If there was a chance to sing, everyone joined in and took a turn to give a song or beat a baila rhythm on an aluminium pot or rattle the hull with a spoon.

Sam tried to imagine a similar group of pampered Westerners thrown into a situation like this. He doubted more than half of them would survive. When the apocalypse eventually came, it would be people like this who would be alive to keep the cockroaches company. Sam, along with the rest of his slacktivist, soap-opera-watching, seat-belt-wearing, syndrome-suffering, soft-palmed couch-potatoes would complain bitterly – and then die. Good luck to the Sri Lankans, thought Sam. They deserved whatever benefits they could scratch out for themselves in the West.

Then he remembered the boy in Milan. He could understand why Rohan had left Sri Lanka. Every fare-paying passenger on board shared those same dreams. But Sam had the privilege of a different perspective and knew they were kidding themselves. They were chasing dreams without knowing what their dreams really were. They were punching fog. He wanted to tell them that, if they had used the money their families had somehow managed to put together to invest in a business back at home, their chances of financial success would have been a thousand times higher. But it was no use. They were young and would never believe him. So he smiled and offered encouragement whenever it was possible. He hoped life would be kind to them. Sam would embrace his fate and the Sri Lankans would have to learn to accept theirs. From what he had learned of them so far, he knew they had a head-start on the rest of us who are fortunate and misguided enough to be brought up believing human rights are a right.

In those quiet hours, Sam learned that Lucian had a good reputation amongst Sri Lankans wanting to get to Italy. He was a caring captain, which made him a rarity. The fact that he didn't charge Tamils twice the going rate put him in a minority of one. It turned out there were eight Tamil boys on board. Their need to leave Sri Lanka was far greater than the simple economic forces driving the Sinhalese. They had been persecuted for a generation. Looking around, Sam could see no segregation or racial animosity. This both surprised and pleased him and he wondered if it had anything to do with the absence of politicians on board.

One of the boys told Sam of a boat full of migrants which had once left Negombo. There were over a hundred people aboard and conditions were deplorable. They put to sea and immediately found food and water were in short supply. Illness spread amongst the passengers. They were not allowed out of the ship's hold under any circumstances. There was no proper sanitation and after 5 days one young boy died. His body remained in the stinking slow-cooker of the unventilated hold for a further two days. On the seventh night at sea, the captain called everyone on deck and, pointing to lights on the shore, told them it was Italy. He approached the deserted beach as closely as he could and ordered everyone to jump overboard and swim the short distance to the shore. Dizzy with the fresh air, one by one, they did so. Surprisingly, they all made it to the beach, despite the lack of buoyancy aids. When the last one was overboard the engines revved and the boat was quickly lost in the darkness as it headed out to the open sea. The exhausted migrants clambered onto the beach, helping those who were weakest.

An old man came out of a hut hidden behind some trees at the top of the beach. He carried a kerosene lamp and, when he heard voices by the shore, he came towards them to investigate. The excited boys began a chorus of ciaos to the stranger. He scratched his small, balding head, walked past them, lifted his sarong and squatted in the sand to relieve himself. He was not Italian. He was an old fisherman from Hambantota on the south coast of Sri Lanka. By the time the boys realised they had been cheated, the boat was gone forever and with it the money their parents had mortgaged their homes for.

38

The passage through the canal took twenty-two hours and it had already been dark for three of them when one of the crew threw open the hatches and grinned as he shouted, "Benvenuto!" He waved his arms comically, as he imagined an Italian would. Once more, there was a crush for the ladder. Sam stood aside and enjoyed the laughter and happiness on all the faces.

The stars were shining, the wind had dropped and it was a perfect, clear, Mediterranean night. 'Enjoy it,' thought Sam, 'This is probably as good as it gets.' Someone burst into song and Lucian's mother appeared with an old wooden drum about the size of a barrel lid, laying it down gently on the deck. She and the aunties squatted around it and she led them in pounding out a steady beat. Everyone else danced round the drum in a large circle. Lucian laughed.

After more than two hours of singing and dancing, exhaustion started taking people one by one. Nobody went back below. They lay around on the deck enjoying the night and the company. Lucian's mother and two of the girls went to the galley and produced a celebratory meal using some of the fresh ingredients they had bought in the Gulf of Suez. That night, everyone slept on deck. Sleep came easily. Sam felt something like bliss as he closed his eyes.

Of course, the 'Benvenuto' was premature. It took another six days to reach the Italian coast. Lucian took a northerly route that took them close to Crete. He explained to Sam he wanted to avoid any unnecessary attention off the Libyan coast. If he was forced to land, he wanted it to be in Crete rather than Libya. That made sense to Sam, who was the only one on board to whom the idea of landing in Crete sounded like a holiday. To the rest, it was just another place short of their destination. The Mediterranean was lumpy for the time of year and, despite most on board having taken delivery of their sea-legs by now, a few of them were violently and persistently sick. Sea sickness is unlike any other illness. With any other affliction, the sufferer's only desire is to get better. With sea sickness, their only wish is to die.

The constant moaning and dry retching, combined with the smell of fermenting bile in the bilges, made the crossing unpleasant. Sam spent next to no time below decks. It was unfortunate those affected chose to spend their time below decks, where the horizons were more predictable. Here, the results of their purging were much harder to dispose of and the once intimate space became foul-smelling and poisonous. The deck became crowded because of a growing reluctance on the part of those who could move to stay below.

Lucian allowed this, but Sam noticed, as they came closer to Italy, he began to show signs of agitation. At times, Sam saw he was clenching his fists so hard his brown knuckles turned pale as the blood was squeezed from them. He would fidget in his chair and then suddenly stand up and pace the cabin. At one point, he blasted one of the crew and struck out at him. The boy was wise enough to disappear below deck immediately. The outburst was so uncharacteristic and surprising that the entire boat went silent. Even the engine seemed to pause in its relentless beat. Shock spread through the crew and people tried to slink into what little shadow there was. This was not the way *their* captain behaved.

Lucian's mother saw the concern on Sam's face as he stared at her son. As she breezed past him towards the galley, her lungi hoisted up to her knees, she said one word, quietly, which sent a chill through his body despite the heat of the midday Mediterranean sun.

"Mafia."

"Mafia?" Sam hissed in Lucian's ear. "You are handing us over to them?" It was hard to keep the indignation out of his voice. "What are you thinking of?"

Lucian was surprised by Sam's poorly-controlled outburst. "No, Sam. Don't be ridiculous. I wouldn't do that. Please – you must believe me. I would NOT do that."

Then he went on to explain that on his very first run he had used Italian facilitators who turned out to be Mafioso. They were cold men with lighter skins than his own, but much darker souls. His passengers were whisked away with frightening efficiency. He could only guess the fate of some of the girls and knew many of the boys would be recruited as picciotti, selling drugs... or worse. It sickened him, but he had been powerless to resist. He had paid the Italians what they had demanded, then put a torch to his boat in an attempt at some sort of purification. His old mother had beaten him with a stick until her hands bled. He never protested nor tried to avoid the blows. It had taken a long time for the wounds to heal. But, when the last scab had fallen off and they were both back in Sri Lanka, he had resolved that next time he would do it differently. And there had to be a next time because, if it was not him, then it would be someone else, who might be more welcoming to the cosy embrace of the Cosa Nostra.

Through Sri Lankans living in Italy, he had made connections with another group who controlled the heel of the boot of Italy. His friends had made him understand that business in Italy was impossible without the agreement of some heavy-duty facilitators. These chosen facilitators were happy to allow Lucian to make whatever arrangements he wanted, so long as he paid the necessary landing fees they insisted were due to them. Whenever he landed his cargo, they were there, silently watching, counting. And when the last passenger was ashore they would come to his boat, anchored in a shallow, sandy bay south of a river that wound its way lugubriously through the region's dusty olive groves and vineyards. The farmers and villagers had been blinded by fear and made mute by a generation of intimidation. When he paid the men, they would smile through thin lips and leave without saying a word. They frightened Lucian more than anything the sea had ever thrown at him. This part of his life was a little too close to the edge. Nonetheless, so far, his facilitators had been as good as their word and allowed Lucian's Sri Lankan contacts to provide transport to take his passengers on the three-hour drive to Naples.

This was the only reason Lucian allowed girls on his trips. If the relationship with the Italians ever showed any signs of breaking down, it would be men only from then on. If necessary, he would turn the boat round and head straight back to Sri Lanka without letting the girls ashore. He swore he would never allow another girl to be taken by them. His mother would kill him if he did.

He had recently heard stories one of the boys on that first trip had now risen through the criminal ranks to the position of Lo Sgarro, a mid-ranking killer in the Sacra Corona Unita, and was busy recruiting Sri Lankans to his own filiale. If a Sri Lankan ever came aboard his boat demanding landing fees, Lucian knew he would hit him over the head with a pipe wrench, wrap some heavy chains round his feet and throw him overboard. Lucian, too, was a man of honour.

Sam saw them, standing in the shadows beside a German car and smoking cigarettes. He was shocked by how ordinary they appeared. No sharp suits or rugged, unshaven good looks. No suave overpowering air of self-confidence. Nothing at all Hollywood about them. Just a couple of working class guys you might expect to see at any weekend Napoli game – with a bulge under their jackets Sam was certain would not be a season-ticket and a ciabatta. They watched and didn't interfere.

Everyone was ferried ashore in small groups, in two dinghies, rowed by men who looked like farmers. A windowless van and a box truck were parked at the head of the beach. Two Asian men hurried across the sand to hustle the Sri Lankans into the backs of the waiting vehicles. The Sri Lankans in Naples formed a tight community that was supportive to both its members and new arrivals. Jobs and encouragement were offered to family members and compatriots. There was hardly anyone on Lucian's boat who didn't have at least one family member living in the south of Italy. The men on the beach would spread the new arrivals out amongst safe houses within the Sri Lankan community. Relatives would collect them within twenty-four hours and their assimilation into Italian life would begin.

Almost certainly, work would be as a domestic or low-paid worker in a catering business. If they were lucky, the girls would be employed looking after elderly Italians or small children. Eventually, some of them would marry. It would also be quite normal for some of them never to return to Sri Lanka. The Tamils formed a much smaller minority, but the life they could expect was much the same.

39

Lucian embraced Sam but neither man spoke. To Lucian's mother, who had already started sweeping the deck, Sam put both palms together in an attitude of prayer and, bowing his head slightly to the diminutive figure, said "*Ayubowan.*"

"*Ayubowan,*" she replied, resting the handle of her broom under the crook of her arm as she reciprocated the gesture. Then she turned away and continued with her cleaning. Sam was the last passenger to be rowed ashore.

The second dinghy approached. The only passenger was one of the men Sam had seen earlier, smoking beside the car. He stared long and hard at Sam and the others as the two boats passed. It was night. They were ships.

To the other passengers, the man going in the opposite direction was just another Italian. He could have been selling olive oil, for all they knew or cared. Only Sam knew what he really was, but all the man was doing was counting heads. His fellow passengers were too excited about landing on Italian soil to care about anything else. As the boat hit the beach and they took the two wet steps to the shore, they knew they had made it. When the drivers of their transport welcomed them in Sinhala, they were in rapture.

The air was warm and scented. Insects buzzed around the dull torchlight that the drivers used to herd the new arrivals into the backs of the two vehicles. Sam was invited to sit up front with the driver of the box lorry. He refused at first but, when it was explained to him that having a European sitting there made it less likely they would be stopped, he relented. In the wing mirror, on his right, Sam noticed the lights of two vehicles following them up the farm track away from the beach. When they turned right onto a larger, metalled road, both sets of headlights did too.

There was no break in the night-time pastoral vista of agriculture. The vineyards and groves of olive trees looked peaceful and silver in the reflected moonlight. This was the bella figura the tourists loved. The darkness obscured any monotonous repetition. In the soft, honeyed focus of the moon it was chocolate box beautiful. Sam felt sorry for those behind him who could see nothing of it. There was none of the usual singing and drumming that any gathering of more than three Sri Lankans spontaneously burst into. Maybe the drivers had warned them to be quiet.

After an hour and a half, they started down a winding road which descended quickly into a round-bottomed valley. There were a few houses beside the road. It was impossible for Sam not to recognise the similarity of some of them to highland crofts. Broken-down vehicles on stacks of concrete blocks, JCBs parked beside porches, agricultural sheds with junk heaps of used building material piled up beside them. All signs of the carelessness that an abundance of space inevitably invites. A cluttered luxury beyond the comprehension of any town dweller.

Scattered amongst the houses of those who worked the land were a few ghostly, white-walled bungalows with manicured lawns and tiny, pointless walls. Just like in the highlands. Sam knew these were the homes of incomers.

After two hours, any signs of agriculture were left behind. The houses turned into villages and the villages into towns. The only break in the continuity of human habitation was when the road brushed close to the side of a steep hill. The driver turned on the radio. It played some Italian folk music.

He had imagined Naples would be something like San Tropez. A quaint, Mediterranean fishing village whose reputation had grown too big for its boats. So it took him by surprise when, rounding a bend on a hill descending to the coast, the city spread out in front of him as far as his eyes could see. It was vast. Naples may well once have been that sleepy little village Sam already felt nostalgic for, but today it was a vast city with over four million inhabitants. It sits comfortably in the top ten most populous areas in the European Union. The port is one of the most important in Europe, handling more passengers than anywhere else on earth, other than Hong Kong. If you wanted to lose a few dozen Sri Lankans quickly, then Naples was probably the best place in the world, outside Colombo, to do so.

The huge ancient centre is a metropolis of alleys and crumbling buildings dating back hundreds of years. It is a city which was never planned, but rather evolved, and is one of the oldest continuously inhabited cities in the world. That sort of history makes hiding child's play for the average minority community. To make Naples sound like a larger version of anywhere else, though, would be to ignore its recent history. The economy of Naples has grown rapidly and it was through the results of this industry, and the low-cost housing of the people who serviced it, that the two vans now drove.

The driver turned right onto a main road that skirted quarters of desolate urban poverty. There were dilapidated apartment blocks with occasional localised signs of heavy fortification. Drug bazaars, more than likely controlled by the Camorra. Sam pitied any Sri Lankans who would be dropped here. But, mercifully, the driver continued through the empty streets and eventually pulled up in a narrow, litter-strewn lane, hidden by small trees and overgrown bushes. Four cars were waiting with their lights turned off. It looked like it might be the venue for dubious sexual liaisons of a nocturnal and voyeuristic nature. But Sam could see behind the wheel of each car sat a nervous-looking Asian man. They were out of their personal comfort zones and were desperate to leave as quickly as possible.

Sam remained seated when they pulled to a halt. The driver quickly slipped out of his seat and went to unlock the back doors of the lorry. A mumbled conversation in Sinhala ensued and the suspension gently rocked as people jumped out of the back. After two minutes, the driver returned and drove off quietly down the lane. Sam could see in the side mirror the other cars leaving. And just like that, a new cohort of Sri Lankans disappeared and joined the diaspora. One more similar stop twenty minutes later emptied the lorry.

"Tamils," the driver explained. He looked at Sam and suddenly seemed surprised he was still there.

"Where do you want to go?"

Until that point, Sam had not clearly thought about it. Where did he want to go? For almost a month he had been denied the responsibility of making decisions. It was the first time since childhood that he had been so carefree… and he had enjoyed it. It had left him free to think. What he had done, in this unplanned decision-making hiatus, was, deliberately, to try and not anticipate the future. He had meditated instead on potential adversity which had left him empowered and relaxed about whatever was to come next.

The driver wanted Sam to decide quickly. After delivering a consignment of illegal immigrants, hanging around is probably high on any list of what *not* to do.

What did he want to do? What? Did he want to return to Skye?

Over the last four months, he had grown into tranquillity. He knew this had been achieved as a consequence of pursuing reason and virtue. Tranquillity itself was never the goal because it was not self-sustaining. The only real goal was virtue.

He wanted to carry on what he was doing. Letting life take its course and enjoying whatever was around the corner. It was precisely the opposite of taking life by the balls and wringing everything out of it. It was more pastel-coloured. He wanted to let life to wash over him and soak in it. That meant meeting people and embracing their differences. And most of all, acting with virtue and taking pleasure from knowing that his actions were good.

After a moment's reflection he gave the driver the only answer he could.

"It doesn't matter."

ACKNOWLEDGEMENTS

Writing a novel is an achievement. Writing a first novel is ridiculous. The amount of hand-holding needed to make this book came as a shock. I wrote the first draft quietly. It was lonely. My wife accused me of staying up late at night to watch iffy porn. Therssy, I was writing.

Andrew Lane (The Piano Man) was the first to read my manuscript. He was heroic. It was rubbish. Andrew taught me how to tell a story and that showing off is silly. He did it with good grace and extraordinary patience. Without Andrew, this book would not be.

Martin's diligent critique went a long way to fine tuning the script. Then he spoiled it by telling me my book filled a much-needed gap. Thanks bro. Thushy was amazingly supportive. She gave me belief in what I was doing. Thushy, I love you.

Fifteen edits later, I took the finished manuscript to Perera Hussein Publishing House. Ameena Hussein gave me a long list of suggestions where it could be improved. I was staggered by her insight. She taught me the beauty of economy. Then Sukanya Wignaraja expertly led me through the final edits with a professionalism that was a joy and a privilege to be on the receiving end of. With Sukanya's guiding hand, I learned there is no great writing, only great editing.

To the people of Marawila, I owe the greatest thanks of all. For your generosity, for your stories and for letting me share your lives and *kassipu* over the last 30 years.

Amen.

Gavin Major is a writer, a lousy fisherman, a successful retailer, a sometime boat-builder and has been a human being for most of his life. He lives in Sri Lanka and on Skye with his wife, when she will have him, and children who come and go. But he dreams of the simplicity of the road and most of the time lives in a world of his own. And he is quite happy there.